ALMOST IMMEDIATELY, HE HEARD THE SOUND.

Footsteps. Running. Coming this way.

He released Jenore's hand and said, "Run. Run home now," even as he turned to meet the rush from the darkness. *Clear noncombatants from the killing zone* said his training. *Turn toward the attack and engage the enemy.*

The light was too dim to see them clearly. There were six or seven young men, Alwan Foulaine's followers almost certainly, closing rapidly, running down the beach toward them. He could make out straight lines, lengths of wood possibly, or more of the metal bars.

He heard Jenore say something and said again, over his shoulder, "I am fine. Run!"

Then he was in action. They would expect him to run or perhaps to stand his ground. But he had not won a thousand fights by doing what the opponents expected. He ran toward them, as silently as he could manage on the shingle but counting on the noise of their own passage to disguise his. He held the rod in both hands, arms extended before him at head height, aiming for the middle of the dark knot of attackers.

He hit one of them hard. Bone cracked, blood splattered Conn's face and he heard a sob of surprise and pain. *Nose broken*, he thought. His momentum carried him past the injured man, whose knees had folded under him, and into the path of another who was coming close on the first one's heels.

Conn kept the rod extended, letting it ride up and over the first target so that it struck the next man in the forehead. The impact was less but the second man went down without a sound except for the clatter of his cudgel on the stones. Now Conn was through the pack and turning to follow them.

His stratagem was working. Those still on their feet would have thought that those who were down had stumbled. They could hear Jenore ahead of them, running for home as fast as she could without any attempt to silence her steps. They continued after her . . .

PRAISE FOR
Matthew Hughes

"If you're an admirer of the science fantasies of Jack Vance, it's hard not to feel affection for the Archonate stories of Matthew Hughes."
Locus Magazine

"Matthew Hughes's *Template* is many things—including a template others should follow to produce outstanding writing. Hughes has been the best-kept secret in SF for far too long: he's a towering talent, and *Template* is his best work to date. Bravo!"
Robert J. Sawyer, author of *Hominids*

"Matthew Hughes stands out as a success . . . if droll dialogue, curious customs, exotic scenery, clever plotting and wry cosmopolitanism are your bag, then Matthew Hughes is your man."
Paul Di Filippo for Scifi.com

"Hughes mixes his science and fantasy well and manages well in the difficult balancing act required to create believable stories mixing the two genres."
Science Fiction Weekly

"Matt Hughes's boldness is admirable."
The New York Review of Science Fiction

"Hughes serves up equal measures of wit, intrigue, and seat-of-the-pants action and even dabbles a little in Jungian psychology . . . "
Booklist

"Hughes writing style is atmospheric and witty; the story keeps moving in interesting places; surprise plot twists; it's just plain fun.""
SF Signal

"Matthew Hughes dips his ladle deep into the age-old stuff of folk- and tall tales and brings up a surprising long drink of cool, tasty water."
The Magazine of Fantasy & Science Fiction

"Hughes's writing is both supple and subtle here; his dialogue is allusive and amusing in that dry, understated style that he shares with Vance, and his descriptions are precise and specific . . . we need more Hughes novels, and a world with a legion of Hughes fans would be a wonderful thing."
Andrew Wheeler, Science Fiction Book Club

THE PLANET STORIES LIBRARY

Sos the Rope by Piers Anthony
Steppe by Piers Anthony
The Ginger Star by Leigh Brackett
The Hounds of Skaith by Leigh Brackett
The Reavers of Skaith by Leigh Brackett
The Secret of Sinharat by Leigh Brackett
The Sword of Rhiannon by Leigh Brackett
Infernal Sorceress by Gary Gygax
The Anubis Murders by Gary Gygax
The Samarkand Solution by Gary Gygax
Death in Delhi by Gary Gygax
Almuric by Robert E. Howard
The Swordsman of Mars by Otis Adelbert Kline
The Outlaws of Mars by Otis Adelbert Kline
The Dark World by Henry Kuttner
Elak of Atlantis by Henry Kuttner
Robots Have No Tails by Henry Kuttner
Worlds of Their Own edited by James Lowder
The Ship of Ishtar by A. Merritt
City of the Beast by Michael Moorcock
Lord of the Spiders by Michael Moorcock
Masters of the Pit by Michael Moorcock
Black God's Kiss by C. L. Moore
Northwest of Earth by C. L. Moore
Before They Were Giants edited by James L. Sutter
Who Fears the Devil? by Manly Wade Wellman

STRANGE ADVENTURES ON OTHER WORLDS
AVAILABLE EXCLUSIVELY FROM PLANET STORIES!

FOR AUTHOR BIOS AND SYNOPSES,
VISIT PAIZO.COM/PLANETSTORIES

Publisher's Cataloging-In-Publication Data
(Prepared by The Donohue Group, Inc.)

Hughes, Matthew, 1949-
 Template : a novel of the Archonate / by Matthew Hughes ;
cover illustration by Kieran Yanner.

 p. : ill. ; cm. -- (Planet stories ; #27)

 Originally published: England : PS Publishing, 2008.
 July 2010.
 Contents: The human canvas / by Jay Lake -- Template.
 ISBN: 978-1-60125-264-7

 1. Fantasy games--Fiction. 2. Adventure and adventurers--Fiction.
3. Science fiction. I. Yanner, Kieran. II. Lake, Jay. Human canvas. III.
Title.

PR9199.3.H763 T46 2010
813.6

 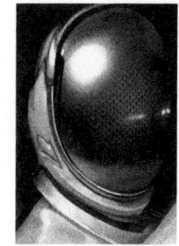

TEMPLATE: A NOVEL OF THE ARCHONATE

BY MATTHEW HUGHES ♦ COVER ILLUSTRATION BY KIERAN YANNER

THE HUMAN CANVAS
by Jay Lake. 8

"The realization of Hughes's universe is a delight, filled with incidental conceits and pleasances that ornament the setting while providing substance to both plot and character. His manifold lapidarian fantasies serve to capture the mind's eye as the reader passes them."

TEMPLATE 10
When professional duelist Conn Labro escapes indentured servitude as the star player of Horder's Emporium, he abandons the gaming world of Thrais and sets out on an interstellar journey filled with murder, deceit, and self-discovery.

PLANET STORIES is published bimonthly by Paizo Publishing, LLC with offices at 7120 185th Ave NE, Ste 120, Redmond, Washington, 98052. Erik Mona, Publisher. Pierce Watters, Senior Editor. James L. Sutter and Christopher Paul Carey, Editors. *Template: A Novel of the Archonate* © 2008 by Matthew Hughes. "The Human Canvas" © 2008 by Jay Lake. Planet Stories and the Planet Stories planet logo are registered trademarks of Paizo Publishing, LLC. Planet Stories #27, *Template: A Novel of the Archonate*, by Matthew Hughes. July 2010. PRINTED IN THE UNITED STATES OF AMERICA.

THE HUMAN CANVAS
by Jay Lake

Matt Hughes has built a career in part out of writing Archonate books. Over the past decade he's had a number of novels published, as well as varied shorter works. *Template*, the book which you now hold in your hands, is the latest and probably the best of the works so far.

Hughes is a funny, thoughtful man. He is gentle and unassuming in person—the Canadian ideal, perhaps—with a sweeping view of the Universe as broad as anything ever created by our field's grandmasters. I'm not talking about elaborated rhapsodies in astrophysics *a la* Greg Benford, nor Greg Bear's tightly-realized convolutions of biology and destiny. Rather, Hughes's canvas is the human experience itself. His years as a speech writer and political aide have given him a wealth of perspective on which to draw when elaborating both characters and the cultures in which they find themselves embedded.

For all that familiarity with the hearts and minds of his characters, Hughes chooses to work in a future as distant and disconnected as any Vancean saga from the workaday world in which we live. Our own present times barely poke up in *Template* in any discernible fashion. This is a brave eschewing of a narrative technique quite often employed to anchor a contemporary audience in a tale set a far distance across time or space. It also deprives readers of the clue-spotting which is a favored game of so many fans of far-future science fiction. There is no "Statue of Liberty in the sand" moment in these books, no point at which the light dawns and we can draw the line from today to tomorrow and beyond.

This distancing in Hughes's approach to his work creates a sense of difference which must be taken in and adapted to immediately on the first encounter, much as a new cuisine might be. It requires both investment and trust from the reader. Such commitments are easily given to the smooth, confident style that characterizes Hughes's writing. Still, this is one of the things which places the Archonate books firmly inside the canon of science fiction for good and all—a dependency on the reading protocols which are virtually unique to our field. That he does this with very little of either science or technology, while remaining firmly science fictional, is testament to the larger qualities of Hughes's auctorial art and craft.

Envision this dyad: a canvas too broad for the spread of a large man's arms; and a paintbox of colors which do not exist in the street outside your front door. Taking these together, you have a sense of the style and substance of Hughes's work, the man's sheer range of imagination. From this dioscuric pair he fashions a brightly-tinted matrioshka array of plots, places and passage of arms, turning through exotic locales and accessible emotional pathways, always with people at the center.

The realization of Hughes's universe is a delight as well, filled with incidental conceits and pleasances that ornament the setting while providing substance to both plot and character. His manifold lapidarian fantasies serve to capture the mind's eye as the reader passes them. The Mordene family foranq, for example, dances lightly with the reader's imagination. It is a great barge built and expanded across the generations of a sailing clan, a towering confection of naval architecture and folk art featuring "carved towers and minarets, painted arches and domes, most in white and gold, like a city from a children's tale but shrunk down to manageable dimensions and set upon a floating hull." Within are kitchens and dance halls and reliquaries and portraits of Mordenes down the generations. Yet this jewel, the lovingly described symbol of a family's victory over the ravages of time, is present on perhaps half a dozen pages within the book. Hughes lavishes the same frenzied level of detail on passing political systems, cultures and technology at every step in the narrative.

As rococo as the novel may be, ultimately *Template* owes more to Hari Seldon than Gully Foyle. The plot is advanced by machinations of men long dead yet still reaching out from within the graves of time. The will and deeds of these offstage protagonists are carried forward by proxies who themselves are often unconscious of their roles in the progress of events. Even with this very classic "invisible hand" plot in play, the novel's underpinnings are also profoundly modern. Identity paranoia and the price of progress lie at the core of the tale like twinned worms coiled round the heart of a dying prince. In at least one meaningful sense, the central question of the novel is quite literally that of who shall wear the coronet.

Hughes's first Archonate work was the novel *Fools Errant*, published in 1994. He has produced fifteen short stories and seven novels in this setting, not as a series *per se*, but as ventures into the world of his mind. I cannot say for certain if there is an overarching plot bridging the body of his work, but there certainly is a set of overarching themes. This is a Canadian sort of universe, bereft of the assumptive exceptionalism so embedded in American culture and literature, instead replaced with a constellation of norms which overlap and intertwine. People are in and of the world, and find their way through it. Like all good fiction, Hughes's work succeeds not for its strangeness, but for its familiarity. The hero's journey is our own journey, after all.

Template will be far from his last Archonate work, I should hope, with this voyage into the future extending into the decades to come for the profit of us all. Come sail his literary foranq and be amazed.

Jay Lake
November 2007

JAY LAKE *is the award-winning author of such novels as* Mainspring, Escapement, *and* Green, *as well as more than 250 short stories. He is a winner of the John W. Campbell Award for Best New Writer, and a multiple nominee for the Hugo and World Fantasy Awards.*

Chapter 1

The tall skinny one and the one with the shaved head kept circling to Conn Labro's right. When they came at him their attack was well coordinated, the points of their epiniards darting in at different angles, aimed at different parts of his body. Now they came again and Conn timed the double parry exactly, riposted against the skinny one so that he had to block the thrust in a way that hindered his partner's recovery.

But it was the third opponent who bothered him. The fat one kept circling widdershins to the others only to leap into the fight seemingly at random, not thrusting but flailing with the long thin epiniard while shouting what sounded like nonsense syllables. Conn would have to duck or leap back in an ungainly manner. Then the other two would come smoothly in and he would have to flick and click, parry and thrust again, trying to find their rhythm then turn it against them.

He soon realized that there was no rhythm to be found. The fat one was actually very good. He was capable, as very few are, of a truly asymmetrical attack, able to resist the unconscious urge to find a rhythm with his partners.

It was turning out to be an interesting contest. Conn surmised that the three must have practiced against a simulation based on some of his past fights. He knew that his employer, the impresario Ovam Horder, sold such artificial experiences to those who could never afford the fee required to meet Conn in the flesh or by remote connection. The trio must have augmented the simulation by factoring in other matches recorded from public performances, then using sophisticated means to meld all into one.

Now here came the two coordinated attackers once more, but this time there was a tiny disharmony to their movements. The skinny one was a quarter-beat behind his partner, meaning Conn must extend his parry an equally small interval of time past perfection before binding the skinny one's blade and sliding the point of Conn's epiniard over the wrist guard.

As he executed the move, he expected the fat one to come in swinging and burbling from his blind side. Instead, as Conn turned his head enough to bring the third man into his peripheral vision, he found the rotund attacker silently sliding toward him, crossing the smooth floor on his plump belly, the point of his weapon aimed at Conn's ankle.

Again, Conn had to make a less than graceful escape, leaping clear over the supine swordster, only to find the other two rushing at him once more. But they came on two different tangents this time, their flexible blades whipping and thrusting from all angles, so that Conn must exert near maximum speed to beat off the attack. And meanwhile, the fat one was coming in between the others, but this time he was actually on his knees, again aiming for Conn's ankles.

Conn felt a flash of irritation and automatically summoned the mental exercise that dissipated the feeling. He heard Hallis Tharp's voice speaking from his memory: *He who loses his temper loses all*, and again he spoke within his mind the syllables of the Lho-tso mantra that restored calm.

He flicked his point at the fat one's eyes, knocked away the bald man's thrust and sidestepped a slash from the thin one. He had to give the three of them credit for a novel strategy: they had known they could not win on skills—they were adequate swordsters, but even three of them were no match for one of Bay City's premier house players—so they had instead closely analyzed Conn's temperament. They must have thought that if they could annoy him enough, if they could bring him to anger . . . .

The three were preparing for another attempt. He saw their eyes signal to each other as they readied themselves, and he looked closely at the fat one. And there it was, plain to be seen: the calculation behind the seeming randomness, and the way the man looked at Conn from the corner of his eye, weighing up the results so far.

Conn realized how the bets must be laid. That was why their attacks lacked true brio and why the fat one behaved like a clown. They were not out to win, nor even to draw, which would have been the best they might expect. Instead, they were intent on annoying and frustrating him to the point where he departed from his legendary equanimity.

He smiled. The moment his lips showed his amusement he read the signs in the others' faces and knew he had won. They stepped back and lowered their epiniards. "Will you continue?" Conn asked.

"To what point?" said the fat one.

"It was a good attempt," Conn said, lowering his weapon and officially signaling to the house integrator that the match was over. The three contestants had chosen for the setting of their duel a deserted stretch of Bay City's docks at night, and now the warehouses and waves disappeared. He stood in one of the private rooms of Horder's Unparalleled Gaming Emporium.

"Where did we err?" said the skinny one.

Conn thought for a moment. "Too much foofaraw in his style," he said, indicating the fat one. "Or too much deliberation behind the zaniness. The incongruity was just a little too sharp to be convincing."

The skinny one spoke to his plump colleague, "I told you it would not be so easy."

The fat one shrugged. "Still, we have gained an important insight and we have a fine tale to tell over ale at the tavern tonight."

"But the insight has come at no small cost," said the thin pessimist. "I said we were wagering more than we could afford to lose."

"But you agreed the plan was sound."

"No, I said any plan appears sound until it leaves its creator's desk and confronts the tap-tip-and-tup of phenomenality."

The plump man's brows contracted. "I remember a different set of remarks altogether."

"I take no responsibility for your memories," said the thin man. "In any case, we did not lose so much that we now face indenture."

"Whatever," said the tall one, reaching into his pouch and producing a card. "We will pay what we owe."

"Not to me," said Conn, waving away the card. "Your debt is to Ovam Horder. I am not empowered to receive for him, only to game as he directs."

"I apologize," said the man, putting the card away. "But we will include a gratuity to express our thanks for the experience."

Conn bowed. Then he pressed a control at his waist. The three men disappeared. Somewhere, the skinny man was inserting his card into a reader which would conduct one end of a long-distance financial transaction with Conn's employer. The details were no concern of his.

The three hunters might be anywhere on the planet or even in one of the orbital communities that glittered in the night sky of Thrais, a modest-sized planet midway along the arm of the galaxy known as The Spray. Conn was where he almost always was during working hours: in a small room whose walls were densely packed with percepts and sensors that connected to the main integrator of Horder's Gaming Emporium.

Horder's enterprise was among the foremost of the many sporting houses along high-arching Blue Sky Concourse, a hill-climbing thoroughfare that rose to the commercial acropolis of Bay City, the planet's commercial capital. Gaming was the most significant industry on Thrais, where the citizens shared a passion for risking sums large and small on contests of skill or turns of chance.

The gaming business also drew contestants from other worlds, even sometimes from Old Earth far down The Spray. Some contestants came with their brains packed with elaborate systems they believed would overcome house odds in games of luck, others brought finely honed skills to try against house players like Conn.

Most went away with their purses lightened. A few risk-addicted plungers bet more than they could afford, gaming on credit extended by Ovam Horder and his ilk. These unfortunates never departed the planet again. On Thrais, said the law, if your purse could not settle a debt, your person would. The most unsavory tasks, such as the removal of street waste, were performed by indentured bankrupts. On some mornings, the waste would include the body of a plunger who had chosen to "stand out" from one of Bay City's tall buildings rather than face a life of indentured service.

Not all indentures led to insalubrious occupations. Many of Thrais's professionals—physicians, intercessors, organo-architects—had come to the planet driven by a pathological need to fling themselves into games of chance in which they lacked the skill or judgment that brought victory. They exchanged the grip of a gambling addiction for the grasp of an indenture contract, their debt being sold to whichever of the planet's several autonomies needed practitioners of their vocations. Free Thraisians supported the system wholeheartedly. They acquired many of the skilled professionals a developed society needed without the expense of educating them.

Occasionally, a bankrupt whose talents were almost, yet not quite, good enough to best the top house players would see his losses translated into indenture to Horder or one of the other sporting house owners. The new house player would spend the rest of his days contending against gamesters whose abilities were adjudged to be beneath his own. Each new indentee began his service clutching a fragile hope of amassing from gratuities the funds to regain freeman's rank; but as the days wore into years the scant hope would grow ever thinner, until one day its bearer would notice that it had evaporated, leaving only a faint mark on his inner being.

Conn was not one of those forcibly recruited from the ranks of the failed; he had been delivered as an unwanted infant to the doorstep of Horder's Gaming Emporium. A scan of his still developing synaptic articulation promised that he might, with training, become an exceptional house player. An account was opened in his name and regularly debited through the years of his upbringing until, by the time he was ready to begin his career in the games rooms, he was irredeemably obligated to Ovam Horder.

In theory, the sums he had won for his employer had long since repaid the debt. But on Thrais theory ran a distant second to practice. As soon as Conn had begun to win substantial purses—remarkably early in his career—Horder had taken advantage of a loophole in Thraisian law which allowed employers to use the debited funds indentees owed them to bet against their own house players. Every time Conn won for Horder, he lost for himself. But he could not offset those paper losses by betting on his own performance. Another cynical wrinkle in the planet's jurisprudence forbade it.

Stripping off the head-to-toe suit of pliofilm that he had worn to be challenged by the three duelists, Conn dressed in modest tunic and britches and pulled on knee hose and half boots. He adjusted the house player's insignia he wore at his collar, straightening the several hanging beads that testified to his proficiency, then spoke to the wall beside him. "I will go now to the Capricotte Salon and play paduay with the old man."

"Hallis Tharp has not come today," replied the emporium's integrator.

Conn was surprised. "He always comes the first day of the week."

"Today he has not come."

"Have you contacted him to find out why not? Perhaps he is ill."

"Yes. There was no reply."

"Did you contact any of his neighbors?"

"What would be the point of that?"

The house integrator exactly reflected the views of its proprietor. Horder stood to gain nothing from inquiring after the welfare of an old man, therefore no inquiries would be made. Likewise, there was nothing to be gained by Conn in seeking to know what had befallen his regular partner—opponent was not quite an accurate term—at the gentle game of paduay. Yet he felt an unaccountable urge to find out.

"Summon an aircar," he said. "Charge it to my account."

"Your time has been reallocated," said the integrator. "A customer has engaged you for a full-flesh contest of epiniards."

"Who is it?"

"He gave his name as Hasbrick Gleffen."

"He is not local." Conn knew all the Thraisians who might seek a full-flesh encounter.

"No, an offworlder. He has pre-paid from a bank draft from Old Earth."

The integrator's remark recalled a disremembered fact to the front of Conn's mind. "Hallis Tharp paid in advance, years ago," he said. "Is his permanent contract for my services still in force?"

The integrator made no reply.

"Is not our paduay session already paid for?" Conn insisted.

There was a pause, then the integrator said, "Yes."

"Then I am on the old man's time. Summon the aircar."

"I cannot. You must speak with Ovam Horder."

"Connect me."

A moment later his employer's overfleshed face appeared in the air before him. Conn made no ceremony but stated his intentions in a cool way.

Subtle marks of vexation disturbed the smooth hummocks of flesh that were Horder's features. "It would be better if you stayed to deal with the offworld contestant."

Conn was surprised to discover that his first reaction was to consider open defiance. He had leverage, if he chose to use it, but had never yet found himself in circumstances that warranted an all-out clash. As one of the most capable house players on Thrais, ranked grand master in a variety of competitive arts, he was regularly approached by other sporting houses. Any other indentor could purchase his contract by paying Horder the total of his accrued debt plus a percentage. But the transaction required Conn's concurrence.

The situation made for an interesting relationship between Conn and Horder. Within a certain range, the valuable player could extract concessions from his proprietor. The limits of Conn's leeway had never been fully tested, and the present disagreement over the fate of an old man ought not to constitute grounds for serious head butting. Yet he was strongly motivated to find out about his missing paduay partner, though he could not account for the source or strength of the impulse.

TEMPLATE

In less time than it took him to blink he sorted through optional strategies in response to Horder's statement of preference and chose to slip the confrontation rather than respond to it.

"I am concerned about Hallis Tharp," he said. "If I can allay my disquiet I will be better able to acquit myself against this offworlder in a live contest."

"Hmm," said Horder.

"To what degree is the bout with this Gleffen?"

"Blood or breakage."

"Do we know his form?"

"No," said Horder. "He claims to have trained at a private school. There is a whiff of aristocratic amateur about him."

"Then he may be good. I will need to be at my peak, without distractions," said Conn.

"That is so."

Having moved his opponent to weaker footing, Conn increased the pressure. "And besides, our paduay sessions are always lengthy, whereas a live contest is usually brief, once the formalities are over."

"True."

"So I could take an aircar to the old man's house, ease my mind about him, and return in ample time for the contest."

Horder moved his porcine features in a way that signaled the matter was of no concern. Conn recognized that his employer was conceding defeat without acknowledging that there had ever been a contest.

"Why do you care about that old man?" Horder said.

"I do not know. It puzzles me."

The proprietor affected a look that said the issue was beneath his notice. "Return soon. I will entertain Gleffen with accounts of your victories."

"That will either unsettle him or impel him to greater efforts," Conn said.

"The latter, I hope," said Horder. "He may feel an urge to increase his wager."

The aircar collected Conn on the third floor landing stage of the gaming house, which reared up fifteen stories from the ground level arcade, through several tiers of private gaming rooms of various dimensions to the employees' living quarters on the upper levels and Horder's luxurious penthouse. The roof, artfully landscaped and covered by a retractable transparent dome, was for private contests such as the scheduled bout with Hasbrick Gleffen, where the contestants met, not through remote sensor telemetry, but in their own vulnerable flesh.

Though he had known Hallis Tharp for as long as he could remember, Conn did not know his address. The time that he had spent outside the sporting house since he was delivered to it as an infant would not amass to a single day. But when he gave his paduay partner's name to the aircar it consulted its records and lifted off. Conn clung to a stanchion and shifted his feet on the impermeable floor as the vehicle banked and accelerated. If Ovam Horder had ever deigned to hire a public conveyance he would have summoned a spotlessly clean phaeton with plush seats and deep pile carpeting. But even a renowned house player rated no more than a utilitarian flying platform.

The aircar inserted itself into the east-west flow of aerial traffic and hummed toward a row of vast but anonymous residential blocks that indented the skyline in the Skrey district. The most charitable characterization of the area was that it was Bay City's least fashionable suburb; it would be more accurate to say that it was simply not fashionable to any degree. Its inhabitants pursued lives of desperation, never farther away from indenture than one missed rent payment.

The vehicle let Conn off at a ground floor entrance of a massive edifice built of synthetic stone, whose designer had conceived of it solely as a box in which to keep people. Every line was straight, every angle at ninety degrees and every surface unadorned. The building's entry was heavily fortified by metal bars over transparent shatterproof doors whose surfaces had been occluded by daubed initials and symbols. Conn knew that parts of Skrey were afflicted by criminal organizations, the residents being able to afford only the most rudimentary police services.

"Remain until I return," he told the aircar.

"If it is in my interest," the vehicle replied.

"I will pay a ten percent premium."

"Agreed, but the contract is void if unsavory elements interfere."

There was a who's-there set into the wall beside the building's entrance. Conn identified himself and told it he wished to see Hallis Tharp. Time stretched through several long moments while he waited, then the who's-there said, "He does not answer."

Conn said, "You did not say he was not at home, only that he did not answer."

The device made no reply.

"Is he there or not? He may be ill."

"I am empowered to violate residents' privacy only in an emergency."

"Then consider this an emergency. Examine Hallis Tharp's residence and tell me what you see."

There was a briefer delay, then the who's-there said, "Hallis Tharp sits in a chair facing the window."

"Compare him to the last image you have of him. How does he now seem?"

"Parts of him are missing," said the device. "Also, he does not appear to breathe."

A pang passed through Conn. He could not account for it. "Let me in."

"I should summon the incumbent," said the who's-there, referring to the neighborhood's resident agent for police services.

"Who will pay his fee?" said Conn. "Hallis Tharp is in no condition to meet the obligation."

"His estate must pay."

"Do you see any valuable possessions in his room?"

"No. His circumstances are sparse."

"And death tends to diminish his worth as an indentee."

"That is so."

"So your proprietor, the building's owner, will be liable for the incumbent's charges," said Conn. "Is he likely to welcome them?"

"No. He prefers not to incur obligations."

"Then let me in. Perhaps this matter can be resolved without complications."

The door buzzed and swung open.

"Which unit?" Conn said.

"West fourteen-eleven."

"Is it locked?"

"Yes."

"Then unlock it and show me the way."

The tiny lobby had a sour and musty smell. There was an ascender but when Conn placed his hand in it he felt no uplift. He climbed the stairs to the fourteenth floor then followed the building's baseboard lighting directions through a labyrinth of corridors and passages that brought him to a cul de sac and a bare metal door in a wall whose paint was peeling. He pressed the control stud and the door slid sideways into the wall. He stepped through the opening and it closed behind.

Hallis Tharp was bound to an unpretentious chair under the light from the room's single window. There was blood in his disordered white hair and bruising on his face. His age-spotted hands lay upturned in his lap like two small dead animals. Some of the fingernails were missing.

Conn examined him. None of the injuries were life threatening nor did they seem to be extensive. But the old man's mouth drooped on one side, as if he had suffered a massive stroke. Conn suspected that he had died suddenly in the midst of the torture. It must have been a disappointment to whoever had subjected him to such mistreatment.

"Integrator," he said to the air, "who has visited Hallis Tharp today?" There was no response. He realized that the building's system had to be manually activated and looked about for the control. He found it on a wall. It required the insertion of a coin before it would respond. When the connection was made he repeated the question.

"He has had no visitor today," said the integrator.

"Nonsense." Conn put his hand on the old man's neck. The flesh was still slightly warm. "His assailants left here not long since."

"I saw nothing."

Conn examined the percept set in the room's low ceiling. "Does this detect only visual light?"

"And high-temperature heat sources, in which case the fire suppression system activates."

Elision suits, Conn thought. Their fabric bent light around itself, letting the wearer move about unseen. He had used their virtual equivalents in contests. He corrected himself: he had been automatically assuming it would require at least two attackers to catch and immobilize the old man without drawing attention; but an elision suit would allow a single capable man to do the work.

He might even still be in the room.

Conn assumed a defensive posture, turned this way and that, tilting his head at various angles to examine the room from the corners of his eyes. Looked at straight on, the light-bending suit conferred invisibility, but peripheral vision would detect a shimmer of motion. He saw nothing.

His rotation had left him facing away from the door, so it was the *swish* of its opening that spun him around. A young woman, slight of figure and dark of hair, stood in the doorway, her startlingly green eyes wide as they moved from Conn to the corpse in the chair.

She dropped the bag she had been carrying, spilling vegetables and packages across the threshold, and fled. Conn pursued her and caught her at the door of another room that was opening to her touch. She fought him energetically but naively until he applied pressure to a point on her throat.

He carried her into the room, giving it a quick inspection before he placed her on a rudimentary couch made of sturdy cartons and foam insulation. The space was as tiny and almost as bare as Hallis Tharp's, but brightened by a colored print of a landscape affixed to the wall. Conn glanced at it, drew an impression of trees, rolling hills, a gabled white house, a mottled blue sky. *Offworld*, he thought. There was a tattered poster on another wall advertising Chabriz's Traveling Show, an itinerant exposition that had broken up on Thrais some time before.

The young woman gave a sharp intake of breath and regained consciousness. In one blink her eyes went from dazed to panicked. She made to rise from the couch but Conn was beside her, one hand pressing her down with a grip intended to remind her of how their former struggle had ended.

He was adept at reading eyes. It was a necessary skill in his profession. He saw fear mingled with outrage, then saw both transpose into sorrow. "Why did you kill Hallis Tharp?" she said.

"I did not."

"I saw what you did to him! Why would you do that?"

"I did not," Conn repeated. "We were to meet today. When he did not come I grew concerned. I came and found him dead."

Her eyes changed again. "You are Conn Labro," she said.

"Yes." He was surprised but did not show it. "Who are you?" he said.

"Jenore Mordene. Let me up."

He saw that she was no longer afraid of him and that she intended neither to fight nor flee. He relinquished his grip. She rose and crossed the room to a small cupboard, opened it and withdrew a large, flat box of polished wood. Conn recognized it immediately.

She said, "He said if anything ever happened to him that you would come and I was to give you this."

Conn took the familiar object but did not open it. He sat on the couch and rested the box on his knees. He was conscious of a powerful sense of loss, as if he had been thrashed in a contest. The emotion confused him, seemed out of place.

Her voice broke into his thoughts. "What is that thing?"

Conn looked up. "His paduay set. We played for two hours each week at Horder's Gaming Emporium."

She looked at him as if he had told her that the old man orchestrated moonbeams. "He played games? How could he afford the stakes? He lived on one meal a day and that no more than soup."

The issue had never occurred to Conn, but he thought about it now. "We did not wager on outcomes. And he bought a lifetime contract for my services when I was still a child and not costly."

"But why?"

"He did not play games with you?" he asked.

She gestured to the window. "In Skrey, people have more pressing business than trying to defeat each other in artificial settings. Real life is contest enough."

"Paduay is not a contest," he said. "The game is about cooperatively opening and closing spaces, theoretically without conclusion. It is unusual in that each player's goal is to prevent the other from being unable to continue."

"And he played this every week?"

"Our current match has been going on continually for almost two years. I can show you the dispositions."

"Spare me," she said.

Conn ignored her. He would open the set. But when he set his fingers to the catches that would unlatch the box he felt a strong urge not to see again the miniature pieces, the grids of straight and curving lines that could intersect each other in a variety of different spatial dimensions, depending on which of several modes the players invoked.

It was an unsettling burst of emotion. His analytical function recognized that it was tied somehow to Hallis Tharp, not just to the old man's death, but to their long association: all the Firstday mornings they had sat on opposite sides of this apparatus of wood and metal, ever since Conn's boyhood. It was not a memory he now wished to explore.

He handed the paduay set back to Jenore Mordene. "Here," he said, "I will have no further use for this."

"But he wanted you to have it."

"It does not matter what he wanted. He no longer exists."

She took the box and held it to her breast. "I don't understand you people," she said. He could see that she was resisting tears. For some reason, her emotion made him uncomfortable. He stood up and said, "Well," then turned to the door.

"What are we going to do about him?" the woman asked, her moist eyes indicating the wall beyond which the old man's corpse sat in the chair.

"What was your relationship to Hallis Tharp?"

"We were friends."

The term had several meanings on Thrais. When applied to the connection between a solitary old man and a young woman, it was usually a euphemism for intimate transactions that the participants preferred not to discuss in bald language.

Conn nodded then saw the expression on her face change again to anger. He had somehow offended her.

"Not like that!" she said. She folded her arms across her chest and gripped her elbows. "What is the matter with you people? Do none of you know what friends are?" She flung her arms wide and said, "Does it always have to be about this?" She touched the first two fingers of one hand to its thumb and rubbed them quickly together.

Conn was not sure what the gesture signified. He was moved to inquire but at that moment his communicator called for his attention. It was Ovam Horder.

"Where are you? Hasbrick Gleffen inquires if you are ready to engage him."

"Has he arrived?"

"Not yet. But he wishes to arrive at the contest venue before you do."

"That is contrary to etiquette," Conn said. "He has challenged me and should enter after I have agreed to receive him."

"He is an offworlder. Perhaps this is how things are done where he hails from."

"It might be intended as a subtle insult."

He heard Horder sigh. "I will levy a surcharge and credit it to your account."

It was a reasonable response. Conn said, "Very well. I am on my way." He put away the communicator.

"Wait," said Jenore Mordene. "What are we to do about . . ." Something impeded her speech and she gestured toward the hallway.

"Was he a member of a funeral society?"

She shook her head. She seemed to be resisting tears.

"Then the building will summon a recycler. They will take care of things."

"They will want to be paid," she said, and he detected an uncalled-for bitterness in her tone.

"Sell the paduay set, if you wish."

He saw her hands tighten on the box. "No."

"There will be enough value in his . . . attributes to cover the recycler's cost."

"His attributes?"

It was not a subject usually discussed in blunt terms. "His materials," Conn said. "What he is made of."

She made a gesture that again he found hard to interpret, but he had neither the time nor the inclination to seek a clarification. "I must go," he said and made for the door.

"Wait," she said.

He stopped and turned, puzzled. She indicated the paduay set in her hand. "How can you not want this?"

"I cannot imagine playing paduay again," he said. "My time is too expensive and the demand for the game is scant."

She appeared to be about to say something else, but instead she turned to the window and gazed out at the harshness of Skrey.

The aircar was no longer at the curb. It had elevated itself to a height several stories above the street, out of range of a half dozen bubblers congregated around the building's entrance. The young men looked Conn over as he stepped through the portal, their faces and body language equally obscured by the semitransparent armor of synthetic material which covered their entire forms like suits of overlapping bronze bubbles.

Conn looked back at them impassively. He had fought in the armor and against it many times. Well-bred gamesters enjoyed taking on street toughs, at least in virtual encounters. He knew the bubbler's strengths and weaknesses and had no doubt that he could deal with a group of young amateurs. They rarely fought amongst themselves, or even against other gangs, reserving their violence for those in the neighborhood who did not pay for their "protection."

For their part, the bubblers noted the insignia and rank beads on the collar of Conn's tunic and formed the collective opinion that something much more interesting was probably happening down the street and around the corner. They moved off, though at a deliberately leisurely pace. Conn summoned the aircar and boarded it.

As the vehicle took him back to the center of the city his communicator chirped. It was Horder again. "The offworlder is finicky," Conn's employer said. "He wishes to know exactly how long before you arrive at the arena. Meanwhile he insists that I be here in the third garden to dance attendance upon him."

Conn had to juggle the communication device in order to retain his grasp on the car's stanchion while the vehicle wove through traffic in three dimensions. "He is rude," he said, "even for an offworlder. I have heard no good reports of Old Earth and this man's conduct confirms my view."

"You are right," said Horder. "I will double the surcharge."

"No," said Conn. "Say to him that I am in transit now. I will be in the third garden shortly. We will omit the formalities and I will teach this one a lesson."

"I would prefer you to be of tranquil mind. He may be good. If you are injured, several upcoming engagements would have to be canceled or postponed."

"I am calm," Conn said, reflexively applying the Lho-tso technique. "This man will not leave Thrais as 'one of the few.'" He referred to the scant handful of combatants who had bested or tied Conn in full-flesh combat. It had been a long time since there had been a new addition to the select group. "I am, however, more motivated than usual today."

"I see. Did you find the old man?"

"I found him dead."

"Ah," said Horder, "that will free you up for two hours a week."

"Yes."

"I will contact Gleffen immediately and tell him I am in the third garden and that you are expected soon." He broke the connection.

The aircar swooped and sashayed through traffic that grew denser as they neared the city center. Conn could see the Emporium. The day was warm and moderately humid, as were most days in Bay City—the metropolis sprawled around the littoral of a sheltered bight of the Serpentine Sea close to Thrais's equator. Horder would have ordered the roof dome retracted as soon as the two suns cleared the surrounding towers.

The third garden was an elongated oval floored with short grass and shaded by mature heaven trees. It would be cool and fragrant at this time of the day, perfect for the lightning-quick exchanges that characterized a duel by epiniards. Conn decided he would absorb the first few passages passively, to take the measure of this Hasbrick Gleffen. Then, if he found that the man's fighting skills did not excuse his personality, he would teach the offworlder a grim lesson.

He recognized that he was allowing himself to become irritated and reflexively performed the mental exercise that expunged the emotion. When his clarity of mind was restored, he sorted through his thought processes and was mildly surprised to discover that the irritant had come from more than just the Old Earther's arrogance; it also had something to do with what had happened to Hallis Tharp. There was irony in that, Conn knew: strong emotion had often been one of the old man's topics of conversation while they traded moves in the gentle game of paduay. Conn could replay Tharp's voice in his head: *He who loses his temper loses the contest*, was one of his frequent observations, usually followed by, *You must never give in to anger*. In Tharp's view, for Conn to accede to any overwhelming passion was an error, but anger was the worst of all.

The aircar dropped lower, slid around the Hi-Flite Tower and angled down toward Horder's Emporium. Its brakes deployed to slow its descent and Conn had to grasp the stanchion tighter as the vehicle juddered and bounced. He saw the canopy of trees above the third garden and, through a gap in the foliage, the foreshortened figure of Ovam Horder pacing in apparent agitation, his hand to his ear as he spoke into his communicator.

The car decelerated further, aiming for a landing stage near the roof's center. As it positioned itself for a vertical descent to the hard surface, Conn caught a flash of intense light from the corner of his eye. In less time than he could have formed words to express it, his mind told him that a line of incandescent air had arrowed down from the sky to strike the third garden.

His head turned instinctively toward the movement, but instantly the smeared window of the aircar was rendered opaque by a glaring explosion. Even as it faded, leaving spots of red and black in his vision, he saw the heaven trees in flame and bursting outwards. Then the shockwave of the blast struck the aircar and flung it out and away from the Emporium.

Conn was thrown against the unpadded walls, battered and tossed like a pea in a rattle as the vehicle tumbled through the air for long seconds before its stabilizers could restore equilibrium. When it finally settled, he was sprawled on the hard floor. He checked himself, found no broken bones, but the shoulder of the arm that had been curled around the stanchion had been wrenched almost out of its socket and a cut on his scalp was pouring blood down his face.

Then he looked toward the Emporium. The third garden was surrounded by charred and blasted trees, stripped of their leaves and blossoms, many of them tilted outwards and leaning against each other. And where the grass had been, where Ovam Horder had been, was a roil of flame and black smoke.

Chapter 2

The fire was soon out. Ovam Horder had paid for Platinum Plus service, so within minutes of the event a flying platform had positioned itself above the Emporium, its precipitators wringing the surrounding air of its water, which was mixed with suppressants and directed onto the inferno.

Damage was confined to the roof and the executive offices below the third garden, where the Emporium's second in command and its owner's sole heir, Saffraine Horder, had been tallying quarterly returns. She had been as thoroughly incinerated as her father, leaving the proprietorship a problematical affair. There were apparently relatives on New Ark, a planet farther down The Spray, and the Arbitration—the facsimile of central government on Thrais—was making efforts to contact them.

Horder had paid even more for security services—Platinum Double-plus—and his death did not cancel the contract, so Conn Labro was soon brought to a small room in the basement of the First Response Protection Corporation where he was subjected to a full-spectrum interrogation. FRP's senior discriminator, Hilfdan Klepht, a lean, long-nosed man with eyes that drooped but missed nothing, handled the session personally.

Conn told him all that he knew; the drugs and induced hypnosis of a full-spectrum inquisition left him no option. Klepht questioned him intently not only about the challenge from Hasbrick Gleffen but about his finding of Hallis Tharp's corpse and his interview with Jenore Mordene. She too was brought in for questioning, Conn gathered from questions he was asked in his second session with Klepht. Tharp's body was also recovered from the recycling center and examined minutely.

Klepht turned out to be a follower of Conn's career, having watched many of his more celebrated bouts. The discriminator soon eliminated the player from suspicion and even satisfied some of Conn's curiosity about the investigation.

23

The weapon that had destroyed Ovam Horder had been an impedance pulse generated by a private spacecraft in orbit above Thrais. The ship had immediately departed at top speed, making for the nearest whimsy, through which it had leaped to who knew where. Its drive signal had been captured and recorded, so if it ever appeared above Thrais again without having retuned its engines, it could be recognized and apprehended, but Klepht agreed with Conn that such an eventuality was unlikely.

They speculated together about motive. Conn suggested that the villain might have been one of Horder's competitors who wished to acquire some of the murdered impresario's assets, perhaps even Conn's own indenture contract. "He was, after all, careful to make sure I was not in the target area."

Klepht discounted the theory as amateur. "There is a longstanding mutual agreement among the gaming tycoons, backed by serious sanctions authorized by the Arbitration, to forbid such an action. If one them ever tried it and was found out, he would lose everything, including his own freedom. You know as well as I do that the professional gambler never risks what he cannot afford to lose."

The discriminator steepled his fingers. "My experience of these affairs, which is long and varied, teaches that the simplest explanation is usually the correct one," he said. "Ovam Horder was a taker and collector of wagers. Most were of a small to moderate size but some were large and a few were gargantuan. Someone may have reasoned that, rather than pay Horder, it was more economical to absorb the costs of hiring a person who had the required ship and weapon and was unencumbered by qualms about using them." Klepht said he would delve into the Emporium's official books, but he believed that Horder had kept some transactions in a private ledger that never left his person. "It was, of course, consumed with him. So we may never know, unless someone someday publishes a last laugh."

The posthumous confession was an institution on Thrais. One who had gotten away with taking secret revenge on an enemy would arrange for the details of the operation to be made public once the perpetrator was safely dead. The stories were published in a special section of the newsfeed and were popularly believed to be truth, although sometimes several dead revanchists claimed responsibility for the same outrage. Their competing claims could lead to furious exchanges of opinion in the letters section, occasionally resulting in duels. Sometimes, if there was a paying client, a police service like FRP would reopen a case in light of the details contained in a last laugh and make an official determination.

"So you do not believe that I was any part of the scenario?" Conn said.

"I do not," said Chief Discriminator Klepht. "Still, if you encounter any unusual circumstances, you could keep us informed."

R epairs were made to the roof and operations at the Emporium continued much as before, the staff processing clients and accounts under the supervision of a trustee from the Arbitration. Weeks went by before news came that Ovam Horder's relatives, a pair of elderly aunts who lived on the southern continent of New Ark and grew meatflowers for export to connoisseurs, had been located and apprised of their inheritance.

The two spinster sisters declined to travel to Thrais and take up the reins that had been blasted from their nephew's smoldering hands. They contracted with an auction service to sell Horder's assets and send them the proceeds so that they could build new beds in which to grow the heavy-lobed blossoms which were their passion. As one of the Emporium's prime assets, Conn Labro's indenture contract was listed by an individual lot number. Many of the lesser-ranked players were sold as pairs and trios, and the foot soldiers went in batches.

The sale was conducted in the first basement of the Emporium, a vast, brightly lit space in which team sports like hack and hussade were usually played. The open center was ringed by bleachers from which aficionados could cry encouragement or hurl abuse. Today they were filled with an assortment of bidders: Horder's competitors, come to acquire prime stock; job-lotters who would sell their purchases to downstream buyers; and sentimentalists who craved a keepsake of time spent on the premises. Some of the bidders had not come in person—their representatives sat in the front row, communicators at ears and lips, ready to bid on command—but every first-ranked sporting house owner was present. Conn noticed Discriminator Klepht, unremarkable in a nondescript daysuit, seated among the ordinaries, his calm eyes winnowing the crowd.

Horder's goods were auctioned in inverse order of value, the minor items going first. The auctioneer, a stocky man dressed in clashing colors, with a perpetually roseate face and tufts of ginger hair that sprang from his bald skull like islands in a pond of skin, was expert in his profession: he would build drama and tension to the ultimate, knowing that raising the bidders' passions would raise their bids.

Conn's contract was third to last on the sale docket, making his services the most valuable asset of the Emporium after its custom-grown integrator and the building itself. He sat in the showing area, watching as former colleagues were ordered dispersed across the face of Thrais, a few even bound offworld.

As always, his mind was a calm, cool place, and he found interest in reassessing other sporting house's strengths and lacks now that they were acquiring Horder's well-balanced stable of talents. After today, the relative statures of the various game emporia would change, but the crucial decider would come near the end of the auction when he and Horder's integrator—rich in strategies and hard-won experience—went to new owners. If the two of them were bought together by a house that already possessed a strong cadre of players, it would alter the dynamics of a number of professional leagues and excite legions of enthusiasts and bettors. The auction had proceeded to where the cream of Horder's stable were on the block. Conn was watching a tense bidding competition for Abel Caspriano's contract between Gedreon's Myrmidons and The Red House when a boy approached him with a communicator. He took the device and activated it.

"It is Jenore Mordene," said the voice. There was no image, but his memory immediately offered him the sight of her as she had been in her small room, holding Hallis Tharp's paduay set in her delicate hands, her green eyes filled with unshed tears.

"What do you wish of me?" he said. He had divided his attention to speak with her while continuing to follow the struggle for Caspriano. Now he became uncomfortably aware of a third stream coursing through his mind, but this was not a stream of thought; instead, it was a surge of emotions, mixed and inchoate—sorrow, anger, abandonment, hate, loss—all tumbling and tangling against each other in a maelstrom of feelings such as he could never remember having experienced before. He was required to calm his inner sea, exercising techniques that he had employed since boyhood.

"I'm sorry," he said into the communicator when he had reestablished his characteristic stillness. "Please repeat that."

The woman told him that she had lost a day's pay while being held for questioning by Hilfdan Klepht, then had been fined another day's wages for not giving notice to her employer that she would be arrested and unable to report her impending absence. The loss of income meant that she had faced eviction and a subsequent likelihood of either being seized by the local bubblers and forced into prostitution or convicted for vagrancy and sold.

"The only thing of value I had was Hallis's game. I took it to the pledgeman. While he was examining it I found something with your name on it."

"What was it?"

She described a thin wafer of anodized metal the size of her thumb. On one side was the logo of a security house; on the other was a strip of adhesive with the name *Conn* printed in Hallis Tharp's spiky hand.

"It is a key," Conn said. "I will come for it as soon as I am able."

"I'm at home," she said. "I'm sorry about the game."

"It does not matter," he said, but even as he spoke he had to put down another welling of emotion that denied the meaning of the words. He broke the connection and applied the exercises again, but the necessity of doing so caused him to wonder at the complexity of his own being.

Caspriano went to Gedreon, representing a significant strengthening of the Myrmidons' capabilities in both squad-level combats and abstract strategic planning. Conn speculated on what it would be like to face his old colleague; it seemed likely he would, since the price Caspriano had brought surely left not enough in Gedreon's coffers to bid for Conn Labro.

The auctioneer called Conn's lot number and a murmur went through the crowd. Conn rose and made his way to the platform in front of the podium and stood while the glib voice above and behind him recounted his accomplishments and suggested pointedly that further remarkable achievements could be expected. The figure at which he opened the bidding was substantial enough to bring audible gasps from the crowd, but it was soon surpassed as the cream of Thrais's sporting impresarios weighed in.

The bids came quickly at first then slowed as lesser luminaries reached their limits and dropped out. Now there were four buyers still in play:

TEMPLATE

Gombar Palray of the New Colosseum, tugging with plump fingers at his pendulous lower lip as he gauged the competition; Tadeuz Kopt of Big Circle Engagement, cool as the ice his eyes resembled; Wagram Eig of The Red House, looking as if he had scored a point— Conn hypothesized that Eig had bid up Teck Gedreon over Caspriano to eliminate a competitor for the prize he truly sought; and a compact, competent-looking man in gray and umber who sat in the front row. He had not bid before.

As the bidding continued Conn assessed the different situations that would ensue if each of the three known contenders for his services was successful. On the whole, he would prefer to go to Big Circle: the house's existing complement, including two of Horder's better players acquired today, would mesh with Conn's own abilities to offer opponents a varied and flexible field with significant depth in every genre of conflict. But scarcely had he formed the opinion than it was rendered nuncupative. Tadeuz Kopt waved away the auctioneer's inquiry and left the bidding to the other three. Two rounds later, Gombar Palray also went to the sidelines, leaving only Wagran Eig of The Red House and the anonymous bidder still in play.

Now Conn focused on the person in gray and umber, whose turn it was to bid. The man was lean of feature with slitted eyes that focused on the air before him as if there was no one else in the room. His hands barely moved as he made the bid.

The auctioneer went to Eig and in a dozen tiny tells and cues Conn could read the thoughts behind the fat man's supposedly impassive face. Eig had already achieved part of what he had come for: Conn Labro had not gone to any of his top league competitors. The man in gray and umber must be bidding for an offworld client; if he took Thrais's best professional player out of competition it would be a loss for the world's gaming industry, but it could be a meaningful improvement in The Red House's competitive position.

The bids had been rising by five percent increments. Eig held up his hand, fingers spread, to signal that it should do so once more. The man in gray and umber looked at his timepiece and the scalp beneath his close-cropped blond hair rippled as his brows drew down. He looked at the auctioneer and displayed all ten fingers, indicating a bid ten percent over Eig's last. There was a gasp from the crowd, even from some of the major luminaries, that was followed by a rhubarb of comment when the man flashed both hands again; the bid was not ten but twenty percent above Eig's.

Conn saw the Red House proprietor's eyes widen slightly, then the fleshy lips made a moue of acceptance. Eig spread his hands, palms down, and the matter was settled. The auctioneer closed the sale and waved Conn toward the recorder's stall behind the podium. The man in gray and umber came to join them. As Conn crossed the floor he glanced toward Hilfdan Klepht and saw the discriminator watching the man's progress with a thoughtful mien.

The formalities were brief: the purchaser produced a draft on the Thrais branch of an interworld transaction exchange. The recorder transferred the purchase price and added the auction service's fee then annotated Conn's indenture contract so that it declared his services to be the property of Flagit

Holdings, a company registered in the canton of Trintrinobolis on Bashaw, a world renowned throughout The Spray for the discretion of its business law.

The recorder passed the revised indenture under a scanner which advised the Arbitration's integrators of the transaction, and the deal was done. The man in gray and umber, whose name appeared on the contract as Chask Daitoo, folded the document then turned to Conn and said, "A vehicle waits outside. You will come."

"Where are we going?"

"I have some business at the Arbitration then we will go offworld."

"Where offworld?"

"The matter does not concern you."

"I wish to collect a personal effect," Conn said.

Daitoo's face maintained its outward composure, but Conn read other emotions beneath the seeming calm: annoyance, offended pride, well-curtailed fear. "We have no time for self-indulgence."

"It is my right."

Conn saw irritation and arrogance move closer to the surface then noticed that a portion of Daitoo's anxiety leaked from its containment when Klepht's voice said from behind him, "He is correct. He has the right to collect personal property."

Daitoo turned to the discriminator, who had come down from the stands and now seemed intent on inspecting the purchaser's agent closely. The officer also gently took the indenture from the man's hand and gave it an unhurried perusal. "Bashaw," he said in a neutral tone before handing it back.

"Yes," Daitoo confirmed.

"First Response has had dealings with the Bashaw federal police," Klepht said.

"I have not," said the agent. He turned to Conn. "Where is this personal property?"

"The key to it is in Skrey. The property itself is in a security box at Allguard Trust."

Now Conn saw a tinge of something else—avarice, perhaps?—creep into the gestalt of the agent's expression, along with a brief overlay of alarm quickly suppressed. "This was not mentioned in the inventory."

"I did not become aware of the property until moments ago," Conn said.

Hilfdan Klepht was attending to the conversation with interest. Daitoo showed an inclination to be away from the discriminator's presence. "Very well," he said. "We will go to collect your effects then proceed as planned."

As the aircar lifted off from the ground floor landing stage, Conn turned to look back at Horder's Unparalleled Gaming Emporium. He had spent almost every moment of his life since early infancy within its confines. Now, as he watched its bulk dwindle behind him, he felt an unaccustomed sentiment. Curious, he probed at the feeling and a succession of images was presented to his inward vision: his first victory as a junior singleton; his first championship in a worldwide league; his personal training room where he had often worked for hours at a stretch to amplify his skills; the intimate chamber where he had sat with Hallis Tharp, fingers clicking over the paduay pieces while the old man sought to distract him with aimless chatter about worlds he would never see and situations he would never face.

Regret, he told himself, *and a desire to recover what cannot be brought back.* He had experienced the former emotion before, in his youth when he had failed to master an opponent, in his maturity when an able adversary made a gross error and allowed an engaging contest to come too early to a conclusion. The latter emotion had never visited him before. He allowed it to lie upon his consciousness for a few moments but, finding that the experience brought no reward, he employed the techniques that dismissed it back to wherever it had come from.

When they had entered the aircar, Daitoo had instructed it to take them to Skrey. Now, as they slid toward the gray anonymity of that district, he bid Conn tell the vehicle the exact address. Conn spoke the coordinates into the car's ear and there was a slight change of direction. More interesting was the sudden alteration in Daitoo's disposition. It was but the tiniest flex of a minor facial muscle, and Conn caught it only from the corner of his eye. He gave no hint of his perception, instead turning his head as if to gaze out over the parks and precincts of the neighborhood known as the Glebe passing below, meanwhile taking note of the set of Daitoo's features and the increased rigidity of his posture.

He said to the aircar, "Contact Jenore Mordene," and gave her communicator code. The minimal apparatus in her room did not offer a visual connection so after the sound of her coin being deposited in the device it was only her voice that came into the vehicle. Conn told her that they would set down outside her building in a short time.

"I'll meet you downstairs," she said.

Conn sat back and considered what he had learned. The address was of significance to Chask Daitoo. Unless the man was exceptionally proficient at controlling the micro-motions of his facial muscles, and there was no evidence to suggest he was, the name and voice of Jenore Mordene meant nothing—neither had evoked a reaction.

The vehicle landed softly and the two men emerged and approached the building. Before Conn could announce himself to the who's-there he saw motion through the scarred transparency of the door. It opened and Jenore appeared, her hand reaching into a pocket of her utilitarian smock and producing the metal wafer.

He watched her face. She regarded him with the same openness of expression he had seen before: no calculation, no suppressed emotion, although he saw an underlayer of sadness that bordered on despair. Then her eyes went past him to focus on Daitoo, and now he read in her face a succession of reactions: first, mere recognition, as if Daitoo's was a face seen before though not much noted; then mild confusion as she realized that the two men had arrived together at the door not by coincidence but because they were connected; finally, alarm.

Conn was already turning as the last expression registered on Jenore's face. Daitoo was to his left and close behind him. Now the man was moving backwards and his right hand had closed around a compact dark object that Conn realized must have been ejected into his palm from a holster up his sleeve. Daitoo was lifting the weapon to bring its emitter to bear on him.

With an economy of motion, Conn's left arm flicked out to bring the back of his hand into contact with Daitoo's wrist, knocking his aim askew. The energy pistol discharged in a coruscating burst of intensity that struck the wall beside the who's-there. A light sconce burst in an explosion of flaming metal. The sound of an automatic alarm scarcely overpowered the force of Jenore's scream.

Daitoo was well trained and far from inexperienced, Conn thought. The agent was still falling back, even allowing himself to topple backwards as he swung the weapon again toward Conn. The player now read nothing in the agent's face but a professional's concentration on the task in hand.

Conn was still pivoting on his left foot. He kicked out with the right, the hard inner edge of his boot connecting with Daitoo's hand. He performed the motion at full speed so that his leg became a blur, and the force of the impact shattered fragile bones and sent the weapon flying over the aircar to bounce somewhere on the street.

Daitoo's back and shoulders struck the pavement. Though his shock and pain were obvious his eyes never lost their focus on Conn Labro as he rotated his left wrist in a sharp gesture that brought another weapon into his grasp. Conn saw its emitter blink as the man aimed and the weapon automatically charged itself.

Rush a pistol, flee a blade was the rule when outmatched by an opponent's equipment. Conn had faced similar situations in virtual combat and had even "died" once in his youth when a cunning adversary had lured him into a cul de sac in a constantly mutating maze. There had been no escape and the distance between hunter and hunted had been too great to cover before the "fatal" shot.

This situation offered equally daunting prospects. If he ran, Daitoo's pistol would burn his legs from under him. If he leapt at the man, the blast would catch him in midair. Jenore Mordene, frozen in fear, could contribute nothing useful to the situation, not even a distraction.

Conn bent his knees, dropping to a squat, and simultaneously threw his head and upper torso to the left. If the movement caught Daitoo by surprise, the pistol's first blast might narrowly miss and in the brief interval before it could recharge, Conn would spring at the agent and end the fight.

But Daitoo was all too clearly a professional. His target was the center of what he could see and Conn could not move fast enough to escape the killing zone. He saw the narrow cone of the weapon's expected field of fire in a tactical image superimposed on his vision and knew that in a moment its rim would blast away part of his torso.

A flash of energy briefly dazzled him. When he blinked his eyes clear Chask Daitoo's head had become an incandescent lump that was already fading to ash and stinking vapor. He heard the whine of gravity obviators and looked up to see an FRP patrol car descending from rooftop height. A uniformed constable was at the controls and Hilfdan Klepht was retracting the vehicle's main armament.

"I was interested to see where things went after the sale," the discriminator said after he had led Conn and Jenore a little distance from the body.

"I am glad to have engaged your interest," Conn said.

The constable brought Klepht the contents of Daitoo's wallet. It contained identification that the discriminator soon dismissed as forgeries—"though professionally done and good enough to pass in the short term"—as well as a sealed envelope and a ticket on the afternoon departure of the *Dan*, a ship of the Gunter Line's interworld service.

"Where was he bound?" Conn asked.

"It is an open ticket. The *Dan*'s first stop is always the sector hub at Holycow. After that, there is a wide range of options, although he was supposed to be acting for a company on Bashaw." Klepht tapped the end of his long nose. "Of course, you realize that he intended to travel alone."

Conn nodded. "I had already come to that conclusion. He apparently meant to kill me."

"The question is why?" said Klepht, opening the sealed envelope. He scanned its contents and said, "And here is the likely answer."

It was the last will and testament of Hallis Tharp, who had left all of his possessions to Conn Labro. "It now becomes clear what this was all about," the discriminator said after a moment's reflection.

"Not to me," Conn said.

"Hallis Tharp has left you the contents of a locked box at Allguard Trust. Your employer can seize those assets and apply them against the amount owing on your indenture contract. Obviously, Tharp owned something this Daitoo wanted, something Daitoo knew or suspected was in the box. Unable to get it from Tharp, he killed him so that you would inherit. He then killed Horder to bring your contract onto the market so that he could buy it. The Arbitration would transfer ownership to him and he would have what he wanted. Then he would kill you and go offworld to claim whatever reward was in the offing."

"You don't think he wanted it, whatever it was, for himself?"

Klepht signaled a negative reply. "Chask Daitoo, or however he was really called, has all the markings of a hired man, though an expensive one. Whoever sent him could afford his fee, the price of your contract, and the private spaceship he used when he killed Horder."

"What could be worth so much death and pain?" Jenore said.

"Why, something valuable," the FRP man said. "Death is a small coin to some, especially when it is someone else's death." He handed Conn the will. "I suggest we open the box and see."

Conn had another question. "He intended to kill me after securing what he was sent for. But why did the sight of Jenore Mordene prompt him to act prematurely?"

Conn could hear that there was still a tremor of shock in Jenore's voice as she answered. "I have seen him before, though we've never spoken. He lives in a room a few doors down from Hallis Tharp and me," she said. "Or he did. Now that I think of it, I have not seen him since Hallis was killed."

"It fits neatly together," Klepht said. "He did not know of Jenore Mordene's connection to you. When he saw her, he realized that she might say something that would cause you to link him to the Tharp killing and put you on your guard against him. That would make you hard to kill, and dangerous. Now we know it all."

"Except who sent him and what he was supposed to recover," Conn said. He looked over at the remains of his would-be assassin, now being covered by the constable. "If you had used a shocker instead of the patrol car's intensifier we might have wrung some answers from him."

"I would have needed a few seconds to come within shocker range," said Klepht, "by which time any answers would have been of little use to your charred corpse." He pulled at his long nose. "Let us go take a look at whatever is in Hallis Tharp's mysterious box. Ms. Mordene will accompany us."

"Why?" she said. "I know nothing of this. I must go to work."

"We'll see."

Upon presentation of the key, the clerk at Allguard Trust led Conn, Klepht and Jenore to a small room then left them briefly before returning with a locked box of a size to hold a pair of shoes. After the functionary discreetly exited Conn used the key to open the container. Inside was a deposit book for an interest-bearing account at the same branch, an object that resembled a large bead and a sealed note with Conn's name on it in Hallis Tharp's handwriting.

Conn opened the note. It read: *Conn: If you are reading this, I am dead. The money is yours and should be enough to buy out your indenture. Take the bearer deed to the Registry of Offworld Properties in the city of Olkney on Old Earth. My advice is to sell it for whatever it will bring. Use the proceeds to make for yourself as satisfying a life as you can manage. I am sorry I cannot do more for you.*

In the same hand but in a different colored ink was an addendum: *Please help Jenore Mordene to get home. She has been a good friend.*

Conn placed the paper back in the box and extracted the deposit book. When he opened it he saw that a single deposit had been made in his name when he was an infant, in a long-term account that paid the Trust's highest rate of interest.

When Klepht examined the book his eyebrows elevated themselves to their uppermost reaches. The initial deposit had been substantial though not a fortune, but twenty-four years of accrued interest had more than tripled the sum. In addition, there had been many small deposits, each attributed to the Horder Emporium's tote. "I believe that some of these dates coincide with your more lucrative victories," he said.

Conn examined the record. "They all do. He must have wagered on me from as soon as I was in competition, though he never mentioned it."

Klepht said, "There is more than enough here to buy out your own contract. You are a free man."

Conn was puzzled. The money had been Hallis Tharp's, enough to let the old man live decently, yet he had subsisted in Skrey on a bowl of soup a day. Or he could have long since bought Conn out of Horder's keeping, if that was his goal. Why had Tharp kept him indentured to Ovam Horder all these years? He put these questions to Hilfdan Klepht.

"Only Tharp would know," the discriminator said. He picked up the bead-like object between finger and thumb and proffered it to Conn. "This may have more information."

Conn could see that it was covered in tiny lines and spirals. "What is it?"

"A bearer deed. One does not see them much anymore. It denotes ownership of property that is located in some place where there is no official apparatus to adjudicate property rights."

"How could there be a place where property rights are not central to the organization of society?" Conn said.

"There are still places where all rights are determined solely by what one holds in one's hands," Klepht said, "be it a bearer deed or a well-aimed weapon. Especially out in the Back of Beyond."

He handed the deed back to Conn. "Apparently you now own property. Perhaps knowing its type and location will shed more light on your circumstances."

But the illumination available on Thrais was scant. They called the clerk back to bring them a reader but when the bead was placed inside its aperture, the attached screen filled with a jumble of mismatched symbols.

"It is encrypted," said the clerk. "And by a very sophisticated cipher, high up in the consistencies."

"Could Allguard's integrator decipher it?" Conn said.

"No."

"What about yours?" Conn asked the discriminator.

"We are a small and relatively uncouth police agency," Klepht said. "You'd need a force that was used to dealing with more imaginative criminals than we encounter in Bay City."

"Where might I find one?"

Klepht made a noncommittal gesture. "Old Earth, for certain. But that is also where the Registry of Offworld Properties is to be found, and unless I miss my guess, that is where this bearer deed was originally issued."

"Another mystery," said Conn. "It appears that Hallis Tharp involved himself in my life, though whether for good or ill I cannot say."

Jenore Mordene's voice was thick with mingled anger and grief. "Hallis Tharp was your dearest friend," she said. "He spoke often of you and only in the best terms. He admired your skills and looked forward to your weekly meetings."

"Yet he kept me indentured to Horder."

"If he did so, it was because he believed it was what was best for you."

Conn studied her tearful face, looking for some clue that would let him make sense of what she was saying. But he saw nothing to help him. He said, "But how did it profit him to do 'what was best' for me?"

33

He saw a flash of frustrated rage that fell apart and became helpless sorrow. "You people," was all she said, turning away and wiping her eyes.

"It seems you have a choice," Hilfdan Klepht put in. "You can accept what fate has accorded you—modest wealth and legal freedom—and resume your life here on Thrais, perhaps to buy a share in a sporting house."

"Yet someone wanted this bead badly enough to send an assassin for it."

The discriminator knit his brows. "Property is often worth killing for, but in this case the killer was at pains not to let you know of your inheritance. Now that you have the deed, the threat may well lapse.

"On the other hand, it is a bearer deed. It confers title on whoever owns it. Someone, somewhere, values it highly and therefore might think it worthwhile to assemble whatever resources it would take to kill you and relieve you of it."

"I could offer it for sale," Conn said.

"Only as a mystery item. It would not bring much."

"But the highest bidder would certainly be the one who sent Chask Daitoo."

"Doubtful," said Klepht. "He has already shown a flair for subtlety and indirection, not to mention ruthlessness. He might send an innocent who knew nothing and who was scheduled for elimination by other agents before the deed was turned over to whoever was ultimately pulling the strings and levers."

The discriminator pulled his nose again and said, "If you wish to pursue the matter your next step is to go to this Registry of Offworld Properties on Old Earth. There you can discover what the property is and what it is worth. If you then put it up for bids, you may at least narrow the field of candidates who could have sent Chask Daitoo to kill you, not to mention Ovam Horder and Hallis Tharp."

"While advertising myself as a target," Conn said.

"Take action or stand pat. There are risks and rewards to either strategy," Klepht said. "You must weigh and choose."

Conn agreed. "I will think about it," he said and began to do so, sifting and sorting probabilities as he had always done in games of skill and strategy.

The discriminator cleared his throat, "First Response would pay a reasonable fee for information that would allow us to make a definitive conclusion on Horder's death. In the interests of maintaining our closure rate."

Jenore Mordene had regained most of her self-possession. "Do you mean you will not pursue your inquiries offworld?" she said.

Now it was Klepht's turn to look puzzled. "Ovam Horder is dead and his heirs have not offered to contract for a full investigation. For whom would we be acting?"

"How about for the sake of justice?"

"Justice is an abstract concept," the discriminator said, "and mutates substantially with a shift in the observer's point of view. It is often difficult to determine whether or not it has been achieved, whereas a transaction involving specified services for agreed-upon fees allows for far less slippage."

The observation seemed self-evident to Conn Labro, but he saw the young woman turn away with a grim retort left unexpressed. But he had more important matters in the foreground of his mind. "I have decided to take the bearer deed to Old Earth," he said. "I will begin by using Daitoo's ticket to Holycow. Perhaps someone will be waiting there for him. That might give me an opportunity to learn where he came from and who sent him."

"FRP can grant you status as an independent auxiliary agent," Klepht said. "You could then ask for assistance from police agencies that recognize our standing, which includes most of those along The Spray."

They took the deposit book to the counter where the Trust's examining devices accepted that Conn was the owner of the funds. Conn arranged for a credit draft that could be exchanged for local currency throughout the worlds of The Spray. He next contacted the Arbitration, determined the amount of his indebtedness as an indentee and paid it in full. If the holder of his contract ever arrived on Thrais, the sum would be paid over. That was doubtful, of course, since an arrest for the murder of Ovam Horder would immediately follow.

"I will conduct you to the FRP offices and confer auxiliary status on you," Klepht said. "You will have just enough time to catch the *Dan*."

When they reached the street, Klepht waved Conn into the passenger compartment of the FRP aircar. The discriminator then boarded and began to close the hatch.

"Wait!" said Jenore. "What about me?"

Klepht's brow formed the shape of a question. "What about you?"

"Hallis's note asked Conn to help me."

The policeman's puzzlement did not lessen. "The request did not amount to a contractual obligation."

The woman was speechless.

Conn spoke from the rear seat. "We are pressed for time."

"The man died under torture by people who want to kill you," Jenore said. "He left you wealth and freedom. And you don't feel any obligation to carry out his last wish?"

Conn spoke as if to a child. "What have I to gain by doing so? Hallis Tharp did not make the fortune contingent on my aiding you. Nor did he ask a price for resisting torture. The matters are not congruent."

"Have you no heart?" said the woman. "Not one of you?"

Klepht made a gesture that signaled incomprehension and made again to close the hatch.

"Wait!" Jenore said again.

"We cannot wait," said Conn.

"I have an offer to make."

"Then be quick."

"You are going to Old Earth?" she said.

"Yes."

"Have you any idea of the complexity of social relations there?"

35

Conn thought about it. He had heard that Old Earth had some peculiar ways, and his infrequent encounters with visitors from there underscored that reputation. "What is your offer?"

"Do you know the correct style of greeting between a person of indeterminate rank and any of the seven levels of aristocracies?"

Conn admitted he did not.

"Then you will need a guide."

He found himself disliking this woman. "I will hire a menial when I arrive," he said.

"You may not get what you bargain for," she said. "Offworld visitors are often viewed as plums to be picked."

Now Conn was shocked. "Are you saying that contracts are not honored on Old Earth? How does society endure?"

"Some are honored, some are not. Circumstances often dictate behavior. Character can also be an issue."

"How do I know that your character is trustworthy?"

She blinked way a fresh start of tears. "I will help you for Hallis Tharp's sake."

"But he is dead."

"Exactly."

Conn did not understand and had no time to unravel the disconnections that somehow made up the thinking processes of Jenore Mordene. He made room for her in the aircar and she climbed in. The vehicle ascended and headed for FRP headquarters. "We can establish terms once we are on board the *Dan*," he said.

"Whatever," she said. "But we must also stop at the pledgeman's and recover the paduay set."

"Pointless," said Conn. "A waste of time."

She set her jaw and said, "It is one of my terms."

From the front seat, Klepht said he would send a constable to collect the object while they were commissioning Conn as an auxiliary. He spoke into the communicator and gave orders then turned to regard Jenore Mordene. "Are there many like you on Old Earth?" he asked.

"I am not much out of the ordinary," she said, "except that I had an urge to go offworld."

"Remarkable," said the discriminator.

Thrais had not been one of the worlds settled during the first wave of the Effloration, as the advance of human settlement along The Spray had come to be known. The long wraithlike arm of the galaxy, now home to the peoples of The Ten Thousand Worlds, had offered more hospitable places than Thrais's largely grim terrains and for millennia the planet had attracted only eccentrics and enthusiasts for modes of life that challenged their capabilities, even to the point of lethal danger.

It was a dry world. Most of it was rocky desert and most of what was not desert was chill tundra. Its flora and fauna were scant and thorny. Only along the equator, where the Serpentine Sea undulated like a fat snake, was the climate within tolerable norms. Except for occasional dust storms, the weather was predictable and water was in reliable supply, so it was to the southern edge of the largest northern continent that the Transactualists came in a flotilla of spacecraft and established the settlement that grew to become Bay City. Here they could put their philosophies into practice without hindrance or oversight.

Transactualism was a utilitarian system that held that existence conducted under rules of zero-sum accounting offered a high degree of orderliness, a characteristic that the system's adherents prized above all. They rejected abstract concepts in favor of quantifiable realities and erected a framework of laws and customs that allowed the citizens of Thrais to live in freedom from all obligations except those they had willingly and knowingly agreed to honor.

All were at liberty to strive for whatever benefits moved them, each receiving according to the value that another might place on his abilities in an agreed-upon transaction. Nebulous concepts such as "the public good" or "the common weal" were swept away by the brisk winds of the open marketplace; all goods were private and could be bought or sold freely. On other worlds, it might be fashionable to make distinctions between animate and inanimate goods, between human and nonhuman. On Thrais, these arbitrary differences were not recognized. Freedom was absolute.

As the *Dan* broke into the darkness of space, Jenore stood at the view port, looking back on the dwindling ocher and gray sphere with an expression Conn Labro could not accurately read. The twin suns known collectively as Aumbispero—the name was said to derive from an ancient language and meant "A Man and His Dog"—soon fell behind as the ship increased speed and made for the whimsy that connected this system to that of Holycow. When Aumbispero was a fading point, she turned at last from the view and shook herself as if waking from a dream.

Chapter 3

The *Dan* was not a luxury vessel like the *Itinerator* of the Gold Phoenix Line or the Amboy Fleet's *Grandeur*. It catered to that class of passengers for whom a safe and timely arrival at their destination outweighed the value of the perquisites and pampering experienced in transit. But the ship did offer moderate comforts and entertainments, including a small casino in the lower forward compartment, where passengers could compete against gaming machines or each other.

Conn and Jenore found the gaming room after the latter had insisted on a tour of the *Dan*.

"Why?" he asked when she proposed exploring the ship.

"Curiosity, if nothing else," she said. "Are you not subject to the emotion?"

Conn's upbringing had not encouraged him to examine his motives or moods. His life so far had been a succession of tasks and contests that had grown more complex as he had become better able to meet them. Between assignments, he rested or prepared for the next encounter. He rarely asked himself what he thought or felt about anything, unless it was to check his preconceptions to avoid a complacency that an opponent could use against him.

"I do not think I am curious," he said.

"Do you never wonder about things?" she said. "How the universe came to be, why you are here in the midst of it, and where it all goes from this fleeting point?"

"What would I gain from such speculation?"

She spread her arms, palms upraised. "Enlargement of the spirit, perspective on the meaning of your existence, a sense of wonder."

"And how would these nebulous qualities assist me?"

"They would give you a reason for getting up in the morning."

Conn pursed his lips then relaxed them. "I usually have an even more compelling reason—a full bladder."

He saw exasperation in the set of her lips and brow as she said, "And after you've emptied it, then what?"

"Then one thing leads to another. There is always something to do."

"So you exist because you have something to do? The meaning of life is a succession of chores?"

Conn had not thought about it. He did so now. "Until lately," he said after a moment's reflection, "that has been so."

"And now?"

"Now I must find out who wishes me dead and prevent him from achieving his wish."

"Why?" said Jenore. "So you can continue to fill and empty your bladder?"

It was a good question, he had to admit, and one for which he did not have a definitive answer. "Still," he said, "if life requires a meaning, I will not be able to find it if I am dead. So I had better keep on filling and voiding for at least as long as it takes to deal with whoever wishes to kill me. After that, I can safely consider abstract issues."

She blinked and shook her head as if throwing off a moment of dizziness. "I thought you were strange," she said, "like most of the people I met on Thrais, except for Hallis. Now I suspect you are even stranger than the rest of them."

"On the contrary," Conn said. "It is you who is strange. I have never felt other than at ease, whereas you often seem nonplused."

Her lips formed an ironic moue. "But you're not on Thrais anymore."

She did not amplify her statement and Conn took it for just another one of her idiosyncratic observations. Then she returned to the original subject and again proposed an exploration of the *Dan*, adding, "In case there are any lurking perils that we ought to know about."

The likelihood seemed farfetched to Conn but he acceded to her proposal. Though he anticipated no "lurking perils," it could not hurt to scout the environment in which he would pass the next few days.

The circuit of the ship took less than half an hour. They found three eating places, ranging in style from casual through informal to full-fig etiquette. There were also three drinking lounges with similar variations in the conduct expected of the customers. There was an exercise area, a reading room and an ashram for spiritual exercises. Finally, there was the casino.

Conn quickly inspected and dismissed the gaming machines: they were the kind common in Thraisian sporting houses that catered to a broad clientele, their outcomes decided more by chance than skill. At a long table in the center of the room, players threw multisided dice and bet for and against specific combinations of pips coming up on this or that roll. Conn watched a few passes and determined that the dice were not adulterated, but the game was ruled so that the house eventually won.

In a corner half-concealed behind a curtain six passengers were seated around an octagonal table playing thrash, a game that used a deck of seventy-two numbered cards in six suits, with eight minor and four major arcana cards whose values mutated depending on what else was in the holders' hands. The game could challenge on several levels, depending on the contestants' skills. Judging by the unequal piles of tokens before the various players and the litter of discarded drink containers, the game had been going on for some time while the *Dan* had remained on Thrais to take on cargo.

Conn watched the play for a number of hands, judging the capabilities of the six persons at the table. It was a mixed group: a pair of stolid Argyllians, commerciants by their modest attire and accouterments, who bet conservatively and contented themselves with taking small pots or portions of larger ones; a large and meaty Hauserian pastoralist whose loud voice and expansive gestures as he called plays and slapped down cards declared that he hailed from the wide plains of that big planet's southern continent; a Stig whose segmented thorax identified it as male dominant with female recessant characteristics though currently in the neuter phase; a lean man of mature years suited in metallic gold with violet ruffles whose extravagant coiffure and embedded facial jewels bespoke an aristocratic origin on Old Earth; and a young Divorgian with cropped hair and sober garments who wore the badge conferred upon graduates of the Bodoglio Seminary. Behind the young man sat a fresh-faced woman of about the same age, wearing a simple frock and a placid expression.

The players followed disparate strategies, Conn saw. The Argyllians, seeking no lavish reward, avoided excessive risk. The Hauserian, flushed of face and bright of eye, took egregious chances in pursuit of splendid gains, which occasionally came his way.

The Stig sought its own ends; no one knew why the species frequented human gaming establishments, being apparently oblivious to wins or losses. It was surmised that they enjoyed some aura that the players gave off either telepathically or pheromonically. It did no good to question a Stig on such matters: the first query would cause the ultraterrene to about-face and raise its tail, exposing the glands beneath; a second query would clear the room and require the questioner to undergo a lengthy exposure to harsh chemicals accompanied by prolonged scrubbing.

The Old Earth lord was playing a multileveled strategy, lying back when the Argyllians were on the march and feeding the Hauserian when it was profitable to lead him on. But the aristocrat's energies became most tightly focused, Conn saw, whenever the young seminarian pressed his luck.

"Will you take part?" Jenore asked quietly when they had watched a few hands.

"No," said Conn.

"Do you fear to lose while playing on your own coin?" she asked. "You have ample funds now."

"I would not lose," he said. "And, as you say, I have all I require and so I do not need the trifles I would win."

"The Hauserian bets heavily."

"True, but the gains are small in comparison to what I already have."

He saw that she was regarding him with a quizzical expression. "What?" he said.

"I am trying to understand you," she said.

"Why? We are not likely to compete against each other."

"Have you never heard it said that one's fellow creature is the only proper subject for study?"

"No," he said. "And I doubt it is true."

"You don't think people should study each other?"

"They should if they wish. But I think there are equally rewarding subjects."

She tapped her small chin with one callused finger. "What have you studied?" she asked.

He rolled off a list: strategy, tactics, human and machine response modes, the strengths and weaknesses of a wide range of weapons, used individually or in combinations.

She interrupted him. "These are all related to your former occupation," she said.

"Yes."

"But you are no longer an indentured house player in a gaming emporium. Instead, you are free and moderately wealthy. You can spend your life doing virtually whatever you wish."

"Once I am sure that no one is seeking to take my life from me."

She conceded his qualifier but said, "Once you have that assurance, what will you do with your life? What captures your interest? What, besides a full bladder, will motivate you to rise in the morning?"

"We have already had this conversation," he said. "What are you trying to accomplish?"

"I'm trying to help you."

"Why?"

"If for no other reason, because it is what Hallis would have done."

Her answer puzzled him. She was not Hallis, and in any case Hallis Tharp's motivations remained opaque to him. He turned his attention back to the game of thrash and saw the aristocrat perform a subtle maneuver with the deck of cards. To change the subject, he said quietly to Jenore, "The dealer is cheating."

Her expression showed unexpected emotion, as if she were herself the victim of the Old Earther's malfeasance. "Why do you react so?" Conn said. "You have no stake in the game."

"Have you no moral objection to cheating?"

"I do not understand the question. Cheating is pointless. It renders the outcome of a contest null and void."

"If it is discovered," she said. "Around this table, it may enrich the cheater more than his luck or playing skills warrant."

It was an obvious point and yet it had not occurred to Conn. On Thrais, cheating was extraordinarily rare. He had to cast his memory back to his young years to recall an incidence. At Able Majko's sporting house, The Fast

Pig, a combatant in the melee had been caught using illegally modified equipment in an attempt to advance to the more lucrative rounds that featured combat by pairs. Most of the population of Bay City had come out to watch the felon make amends—not the whole process, of course, but some portion of the seventy-four intervals between the First Apprehension of forthcoming pain and the Micturation upon the Remnants.

The young malefactor did not achieve the full seventy-four. Technically he failed to discharge his obligation to Able Majko by ending the process at step forty-nine, the Revelation of the Tree. When further resuscitation proved impossible—he had already expired four times during the proceedings—the crowds dispersed. It was generally agreed that the penitent had displayed satisfactory energy during the middle passage.

Conn paid closer attention to what was happening around the table. He watched several hands, counseling Jenore to restrain herself while he analyzed the aristocrat's actions. After a while he drew her away and said, "It is odd. In a game like thrash, played for table stakes among strangers, I would expect a cheat to be motivated by gain. Yet his shuffle-and-shift is never aimed at the Hauserian, who wagers extravagantly and does not grumble at losing. More curious still, the sole target of the lord's trickery is the young Divorgian, yet he has brought the most meager purse to the table."

"Perhaps gain is not the motive," Jenore said.

"What else is there?" Conn said. "There is neither rank nor trophy to be won."

"See where he looks."

Conn observed and saw the aristocrat's eyes flick from time to time to the worried young woman who sat behind the seminarian. Beneath the contrived stillness of the lord's face he discerned a sharp appetite. "He desires the woman," he said, "though I see a complex of urges, some of which I cannot name."

"You must help the young couple," Jenore said.

Conn was surprised. "Why?"

Her whisper was fierce. "Because you can!"

"Once again you make no sense."

She placed her fingertips to her brow. Again he saw exasperation underlaid by a sincere intent to assist him.

"Listen," she said, "will you accept that the universe is more complicated and varied than your experience on one world might have equipped you to appreciate?"

He began to think about it but she broke in upon his chain of reasoning as if there was an urgency to the question. "Your preconceptions have already been challenged by the behavior of Lord Cheat'Em, have they not?"

He admitted as much.

"Then I want you to trust me—you do trust me, don't you?"

"I am sure that you mean me no harm," he said, "although some of your attitudes frankly puzzle me."

She blew out a long breath. "Just for now," she said, "I ask you to assume that my 'attitudes' stem from a wider experience of humankind than you have been able to acquire in Ovam Horder's sporting house."

"That is a rational assumption."

"And I want you to believe me when I say that it will be good if you intervene in that game to prevent the dissolute lord from doing what he wishes to do with the young woman."

Conn wanted to ask her what she meant by "good" in this instance, and how it related to his interests, but the expression on her face told him that she had nearly exhausted her capacity to continue the discussion. Still, he could not see how doing what she asked would bring him to harm. "I will trust you," he said.

He was welcomed into the game. "Fresh meat!" cried the Hauserian with a jocular twist of his lips that was not entirely echoed by his eyes. The others responded as their natures dictated while Conn touched his fingers to the receptor at the center of the table, causing it to disgorge a substantial wealth of playing counters and charge the cost to his account.

He had already unconsciously analyzed the play before sitting down. He could estimate within quite close tolerances how each player would react to the evolution of the rounds and could confirm his evaluations by reading the tells and giveaways displayed by the autonomic movements of lips, brows, pupils and sweat glands.

To have simply played to win the maximum from each player would have offered no real challenge. Thrash was a moderately complex game, but the players were not expert—except for the Old Earther. Now that Conn examined him competitively, he became aware that the aristocrat was able to exercise much greater control over the unconscious motions of his face than any amateur. He concluded that the man was a professional gambler. He also saw the means by which he hid his plans and responses: the locations of his embedded facial jewels corresponded with neuronic trigger points; frequent touches by the lord's beringed fingers inhibited the nerves beneath and gave his expression a preternatural stillness.

But the man's eyes gave him away: his pupils swelled whenever he looked at the young woman seated behind the Divorgian. Conn could not fathom what motivated the gambler's appetite; she was plain and graceless and would prove at best an unenthusiastic partner for whatever the aristocrat had in view. It occurred to him that Jenore Mordene was right: her wider experience allowed her to view human behavior through windows that were opaque to his eyes. He settled into the rhythm of the game, won the deal a couple of times then sent it back to the aristocrat. He made the game more interesting by setting himself the task of not only frustrating the Old Earther's attempts to ruin the young man but of determining how each of the players would fare.

He used his own funds and the Hauserian's to keep the Argyllians within their comfort zone, while feeding the seminarian small to moderate gains that rebuilt the stake the aristocrat's fraudulent play had stolen. Then he arranged for the pastoralist to win a substantial pot, which encouraged him to overbet the next few rounds. Within a few minutes the young Divorgian, who displayed no real aptitude for the game, possessed twice the amount he had brought to the table.

Now the plain woman leaned forward, a deep vertical line engraved between her eyebrows, and spoke quietly but forcefully to the young man. Reluctantly—it was all there to be seen in the downturn of his mouth and the stiffness of his shoulders—the seminarian rose from the table, swept the counters into his purse and allowed his companion to lead him from the room.

The aristocrat's eyes followed them out, then flicked back to meet Conn's level gaze. There was a stillness around the table for a moment, broken only when the tree-like gills that branched from the Stig's prehensile neck expanded and lightly fanned the air.

"You have a remarkable facility for the game," said the Old Earther.

"As do you," said Conn.

"The game noticeably changed direction when you joined us."

"Yes. For the better."

The Hauserian herdsman interrupted to let them know his point of view, which likened the ups and downs of thrash to the progress of some animal called a chukkichukki across an open prairie, although with "more jinks and jukes than you could throw a spangbrake at." Neither Conn nor the aristocrat responded nor took their eyes from each other.

"Indeed," said the Old Earther, "your abilities test the conventions of reasonable odds and permutations. One might say you stretch them to the brink of snapping."

Conn's voice was even. "Have you a more pointed suggestion to offer?"

The lord's face remained frozen but there was a hard glitter in his eyes. "I may. Where are you from?"

"I am of Thrais," said Conn.

Now a faint smile ghosted across the aristocrat's lips. "I am told that Thraisians sometimes settle disputes by direct confrontation."

"You are told correctly."

"I am sure you are aware that I am of Old Earth."

"So I have been told," said Conn. "I am not versed in the customs of every obscure world, but I have engaged with a few combatants from your end of The Spray."

The Stig's brachial gills had turned a darker pink and were rippling like fingers massaging the air.

The lord said, "I am called Willifree. My rank is Margrave-minor. I will forgo naming my ancestors since they will mean nothing to you. I have encountered nineteen opponents and defeated seventeen. Two contests ended in draws, but I was young."

Conn was familiar with the style of the challenge—it was common up and down The Spray wherever dueling was permissible—and responded in kind. "I am named Conn Labro," he said. "My rank is now indeterminate, my ancestors unknown to me. Since attaining manhood I have met and defeated one hundred and eighteen opponents in various modes of combat. I have drawn once. If you have something more to say to me, speak on."

That completed the phase known as the Declarations. Several steps should now ensue: the Particulars of Offense, the Rejection of Mediation, the Challenge Ordinary or the Challenge Exceptional, the Concord on Means and Circumstances and the Agreement on Proceeds. Conn waited.

But Willifree abruptly declined to continue. Conn saw calculation and some indefinable emotion in his eyes before the aristocrat looked away. He would have recognized fear had he seen it, and knew that he had not. Indeed, the man had the look of an accomplished swordster; he might even command that indefinable quality called *rif* that distinguished the gifted duelist from those who were merely masters of technique.

The silence lengthened then the Old Earther said, in tones of distaste, "You are not of rank. To engage with you would demean my ancestors."

"A pity," said Conn. "However, I am on my way to Old Earth on a matter of business. I understand titles may be purchased there. Perhaps we will run into each other again and I could offer you satisfaction."

"It is doubtful our circles will ever coincide," said Willifree. He appeared to wish to say something more, but changed his mind. He scooped his winnings from the table, rose to his feet and assumed a precise posture. Then he turned and left the room.

Four players not being enough to sustain play, the game broke up with the Hauserian urging all to regather for a subsequent match. "You just bring 'em on, flat, flipped or flying high. I'll be there with boots, buckles and busters," he said, in what Conn assumed was a reference to techniques and equipment used to herd the domesticated fauna of Hauser's vast plains.

Conn crossed the room to where Jenore had stood watching. She leaned in close, touched his hand with hers and stood on tiptoe to place a light kiss on his cheek. He was surprised by the softness of her lips.

"That was a good thing," she said, linking her arm in his and leading him from the room, "and necessary."

He understood neither observation but he did not extricate his arm from hers. They went to the ship's middle-priced dining room and took a light meal.

The *Dan*'s upper forward lounge offered comfortable seating in a variety of arrangements. Single seats catered to those who preferred solitary contemplation, while groups of chairs and sofas attracted those who enjoyed social discourse.

When Conn and Jenore entered they saw the two soberly dressed Divorgians clustered with the Hauserian pastoralist. Jenore drew him toward them. All offered appropriate gestures and sentiments, followed by introductions.

Ren Farbuck controlled several immense land leases around Sixty Mile Station on Hauser, where he ran vast herds of a native species that had long ago been modified to conform to human digestive processes. The Divorgians were Moat and Clariq Wallader, brother and sister as well as graduate students of the Bodoglio Academy at large for a year of field study.

Conn would have asked what field they were studying, but their entrance had interrupted Farbuck's recounting of an incident concerning an uncooperative employee. Out on the endless plains, there was no Arbitration to settle disputes, Conn gathered; contentious matters were resolved directly between the disputants.

"We came to a point," said the pastoralist, "at which he compared my appearance to the south end of a northbound squajja. There was then no recourse but to the hassenge."

At Moat Wallader's urging, Farbuck described the practice. The two disputants stood face to face at close range. Each held in his right hand a pokkai, a blunt, short-bladed knife, the point of which he set against the opponent's upper chest. The left hand was placed behind the back and the contest began.

"You lock eyes and lean your weight against the other man's blade, starting easily but gradually increasing the pressure as you incline yourself further. Your pokkai presses against his flesh, his against yours. Growls leak out from behind clenched teeth. The pain is glorious. He loses who is first to cry, 'Hold!' or to bring the left hand around to relieve the pressure. Indeed, to move the left hand at all is tantamount to surrender."

"Do you play to first blood?" Conn asked. He was trying to understand the strategy behind the contest but if there was one it escaped his analysis.

"Children play to first blood," Farbuck said, "and sometimes women if the disputants are friends. No man would give in before the pokkai is well seated. Among experienced hassengions, complete transfixion is not uncommon, and he whose back is pierced first is accorded the victory."

"You allow your opponent to push a dull knife right through your upper body?" Conn asked.

For answer, the Hauserian removed his upper garment, a smock of softened and sun-bleached hide, and turned to show three scars in the upper left quadrant of his back. The corresponding area on the front of his body was criss-crossed with scars, most white with age, one still freshly purple.

"I do not understand," Conn said. "What do you gain from the experience?"

Farbuck's eyes flashed. "Honor."

"Yes," said Conn, "you outrank the loser. But what is the tangible gain?"

The Hauserian's face hardened. Conn read anger there.

Clariq Wallader intervened. "He means no offense," she said. "He is of Thrais, where life is understood to be founded entirely upon economic transactions. The Thraisian concept of society is indistinguishable from a marketplace." She turned to Conn. "That is so, is it not?"

"I am of Thrais," Conn said. "And of course life is a matter of economics. What else would it be?"

The Divorgian woman smiled indulgently. "There are other models," she said. "As students of the Bodoglio Academy, my brother and I study the range of concepts underlying the disparate human civilizations along The Spray. We have just spent a few days confirming Raul Hoysin's research on the Thraisian polity. Are you familiar with his works?"

"I am not," said Conn.

"No matter. A fish does not need to know about water in order to swim in it," she said. "Although when the fish leaves the sea, an understanding of air does become advisable."

There was something about her tone that irked Conn. He wondered if he were being belittled. Yet when he inspected her features he saw only disinterest.

"I am not a fish and I have never cared for argument by metaphor," said Conn. "To argue that one thing is similar to another is to focus exclusively on the similarity at the expense of the dissimilarities. The former may be trivial and the latter profound."

Jenore Mordene put her hand on Conn's arm. "She meant no offense," she said.

"I am not offended," he said though even as he said it he wondered if it were true. But no, he could not be offended if he chose not to take offense and now he deliberately made that choice. Evidently, offworlders could build their lives around strange concepts. If he was to function amongst them, he must endeavor at least to be aware of the illusory landmarks that were plain to them though invisible to him. "Please say on," he told the Divorgian. "You mentioned other 'models'?"

She assumed a momentary air of introspection then said, "There are many different ways of being a human being among other like-minded human beings. Societies begin with people banding together in common efforts to solve the most basic problems of life: food, shelter, security. When those needs become routinely provided for, a new priority emerges. Once their bellies are regularly full, their bodies warm and dry, and their lives, limbs and liberties unthreatened, human beings discover a need for a sense of consequence to their existence. The inevitable question arises: what is the meaning of all this doing and saying and being? Equally inevitable is that the answer takes the form of an idea around which they structure their individual and collective lives."

Now Moat Wallader entered the conversation. "My sister and I are preparing a monograph that argues that every society is fundamentally organized around one or another of the cardinal sins."

Conn's was not the only puzzled face among the listeners. "I mean," said the Divorgian, "that every culture, whatever ideals it professes, is in practice built around one of the seven mortal iniquities identified in ancient times: pride, envy, and so on."

Clariq chimed in again. On Hauser, society was based on the sin of pride, she explained. Ren Farbuck and his adversary endured severe pain and a certain degree of fear—after all, the hassenge is occasionally fatal, usually from blood loss or septicemia—for no other reason than that all who knew them, including themselves, would have held them in disesteem if they had quailed.

"Mud on the name, earth on the grave," Farbuck aphorized. "How can it be a sin for a man to defend his honor?"

Conn ignored the comment. "But neither of them gained anything from the transaction," he said. "Nor lost."

The Hauserian shook his head and muttered something Conn did not hear because Clariq was saying, "They did not view the event as a transaction."

"Yet it must have been a transaction," Conn insisted. "All human interactions are."

"They are to those who are disposed to see them as such," the Divorgian woman said, "but not to those who wish to see them as something else."

"A thing is what it is," said Conn.

"No," said Clariq, "some things are what everyone says they are. Answer me this: on Thrais, if someone were to publish a libel about Conn Labro, what recourse would you have?"

Conn answered immediately. "A suit before the Arbitration. It would adjudicate on the basis of the facts, including the intent of the libeler. He would be required to pay me damages, and if he could not pay from his assets he would pay with his indentured body."

Clariq looked over at the Hauserian. "How does that strike you?" she said.

"I will risk a blunt reply: it is disgusting!" said Ren Farbuck. "How can the value of a man's name be assessed in currency? What would you sell your children for, I wonder?"

"I have no children."

"That is not an answer."

"As an infant, I was sold anonymously to my indentor, Ovam Horder," Conn said. "My value depended to some extent on my potential, determined by reliable tests, as well as on Horder's interest in acquiring me. Had I been an unhealthy child I would have had almost no value at all, other than the worth of my essential attributes."

The Hauserian's ruddy complexion had paled. "Parents actually sell their children on Thrais?"

"I assume it was my parents who sold me, since no one ever came looking for me. It is not commonly done, but it is not completely uncommon."

Farbuck stood. "I will leave," he said, "before I am compelled to say something that would inevitably lead to the hassenge."

"Not inevitably," said Conn. "For I see no possible profit in obliging you."

Consternation and frustrated outrage clashed in the Hauserian's face. He found his broad-brimmed hat and set it on his head, turned and stalked from the room on hard-heeled boots without another word or rearward glance.

"Did you hear what he said when you declared that neither had won nor lost in the hassenge?" Moat Wallader asked.

"No."

"It was an observation that some people know the price of everything and the value of nothing. Do you know what he meant?"

Conn turned the statement over in his head. "Is it a riddle?" he said after a while.

"No," said the Divorgian, "but never mind."

Jenore said, "You said Hauserian culture was based on the sin of pride. What about Thrais?"

Both Divorgians spoke as one. "Why, greed."

Conn waited for some clarification. When none was forthcoming he said, "But greed is not a sin."

They looked at him expectantly.

"Greed is a virtue," he said. "It is simply the praiseworthy desire to better oneself. That urge is the foundation of society, the motivating force behind every transaction. If people did not wish to acquire the wherewithal of life, they would not act. Society would come to a halt."

"To you, this is self-evident," said Clariq.

"To any rational person."

"Does Ren Farbuck seem rational to you?" she said.

"He does not rave, though he speaks in riddles."

"He is typical of his culture. Hauserians like the good things of life and spend considerable energy to acquire them. But the true goal of their existence is to acquire repute and standing among their fellows. Ren Farbuck, I believe, would give his entire fortune to preserve his reputation among his peers, or even among those he considers his social inferiors. And give it gladly."

"Then he is mad," said Conn, "and his world a madhouse."

"He might say the same about you and Thrais," Clariq said.

"But he would be wrong."

Jenore intervened again. "Tell us about the man with the jewels in his face. What motivates him?"

"Ah," said Moat Wallader, "I sense you know already."

"Perhaps," said Jenore, "but my companion does not."

Moat made an ambiguous gesture. "He is an adherent of the Immersion. I estimate his rank as not less than Blue-Green Exemplar and possibly as high as Yellow Cynosure."

"I am not familiar with the terms," Conn said.

"The Immersion is an association or fellowship—the less charitable would call it a cult—among the intensely inbred aristocracy of Old Earth. It has chapters up and down The Spray and its members devote themselves to erotic pursuits of extraordinary types. Their goal is to encompass the full depth and breadth of amatory experience and thus enable themselves to break through to a new realm of consciousness they call Prismatic Abundance."

"Why?" Conn asked.

"It is what gives shape and meaning to their lives," Moat said. "They believe that the copulative impulse is the prime human drive. All else is adjunct and afterthought. They must experience every possible variant and many of them devote considerable energy to the search for new varieties, which, when you consider that human beings have been futtering each other with verve and imagination for millions of years, bespeaks a remarkable optimism."

Jenore said, "In other words, their world view is founded on the sin of lust."

"Just so," said Clariq.

"Hence the bejeweled man's strategy at the thrash table," Jenore went on. "He was playing to reduce your brother's purse to the point where you would be vulnerable to his advances."

"Worse," said Conn, "he was cheating."

"Hmm," said Clariq. "He would have been disappointed. We would have applied through the captain to the Bodoglio Seminary for further funds." She looked at her brother and they smiled as at the pranks of a child.

"Did you not hear what I said?" Conn said. "He was cheating. Are you not revolted?"

Moat made a complacent gesture. "It is of no moment. All worked out well. We were able to observe him at close range."

Jenore said, "Suppose the captain had not agreed to advance you funds, and suppose further that Conn had not intervened to undo the aristocrat's scheme. Then what?"

"Then I suppose I would have had to accommodate the man," Clariq said, with a small sigh.

"It might have been painful," Jenore said. "It would almost certainly have had repellent aspects. I expect he has moved far beyond the usual ins and outs."

"Then I would have learned something for my pains," the woman said.

"If you survived them. There are rumors about some of the Immersion's less advertised practices."

"If death became unavoidable, I trust I would have had the presence of mind to appreciate the experience."

"And that would have been consistent with the sin around which Divorgian society is built," Jenore said.

Clariq's thin lips spread in acknowledgement. "True," she said, "I admit that we are all gluttons. We choke ourselves with sensations and experiences of divers kinds. For some it is the sight of sunset on every world. For others, it is all the musics of The Spray. For Moat and me it is revealing encounters with our fellow human beings; we will gorge ourselves on knowledge of the other until our neural membranes burst."

Conn had heard enough. He rose and made a more brusque leave-taking than the informality of the discussion warranted. After a few more words with the Walladers Jenore gave a more amiable salute and followed him.

Up a broad spiral staircase from the forward lounge was a crescent-shaped gallery that stretched across the bow of the *Dan*. Some of the passengers stood to watch the stars flow toward them as the ship continued to build momentum. Soon the alarms would sound to notify the ship's complement that they were nearing the whimsy through which they would plunge, leaving familiar space and time to traverse a region of another kind of reality, emerging eventually—some said the passage took hours, others days, a few found it interminable—into normal space a prodigious distance away.

Very rarely, a ship failed to reemerge. There were fanciful speculations about where—some said it was more appropriate to ask, "When?"—a lost vessel might reappear. Conn had encountered some of the theories: its atoms were evenly distributed across the cosmos; it reemerged, but out of phase with the rest of the universe, so that crew and passengers became sad ghosts vainly struggling to attract the attention and help of those who could not see them; it was captured by the inhabitants of the intermediate realm and worn as jewelry.

Conn had never thought much about the matter. He dwelled on it now, not out of fear or wonder but to take his mind away from the bothersome feelings that had arisen in him during the conversation with the offworlders below. Why did they have to take perfectly simple, blatantly obvious facts and twist them so wildly out of true? It was one thing to recognize perversity. He was aware that fools and deluded folk came in abundance up and down The Spray. But to hold sense in one hand and nonsense in the other while pretending that each had equal weight and substance—why did they do that?

The first alarm sounded, a gentle *bong* followed by the ship's integrator's dignified tones advising that it was now advisable for passengers to return to their cabins, take their medications and lock the doors. Moments later, Jenore Mordene came up the spiral staircase.

"Are you all right?" she said.

"I am fine."

"The conversation seemed to upset you."

"It was foolish talk. People should be more serious about important matters."

She said nothing but laid her hand upon his arm. For some reason it bothered him to read only solicitude in her expression but he did not free himself of her gentle grip. She said, "We should get ready for the whimsy."

"I have never experienced it before," he said. "I was thinking of not taking the drugs."

She sighed. "Keep them handy in case you change your mind. In fact, keep them in your hand. A cabin can seem as wide as a continent."

"Have you been through it often?"

She nodded. "When I was with Chabriz's show, we went up and down The Spray. I have tried it with and without medication. I recommend with, but it's up to you."

"I have heard that it is best to make one's first passage unaltered. One learns about oneself."

Her eyebrows went up. "I thought you already knew all that you wanted to know about yourself."

"Why do you say that?"

"Well, I feel that I know you from what Hallis used to say. Paduay is a leisurely game. The players must come to understand each other's minds in order to keep the game going. He said he never heard you speculate about your origins, who your parents might have been, why they sold you to Ovam Horder."

"There is no need to speculate," he said. "Obviously they could not keep me. I was not defective, else I would not have lived. Most likely they suffered an economic reverse and had to divest themselves of unaffordable burdens."

"They could not have had other motives?"

"What other motives could there have been? I was too young to have offended them."

The alarm sounded again, more strident. She had been about to saying something more but clearly changed her mind. "We should get ready for the whimsy," she said.

They descended the staircase and found the lounge emptying out, the Walladers already gone. They made their way to their adjoining cabins in lower first class and separated. Conn locked himself in and reposed upon the bunk, the medications sac snug in his grasp. He composed himself and waited.

The third alarm came, annoying and insistent, lasting far longer than the other two warnings. Its cessation left a ringing silence. Moments later Conn felt a *tilting* followed by a *stretching* then a series of sensations he could not name. He closed his eyes and saw a landscape of shapes and lights, mutating and shifting across and through each other. He opened his eyes and saw the cabin anew. The ceiling seemed impossibly remote, an astronomical distance away, yet at the same time he felt its presence as if it vibrated only a hairsbreadth from the tip of his nose. There was a sense of unbearable imminence, as if the entire universe stood poised on a pinpoint threatening at any moment to topple and crash in a cataclysm of unimaginable proportions.

He moved his eyes to the reflector above the dressing table. It was flowing like a slow liquid although it did not move and instead of bouncing light from its surface it drew the energy in and transmuted it into a glowing darkness.

Conn closed his eyes again. His mindscape now offered him a spherical mandala, tranquil yet full of immense power. He watched its changes and permutations for a while, resisting the distractions of his sense of bodily position, which told him that his limbs had contorted themselves into impossible arrangements and that his head had ballooned to the size of a small moon.

The sensations and perceptions were interesting but not revelatory, except for one conclusion: he was certain that he had encountered them all before. He reached for a clearer memory, for a sense of time, but all that came was an impression of lying—no, of floating—in a congenial space, of a timeless existence that went on and on, moment by identical moment, for a seeming infinity. He sought for detail but his ability to clarify his mind was compromised by the absurdities that the whimsy was inflicting on his sensorium. He decided that he had experienced enough of the effect and squeezed the sac in his hand, causing its contents to seep into his palm. The swirling globe gradually dimmed and dwindled to nothing, as did Conn Labro.

Holycow was a spectacular world, wide and pastel-colored with eighteen moons in sweeping orbits just beyond the planet's broad glittering rings. It was not far from where the *Dan* had reemerged into mundane space and by the time Conn appeared in the forward lounge, walking shakily as body and mind reacquainted themselves and dispelled the whimsy's aftereffects, the great swirling orb hung enormous in the facsimile windows.

He found Jenore curled up alone in an armchair, cradling a cup of punge in both hands. A second steaming mug awaited him on a small table beside a nearby chair and he took both gladly. They said nothing as they watched one of the planet's moons loom larger; it was the transfer point for vessels heading in several directions up and down The Spray, there being no fewer than six whimsies within range of Holycow. Ships constantly rose and fell from and to the moon's surface, while others connected with orbiting stations, touching only long enough to exchange goods and passengers before standing out for other stars.

It was a while before Conn and Jenore were ready for conversation. By then the *Dan* had docked at an orbiter and the ship's bells were ringing to alert departing passengers to the need to gather their possessions and move toward the exits. They finished their punge and went to collect their goods, but as they were about to depart the lounge they encountered Moat Wallader looking pale and strained.

"Have you seen my sister?" the Divorgian asked.

They had not. The man looked about the lounge and saw no sign of Clariq. He went up the staircase but immediately came back down. "She is not in her cabin. Indeed, her bunk does not appear to have been used and her medication remains on the table."

"We had best summon a steward," Jenore said.

"Of course," the man said. "I am still fuddled from the whimsy." He spoke to the air, "Ship's integrator. Please send a steward."

A uniformed crewman appeared a few moments later. Jenore explained the situation and they repaired to the missing woman's cabin, finding all as her brother had described.

A search of the ship was undertaken while disembarking passengers flooded the passageways. Clariq was in none of the common areas nor in the parts of the ship accessible only to the crew. Stewards went from cabin to cabin, knocking and entering, unlocking those from which there was no reply.

Clariq Wallader was found in a compartment in middle first class. The female steward who made the discovery suffered a collapse and had to sit on the floor of the cabin for some time before she recovered enough presence of mind to call for the ship's security officer.

An order went out to hold all passengers but most of them had already disappeared into the anonymous rush and thrust of the station.

Chapter 4

"She did not suffer," said Second Officer Wochan, the *Dan*'s security officer, a small, smooth-haired man whose precisely cut white uniform somehow made him look even more compact than life had fashioned him.

They were gathered in the station's constabulary office, grouped around a scarred table in the refreshments room. On one side were Wochan and the station's chief constable, a portly man named Soof who clearly placed great importance on the size and grooming of his mustache. When he nodded in agreement with the ship's officer, its elevated points bobbled in counterpoint.

On the other side of the table, Moat Wallader made a noise that might have been a sigh or a groan. Jenore put a hand on his shoulder and when he seemed unable to frame a response to the officer's remark she asked Wochan to go on.

"The perpetrator was behind his cabin door, holding it slightly ajar. When the victim passed he stepped out, pressed the medication sac to her neck, caught her as she fell and took her within."

"I do not understand," Conn said. "Why did he do this?"

Wochan glanced at the distraught Divorgian and said, "At this point, any discussion of motive is pure conjecture."

The chief constable gave a throat clearing rumble and said, "There are indications he was an Immersionist. If so, it is possible he sought to experience certain . . . sensations while in transit between the whimsies. Afterward, it appears that he took his medications and lost consciousness while still on top of her. Part of his body blocked her airway and she smothered."

Conn would have asked more but Wallader groaned again and Jenore interrupted to ask if the man had been identified or if his movements after leaving the *Dan* had been tracked.

The mustache semaphored as Soof indicated no. "He was manifested as Granfer Willifree, a margrave from the city of Olkney on Old Earth. We are almost certain that was a traveler's pseudonym. We do not know what became of him after the *Dan* docked."

Conn had a thought. "Could he have been wearing an elision suit?"

"It is quite possible," Soof said. "Our monitors are calibrated to assist the movement of passengers from debarkation to embarkation and to identify dissident elements when there are delays because of mechanical failure or unavoidable work stoppages."

"Why do you ask about elision suits?" said Wochan.

Conn told them about what had happened to Hallis Tharp under the eyes of a house integrator.

"Are you positing a connection between the cases?" said Wochan. "It seems farfetched."

"Perhaps it is merely a coincidence," Conn said.

"We have Willifree's image and voice," said the chief constable. "We will send them to the Archonate Bureau of Scrutiny on Old Earth. Doubtless he can be identified. Eventually, he will be caught and dealt with."

"We are going to Old Earth," said Jenore. "We could carry a report."

Soof made a sound that mingled disparagement with surprise. "Your enthusiasm is commendable but this is an official matter."

"My companion is accredited as an auxiliary of First Response on Thrais," she said. "We will be contacting the Bureau of Scrutiny on another matter."

The eyes above the mustache weighed Conn briefly. "That is different. Would you be willing to assist?"

Conn saw no reason why he should, but equally he saw no argument why he should not. He disliked Willifree. "I will do it," he said and was surprised when the girl squeezed his arm.

Moat Wallader was descending into a deeper misery as shock wore off and the distraction offered by official proceedings wound down. At a discreet summons from Soof, a matronly woman appeared from an inner room and coaxed the Divorgian to accompany her to something called Travelers' Aid.

"He will indulge himself in grief to the hairline," Soof said. "It is the Divorgian way." The chief constable composed a brief message and appended to it the voice print and image of the suspected Immersionist and gave it to Conn. All rose and made appropriate gestures and suddenly, their business done, Conn and Jenore were back in the station's concourse amid the flux and flow of people from scores of worlds, woven through by the occasional passage of a feathered or furred ultraterrene.

They threaded their way through the crowds, Conn letting Jenore set their direction since she seemed to know the terrain. When he inquired, she confirmed that she had been through the place a few times: beyond passenger transfers, the orbiter offered refueling and provisions for private starships, including the chartered craft that had carried the Chabriz show from world to world.

"There is the Interworld Haulage office," she said after they had made their way to a section of the concourse past the zone where the major lines maintained ornate facilities to accommodate their various classes of passenger. Here the facades and displays were more utilitarian, the staff beneath them clad in uniforms that bore no marks of fashion or efforts at panache.

The woman at the Interworld booth was of middling years and stature, with an experienced face and an uncomplicated coiffure. She consulted a schedule and advised that the *Grayling*, a freighter bound ultimately for Old Earth, was due to depart in a short time and that it had vacant cabins. The fares were more than reasonable compared to the prices the Gunter Line charged.

"Where else does the ship stop on the way?" Jenore asked.

The woman flipped a page and ran a finger down a column. "Firenz, Dusoulier, Bashaw and Huddle," she said. "The first two are station stops. Bashaw is a one-day stand-down for maintenance and refueling. Huddle gets a pass-by if there is nothing to offload or collect."

Conn said, "On Bashaw we could advise Flagit Holdings that I no longer belong to them. We might learn something about Chask Daitoo."

"We did not think to look for anyone awaiting him when the *Dan* docked," Jenore said. "Poor Clariq."

"I looked. No one was holding up a sign with his name on it, which I admit would have been unlikely, but neither did I see anyone who looked puzzled or disappointed."

The girl regarded him quizzically. "You remembered to do that while we had poor Moat to look after and all those policemen underfoot?"

"I was trained from my earliest days to take my surroundings into account."

She nodded as if to herself. "There are long moments when I forget how unusual you are."

Conn was surprised to find in himself an inclination to bridle at the remark. He suppressed the urge and said, "I believe your definition of unusual differs from mine," he said.

"That is true," Jenore said, "but I believe you are unusual even for a Thraisian."

"How so?"

"When it comes to spending money, most Thraisians only have a problem if the outlay benefits someone else. On themselves they lavish as much luxury as their purses will sustain." She gave him a considering look. "You are somehow innocent of an appetite to pamper yourself. It is an unThraisian trait."

"I am far from innocent," Conn said, but at this point the Interworld woman broke into the discussion.

"Do you wish to book passage or not?" she said. "I have other work to do."

"I say yes," said Jenore then added for Conn's ears only, "If anyone is watching for you, they'll likely be keeping an eye on the scheduled passenger ships. The *Grayling* will put in at a nondescript berth where we're much more likely to spot them first."

Conn did not anticipate lurkers either way, but he signaled agreement. He produced his credit draft and moments later he and the girl were on their way to a nearby lounge to await their boarding call.

"This place has not changed since I last came through with the Chabriz company," she said.

Conn gave the most minimal response: a sound made in the back of his throat, not developed enough even to qualify as a syllable.

She looked up at him. "Is something wrong? Are you angry at me?"

He did not answer but pushed open the door to the lounge, finding an unwindowed space with utilitarian furniture and a row of dispensers for those who required unsophisticated food, drink or modest diversions. There were no other passengers. He chose a bench and sat.

He was aware that the way the young woman was gazing at him meant that she expected a response to her question. But Conn was unsure how to answer—indeed, he was, for the first time in as long as he could remember, uncertain of himself.

Identifying the feeling left him even more ill at ease. It was not a condition he was used to. Until now, since earliest childhood, his primary sense of himself had been that of strong competence, of being the principal actor in his own story, even when he was reacting to circumstances imposed upon him by others—Ovam Horder, his trainers, his opponents.

He could always define his goals and establish a strategy to achieve them, could revise the strategy to meet a fluid situation. He had functioned—and optimally, it was universally agreed—within a framework of tasks to accomplish along a clearly visible career path: become a superior contender, strive to rise above his peers, win and hold a preeminent position.

Now all of that was gone. There was no framework, no path, no goal other than to ensure his continued survival and unravel a mystery dropped upon him by the death of Hallis Tharp. The lifelong landmark of his existence, Horder's Gaming Emporium, had abruptly ceased to exist, and he was pitched from its familiar confines into a wider universe that was rife with whole worlds ruled by mass delusion.

And now Jenore Mordene sat beside him, again wanting to know, "Is anything wrong?"

"Yes," he said.

"What is it?"

"Everything. Nothing. I don't know."

Her mouth formed a puzzled smile. "You sound like a typical troubled adolescent."

"I was never troubled as an adolescent. I had more important concerns."

"That, too, is unusual."

He decided he would let his irritation show before suppressing it. "You keep using that word in connection with me. I find your views ill founded."

"I intended an innocent observation, not an attack."

He performed the exercise that restored his equilibrium. "Let us not speak of it. Let us formulate a plan to take us forward."

She made a noncommittal movement of head, hands and shoulders. "At some point, we should establish the terms of our relationship. After what I saw you do to Chask Daitoo, I am fearful about making you angry."

"I was not angry at Daitoo. Some situations are too serious for the luxury of emotion." He was quoting from one of his early trainers—he could not recall who had said the words—but the statement reflected his feelings. "Our present circumstances are also serious and I would prefer to make a plan rather than chatter about irrelevancies."

She made an ambiguous gesture that could not disguise a mix of emotions. He disregarded them and pushed the conversation on. "On Bashaw," he said, "we should inquire about Flagit Holdings, the supposed purchaser of my indenture. There may be something to learn about Daitoo and who sent him to kill me."

"Discriminator Klepht's opinion about the bearer bead might also be tested," Jenore said.

"Yes. We will accomplish those goals on Bashaw then move on to Old Earth. The nature of the property may also tell us much."

"So may an identification of its previous owners. It may also be relevant to know how Hallis Tharp came to possess whatever it is," she said. She chewed her inner lip thoughtfully, then added, "Perhaps it is stolen and someone wants it back."

Another twitch of irritation pulled at his inner balance. "Hallis Tharp was no thief," he said.

Her eyebrows quirked. "Why so sharp?" she said. "So you did feel affection for the old man?"

"Do not seek to distract me," he said. But she had zeroed in on a soft spot that he had not known was there. Her suggestion had called up a flurry of images: Tharp seated across the paduay set from Conn, his aged face animated as he made some irrelevant philosophical observation; the thinness of his shoulders under his threadbare garment that Conn had noticed a year or so ago as Tharp departed the playing room after a session; the way his long, delicate fingers would hold a paduay piece above the board for a last moment before positioning it; those same fingers ruined and torn, illuminated by the uncompromising glare of Aumbispero flooding through the filthy window and lighting the bleak room where he had died.

"Are you sure you're all right?" Jenore was saying.

"I am fine. Let us continue."

"Well," she said, "we can't plan much beyond the things we may discover on Old Earth."

"Yes," Conn said, "beyond that there are not yet any signposts." He rubbed his hands. "Still, it is enough for now. We have a plan."

"That comforts you," she said.

He turned a direct gaze upon her. "It will go better if you do not constantly pick at my crust in search of the inner me. Accept what you see and hear and we will work together more smoothly."

She made a placating gesture. "We are all prisoners of our upbringings," she said. "I was raised to be conscious of the feelings of others."

"Why?" he said.

"A cultural norm," she replied. It struck him that he knew almost nothing about her background. When they had discussed social underpinnings with the Walladers and Ren Farbuck, she had not contributed anything from her own upbringing.

"Where are you from?" he said. "And what is your founding sin?"

"So it is all right for you to pick beneath my crust?"

"If you do not wish to answer, I will not press."

"I will answer," she said. A softness came over her face as if she gazed on a familiar and welcoming scene. "I am from the county of Shorraff on Old Earth." She described an archipelago along the southern rim of the New Shore, a collection of islands and islets set among reedy marshes. The inhabitants lived on the firm ground or in floating communities linked by canals, bridges, boats and stilt-hacks.

"We are prodigious boat builders. The young people fashion light and springy craft called bitsas that glide down the channels as if on oiled glass. There are races and regattas. Winners' ribbons are prized."

She told how in their maturity the Shorraffi poured their energies into the making of great barges—foranqs they were called—intricately carved and ornately decorated over the generations into towering confections of shaped and painted wood. "My family's is white and gold, with a frieze of eyes, in relief and painted red over blue, along the gunwales. Foranqs are mainly for ceremonial use—naming days, birthdays, the exchange of cousins."

She fell silent and let her eyes drift away.

"And your sin?" Conn asked.

"I suppose, like the Hauserians, our flaw is a kind of pride."

"You have some version of the hassenge?" He could not imagine Jenore prodding an opponent with a span of edged metal.

"No," she chuckled, "we kill each other with kindness."

He waited and she went on to explain that in Shorraff status was the goal. Rank was acquired by the degree to which a person's "handedness" was in demand. Growing up, young Shorraffis tried their hands at whatever activities caught their imagination, discovering along the way where lay their strongest aptitudes.

"At the threshold of adulthood, after discussion with our elders and tutors, we undergo a series of trials and explorations called the ratherings to determine where our interests and talents coincide. We then attach ourselves to an acknowledged master or mistress of whatever art or artisanry we wish to encompass, learning by their precepts and examples. Those who show the most promise receive the most attention. They grow and flourish. Those who strike no sparks try other disciplines."

"What was your 'handedness'?"

Her mouth shaped a moue of bygone regret. "I strove to master the plastic arts—pottery, ceramics—but I lacked the quality we call eyefullness.

My shapes and proportions were fashioned well enough, but my glazes and painted scenes never progressed much beyond a child's daubings. So I became a dancer."

He found that he could imagine her in motion. He had noticed a fluid grace in her unconscious movements. "And how did you fare?" he said.

"I was good enough to study under the third best dancer of Shorraff. But it would always have been chorus and entourage for me, with at best the occasional character or feature part."

Then the Chabriz show had come to a town on the mainland to which the young Shorraffis liked to paddle their bitsas. Jenore had gone with her crowd to sit beneath the clouds of canvas and watch the Chabriz troupe at their leaps and saltations.

"They were not so good, we thought. In our youthful arrogance, we did not realize that their art was not in the movements but in the eloquent stillnesses between. Some of us climbed onto the stage and offered our own interpretations."

The crowd had complained and the ushers had shooed away the young mockers. But Anwar Chabriz had noticed Jenore. He caught up with her as her group wandered among the put-and-pitch booths and sausage stalls and offered employment.

"My parents spoke against it, and so did a self-important lump by the name of Alwan Foulaine who fancied he had acquired some rights to my person. But I knew I would never be a first ranker in Shorraff. My handedness as a dancer was good and would have got better but it would never have been great. Chabriz held out adventure, travel, novelty. At the time, these qualities shone with an irresistible luster."

"And now?"

"The glow faded during those long months I sweated for crusts in Skrey."

He asked if she would return to Shorraff once she had guided him about his tasks on Old Earth.

"I will at least visit, to see what has become of my friends and to determine if Alwan grew the paunch that even in youth seemed his destiny." Her eyebrows performed a small shrug. "But I will not fit there. Shorraff will be like a shoe broken in by someone else's foot. It will not flex and bend where I do, and it will pinch."

"So, what then?"

She smiled. "Like you, I will look up the road and see what signposts have come into view."

A reverberating voice spoke over their heads, announcing that the *Grayling* was ready to accept passengers. They gathered their baggage and made their way to the docking port. Formalities were few. Their passage vouchers were checked by a breezy young ship's officer whose neck clasps were left undone. A whistling crewman led them to a suite of small but comfortable cabins forward of the cargo modules. Conn's and Jenore's were adjacent.

"You will find refreshments in the passengers' mess," the matelot said and returned to his duties. They stowed their baggage and found the indicated salon, which was set out with tables and chairs and a buffet offering simple fare. The punge was good and the breads and meats fresh.

There was a smattering of other passengers, none of them remarkable. Conn and Jenore chose from the common board and went to sit at a table in the corner.

"Your Shorraff does not sound that different from my upbringing," Conn said. "The capable are well rewarded. Others struggle as best they can."

Her small pointed tongue cleared crumbs from the corner of her mouth. She said, "You are fitting what I told you into the template of your own experiences without seeing your biases."

"Explain," he said.

"I spoke of status, not reward," she said. "You assumed that money changed hands."

"It is a reasonable assumption. It is how things are done."

"Not in Shorraff. Money is anathema to us."

"That is silly. How do you conduct business?"

"Very well," she said, "and it is not silly at all. My father is one of our best artificers in bone yet he has never taken so much as a bent grimlet. His sole reward is the renown his work brings him."

"He does not work for money?"

"No one does. We see money as a veil that obscures the intrinsic value of things. It reduces everything to the lowest common denominator."

"Again, that is nonsense," Conn said. "Money is a medium of exchange, an economic lubricant, nothing more."

"Then how is it that people buy and sell money, that they speculate on whether it will lose or gain value?"

"All right," he conceded. "It can also be a commodity."

"And does it not corrupt one's perceptions, so that people labor not for the satisfaction of achievement but for the monetary rewards they receive?" she said. "Are there not people right now swinking away at some task solely to get money?"

"But only so they can spend it to get the things they want and need."

"But if they didn't have the money to buy those things, might they not discover that they don't really need them, or even want them, at all?"

Conn waved her supposition away. "This is circular logic. You end up where you started because that is where you aimed in the first place."

"Yet it has served Shorraffis since time out of mind."

"But how do you conduct life's everyday transactions?"

"Like anyone else. People come to my father's workshop and choose a comb or a decorative screen or a figurine. They discuss which of his works 'spoke' to the acquirer. There are certain formal words and gestures and the object changes hands."

"And your father receives nothing?"

"On the contrary, he receives the respect and renown that are his deserved due and the only reward he prizes."

This made no sense, Conn thought. He said, "But suppose a man came in and simply took all of the stock?"

"How could he?" Jenore said. "If the acquisition were not appropriate it could not occur."

"I do not see how it could be prevented. Are there guards?"

She signaled that the concept was preposterous. "An inappropriate acquisition is referred to by a rude word. I will whisper it to you."

She did so. The term meant nothing to Conn.

"If someone performs a . . ."—she fluttered a hand to indicate the obscenity—"he loses whatever status his handedness has earned him. No one will deal with him again. He is discluded, forever outcast. His family disavows him. The best he can receive in Shorraff is pity from those struggling to overcome revulsion."

"Does it happen?"

She looked away. "Rarely. It is not talked about."

Conn contemplated the picture she was drawing in his mind. It was bizarre. "But normally everyone knows exactly what he is entitled to and acquires it accordingly?"

"I said we were governed by the sin of pride," she said. "We know to a minim our exact worth. It is usually no farther from our minds than a Thraisian's knowledge of how much or how little jingles in his purse."

Conn saw a thought occur to her. "Remember," she said, "what Ren Farbuck said about knowing the price of everything and the value of nothing?"

"Yes." He did not say that he was still unsure what the Hauserian had meant.

"For Shorraffis, it is the opposite," she said. "We can judge our own and others' value down to the fineness of a hair. But of prices we know nothing."

"Ah," he said and now he caught the shape of the idea. It was outlandish but he saw its symmetry.

"Of course," she went on, "we do not see our culture as rooted in a mortal sin. We consider our ethos a virtue, expressed in the common Shorraffi saying: *What are we here for if not to help each other?*"

A buzzer sounded. They were approaching the whimsy that would throw them toward Firenz, the *Grayling*'s first port of call. The other passengers rose without delay and departed the lounge.

"We should go," Jenore said. "On a freighter, we will not receive the repeated warnings we heard on the *Dan*."

They rose and returned to their cabins. Before they entered their separate quarters Conn asked a question.

"When you first passed through a whimsy, did you have a sensation that you had done so before?"

Her eyes widened. "Not at all," she said.

"Have you heard of such a thing?"

"Never. Was that your experience?" When he signaled that it was, she looked thoughtful. "Your earliest memories are of Horder's sporting house?"

"Yes."

"Then perhaps we should assume that you were brought there, not from some indigent Bay City family, but from another world."

"It is an assumption that leads to many questions," Conn said.

She stroked the delicate line of her jaw. "The answers to which could be revealing. I have been telling you that you are unusual."

A strident alarm sounded, cutting off Conn's reflexive protest before he could voice it. His last thought as he lay on his bunk and reached for the medicine sac was that perhaps she was right.

The trip was uneventful. At Firenz they wandered about the orbiter inspecting the goods offered to transients. These tended toward fabrics knotted into allegedly useful arrangements, though Conn could not easily envision their end uses, along with jewelry and decorative objects fashioned from the slag which was to be found in great heaps across the planet's second moon.

Apparently an impossibly ancient space-faring species had mined the moon for a rare mineral, bubbling it out of the crust with an unknown energy that cooked the overburden into dark crystals with interesting prismatic qualities. The nature of the energy, the identity of the mineral and the fate of the species were all matters for scientific speculation or mystical wonder.

Jenore was taken by a pair of eardrops. "I have no funds," she told Conn. "Would you buy these for me? Actually, they are for my younger sister, Corali. She would love them. They are rare on Old Earth."

"What would you or your sister do for me in return?" Conn said. When he saw the sentiments that his question evoked he explained, as if to a child, "The transaction must balance. Otherwise it is chaos."

"Have you not heard anything that I or Farbuck or the Walladers have said to you?"

"I have heard it all. I accept that things are peculiarly different in other cultures."

She rested her small fists on her waist, elbows angled out. "Well?"

"I am not of those cultures. I am of my own," he said. "I understand that you wish me to give respect to those foreign ways, though I find them . . ."—he sought an inoffensive word—"outlandish. Equally, should you not give respect to my culture by not expecting me to act in ways that are contrary to my sense of the appropriate?"

She pulled her lower lip between her teeth and contracted her brows then said, "That is fair. What can I do in return for the crystals?"

He remembered the vehemence with which she had rejected his assumption about her friendship with Hallis Tharp and put aside the first thought that occurred to him and that would have sprung into the minds of most healthy Thraisian males. "You said your calling was to be a dancer."

"You wish me to dance for you? Here?" She looked up and down the orbiter's commercial concourse then shrugged. "I suppose there's no reason why not. Can you carry a tune?"

"Do you require one?"

"Dancers without music can be indistinguishable from persons afflicted by nervous disorders. I would not wish to cause a commotion. Sing me your favorite song."

Conn did not have one. Music had never been more to him that a sometimes interesting mathematical sequence. "But Hallis Tharp used to sing a song while we played paduay," he recalled. "It was when I was very young."

An air of loss and regret fell over her. "Sing it," she said.

Hallis had said the song was ancient beyond all memory—about a young man going off to join an army and his mother knowing that she would be dead before ever he returned—and the melody was mournfully simple. He sang it only loud enough for them both to hear. She listened to the first verse, said, "I know this," then began to move with the second. Again he saw the natural fluidity that was hers in any motion, but now it was not the diluted liquidness of the everyday Jenore, the way she raised a cup or turned her head to listen; now it was the full concentrated liquor of flowing form. She glided. She spun. She rose and subsided, opened and closed. Somehow she caught the song's sadness, steeped it through her limbs and torso so that it emerged transformed into moments of resignation set against a soft chorus of undying affection.

Conn watched and sang and as he did so sensations passed through him, feelings he could not name, faint and formless longings, wisps of wishes long forgotten. And with them came a sense of connectedness to Jenore Mordene that he had not felt before for any person.

He broke off the melody and she stopped. "Is it not to your taste?" she said. "Perhaps a more lively song?"

"It was fine," he said and heard a sound in his voice that he covered with a clearing of his throat. "Let us buy the eardrops."

He reached for his credit instrument and made the transaction. Jenore held the darkly sparkling gems in her palms and regarded them for a moment, then slipped them into an inner pocket. "Thank you," she said.

He nodded and turned back toward the *Grayling*'s dock, setting a brisk pace. She hurried to accompany him. "Are you all right?" she said.

"I am fine."

"You seemed . . . upset."

"I was not. I am not."

They hustled along. "I believe I owe you an apology," she said.

"For what?"

"On the *Dan* I browbeat you into playing thrash against your inclination, to help Clariq Wallader. By your lights, it was an unseemly act for you to do something for nothing."

They reached the dock and were admitted to the ship by the same officer who had welcomed them aboard at Holycow.

"It was not for nothing," Conn said when they were seated in the lounge. "I enjoyed the contest once I was engaged."

"Still," she began.

"Put it from your mind," he said. "I was not discomfited." He did not tell her that there had indeed been a transaction, and that he was well satisfied with his payment for routing Willifree: Jenore had stood on tiptoe and kissed his cheek.

The station at Dusoulier waved them on, there being neither goods nor persons to take on board. The next whimsy was not far and Conn was barely over the effects of the medication before it was time to plunge back into unconsciousness. This time, however, he waited again, letting the first waves of irreality pass through him, while he forced his disciplined consciousness to stand back and take note of the sensations. He went farther than he had on the *Dan* and again was convinced that he had experienced this before.

When they were out of the whimsy and falling toward Bashaw he approached the young officer who had seen them aboard. "I have a question about passage through the whimsy," he said.

"You will not be the first," the man said with a smile. "Ask on."

"Are infants also medicated?"

"They are. The dosage is reduced, of course."

"What about unborn fetuses?"

The smile faded and the open face took on the look of a man trying to recall a fact that had slipped beyond memory. "I am not sure," he said after a moment. "I have never seen a pregnant woman on a ship. Perhaps they are advised not to travel." He brightened again. "Let us consult the ship's physician." They did so. It confirmed that women with child were advised to forgo whimsies. The placental barrier prevented the medications from passing all the way through to the fetus. Anomalies could occur.

Two sleeps after, Bashaw grew in the forward observation port. They did not put in at an orbiter but descended to a surface refit facility in the canton of Narv. The passengers were offloaded then taken by surface transportation to an unassuming hotel and advised to be in its lobby and ready to reboard the *Grayling* the following evening.

The small crowd dispersed in pursuit of its members' various goals. Conn acquired a map of Bashaw and said to Jenore, "By this chart the canton of Trintrinobolis is a short flight to the east. Let us see if we can find Flagit Holdings or anything about Chask Daitoo."

"First we should alert the authorities in Trintrinobolis that you are acting as an auxiliary police official."

"Is that necessary?"

"On Bashaw, it is advisable," she said.

The hired aircar was spartan in its appurtenances. It flew low over the low-rise cityscape of Narv, an aggregation of rectangular structures painted or stuccoed in shades of gray and white. Conn saw no curves, no ornamentation, none of the flair for colorful detail or eye-pulling embellishment that characterized Bay City. The vehicles on the roads and in the air about them were likewise sedate in style and paintwork and the people who sat in them or rode the pedestrian slides were similarly bland in aspect.

"It seems an uncommonly dull place," he said to Jenore.

"To the contrary," she said. "It seethes."

Before they departed the hotel she removed the rank and status insignia from his collar and told him to keep them in his pocket. She would not explain but bade him wait until he had met a Bashavian or two.

Conn encountered his first at the squat and foreboding police prefecture near the center of Trintrinobolis. The building was as colorless as any other in the canton but wore an aura of uncompromising conviction that Conn ascribed to the small, heavily barred windows along its foundation. A drably uniformed officer at the reception desk pointed them to the office of Subinspector Fonseca Smit.

Smit was a narrow man, thin of chest and face. He gave an impression of great energy ruthlessly repressed as he minutely inspected Conn's identification and the letter Hilfdan Klepht had given him before bidding them sit in the rigid chairs that fronted his desk of painted metal. The subinspector's own chair was no improvement on the hard seating offered visitors. He weighed Conn with a policeman's long and direct gaze then dismissed Jenore with a cursory glance.

"How may I help you?"

"We are making inquiries into three murders and an attempt," Conn said. "I was the object of the latter."

"You are investigating an attempt on your own life?" Smit said. "That seems a touch dramatic."

Jenore broke in. "We happened to be passing this way and the authorities on Thrais asked us to stop in. Our ship is undergoing maintenance so we have time on our hands."

Some of the stiffness went out of Smit's posture. "Ah," he said, "so the fact that you are both victim and investigator is merely a coincidence?"

Conn read the message in Jenore's eyes and said, "Yes, entirely a coincidence."

"The prefecture would be pleased to offer all possible assistance," Smit said. He activated his integrator and made inquiries about Chask Daitoo and Flagit Holdings. After a moment's examination of the data he said, "The company appears to have been only minimally active until fairly recently, although it kept up its regulatory requirements."

"What is the nature of its business?" Conn asked.

Smit scanned the entries. "Buying and selling, it seems, though without a particular adherence to category."

"I don't understand."

"It is a trading house. It deals in anything that can be bought or sold: property, financial instruments, scientific apparatus, contracts for consulting services, construction supplies."

"Who owns it?"

A look of shock froze Smit's thin features then his mouth made a grim line.

Jenore spoke quickly. "My colleague has spent his life on Thrais with little exposure to other cultures. He means no offense."

Smit gave Conn a hard look. "It is advisable to learn the basics concerning a world's mores before flinging oneself amongst its population," he said. "On Bashaw, ownership is a deeply private matter. One discusses one's holdings only with one's intimates."

Conn made an apology. "What can you tell me about Flagit without straining propriety?"

Smit went back to the data. "It was inactive for a long period. Trading resumed a few months ago and has been brisk."

"Does that signify anything?"

"It might indicate a . . ."—the subinspector lowered his voice—"change in possessorship. That, by the way, is the term to be used in polite company."

"Has there been any trading in indentured service contracts?"

"No, nor would such be allowed. On Bashaw, possessorship of a human being, even through the legal fiction of indenture, is an unthinkable obscenity."

The subinspector was growing uncomfortable at the nature of the discussion, Conn could see. He switched subjects. "What about Chask Daitoo?"

Smit called up the information and read the screen. "He has never been on Bashaw, at least not under that name."

Conn handed over the identifying information on Daitoo that Klepht had supplied. Smit ran it through a reader and gave the resulting information a policeman's confirmatory nod. "Daitoo was, of course, a temporary name. Indeed, he has had so many aliases it is doubtful he even recalled the syllables of his naming day. Certainly, we don't know it, though he seems to have originated on Old Earth."

"He was a professional criminal?"

Smit hummed an equivocal response. "He inhabited the gray penumbra between licit and illicit. Sometimes a mercenary, sometimes a secure courier, sometimes a figure in the shadows when someone met with an injury or mysteriously vanished. Occasionally questioned, never charged, always encouraged by police forces along The Spray to take the next ship offworld. If he is dead, I will add the information to the file and transmit it to other agencies."

"He is dead," Conn said.

"Under what circumstances?" Smit said, as he made notes.

"He died trying to kill me."

Again, Conn saw Smit suddenly stiffening and the warning in Jenore Mordene's eyes.

"You were fortunate," Smit said, his voice tight.

"Yes, I was," Conn said. "Discriminator Klepht was to hand at just the right time."

Smit relaxed. He returned Daitoo's identifying materials and gave them Flagit Holding's address. They bade each other good day in the restrained Bashavian manner, Conn mimicking Jenore's example.

When they were aloft in the aircar, Conn said, "I seemed to be often on the verge of outraging the subinspector, though I do not know why."

"As he said," Jenore replied, "it is well to understand the ways of a world before going abroad among its citizens."

"But what was my offense?"

For answer, she spoke to the aircar. "My companion is not knowledgeable about Bashavian culture. How would you describe your world's way of life?"

The aircar said, "We are simple and unassuming. We make no vain displays. Know that and we are easy to get along with."

Jenore thanked the vehicle and pressed the privacy control. "The prevailing ethos on Bashaw is modesty. The good citizen's goal is to draw no attention to himself. Thus whenever you even hinted at any superiority of innate ability or accomplishment he bridled. To have worn your player's beads would have been like slapping him across the face."

"But every culture makes distinctions," Conn protested.

"As do Bashavians. But they do it in subtle and tactful ways that you and I would scarcely notice. The difference in tailoring between Smit's uniform and the desk officer's, for example."

"I noted no difference," Conn said.

"Indeed, but they do. To them such tiny variations loom as vast as mountains."

Conn made a gesture of mild incomprehension. "What a waste of energy."

"They would say the same about the thrust for riches on Thrais. And be disgusted by the flaunting of wealth and dominance."

Conn looked out at the drab sprawl that was Trintrinobolis and thought there were worse ways of life than the innocent pursuit of money. After a moment, Jenore interrupted his musings.

"Have you identified the fundamental sin of Bashaw?"

He thought for a moment, then said, "Envy."

F lagit Holdings was listed on the barebones directory of a bland two-story edifice in the business district. It occupied a single room down a corridor on the first floor. At the simply varnished door with small painted lettering that listed three other firms, Jenore reached for the opener. Conn stopped her.

"Wait," he said. He took a coin-sized object from his belt pouch and concealed it in his palm. "All right." He motioned her to open the door.

The occupant of the room was a pale-eyed man with thinning hair and a curved spine. He looked up from a ledger on a counter that ran most of the way across the office, then immediately closed the book and placed it on a shelf below the counter. The single word he spoke was "Yes?" but the tone of his voice and the set of his face said the opposite.

Conn stepped to the counter and leaned his elbows on it. "I have a message for the principals of Flagit Holdings, whoever they might be," he said.

He saw no alarm cross the clerk's eyes, only wary calculation. "We are their agents. What is the message?"

"Chask Daitoo is dead." Conn was watching the man carefully. The information brought no reaction.

"Also, the indenture contract of Conn Labro has been paid out and voided."

Again, no agitation showed in the man's expression, only puzzlement. "Who is Conn Labro?"

"I am."

"Are you sure you have the right office?"

Conn reached into his pouch and withdrew the bearer deed. He let the figured bead rest in his palm and showed it to the man behind the counter. "One last thing," he said, "I am taking this to the registry on Old Earth."

This time there was a response, though quickly suppressed. "I know nothing of this. You have the wrong business."

"That is quite possible," Conn said. "The whole affair has been fraught with mystery and misdirection. Still, we will sort things out conclusively on Old Earth."

The pale eyes flicked to the bead and again Conn saw that he had struck something in the clerk that vibrated. He made a breezy farewell and led Jenore from the room.

When the door was closed behind them they went down the hall a short distance. Jenore made to speak but Conn signaled her to silence. He waited most of a minute then marched back to Flagit Holdings, opened the door and stepped into the room and up to the counter.

"I thought I heard you call," he said.

The curved man was speaking into a communicator. He broke off and said, "I did not."

"No matter," said Conn. His hand slid along the counter's edge then he departed.

"Did you hear him say anything useful?" Jenore asked as they strode down the corridor.

"No," said Conn. Then he produced the clingfast, a small listening and recording device of Hilfdan Klepht's that he had placed and recovered from beneath the counter's lip. "But I'll wager this did."

They reentered the aircar and flew toward the hotel. When they were secure in Conn's room, he sat on the hard and narrow bed and activated the clingfast's playback. They heard the sound of a communicator being activated then the pale-eyed man's voice, shaking with agitation, spoke to an unknown listener.

"An offworlder was here," he said. "He called himself Conn Labro." There was a silence while whoever was on the other end of the communicator reacted.

"I don't know," said the clerk. "He said something about a man named Daitoo being dead, then he showed me a bearer deed. I think it was the one."

Another silence, then the man said, "He said he is on his way to the registry on Old Earth."

There was the sound of the door opening and Conn's voice said, "I thought I heard you call." He shut off the playback.

"There is nothing here to take to Subinspector Smit," Conn said, "no apparent connection to the killings on Thrais or the attempt on my life."

Jenore was staring at him. "But the bearer deed meant something to him. And now you have told whoever wants it where you are and where you are going."

"Yes."

"If whoever wants the deed also wants to kill you," she said, "you have just told them where to set the ambush."

"Exactly," he said. "Now all I have to do is survive it."

Chapter 5

Very few residents of The Spray traveled to Old Earth. It was off the main routes, exported almost nothing and took in only a few antiquarians and even fewer voyagers in search of diversion. It was thought a fusty, insular, timeworn place with little to offer the discerning.

The planet's main space terminal, therefore, was a small and ill-attended facility on an island in Mornedy Sound, connected by boat, air and an undersea tunnel to the great city of Olkney. The tunnel had never achieved popularity and carried only self-directed freight vehicles.

The *Grayling* discharged its few remaining passengers at a single-story terminus whose only visible staff was a cargo handler directing an articulated crane. No one paid any attention to the handful of people and one feathered ultraterrene who descended the ramp from the ship's smallest portal. Bashaw had been the end of the line for most of those who had been aboard when Conn and Jenore boarded at Holycow. Only two had boarded at Bashaw: the ultraterrene and a Bashavian in gray worsted who hurried ahead of the others to commandeer the only vehicle for hire. The aircar went aloft and disappeared over the sea toward the mountains of the mainland, their dark peaks distant on the horizon.

"If someone was sending a message to prepare an ambush," Jenore said, "That man is carrying it."

"Yes."

"Then why not stop him and learn what he knows?"

"He probably knows no more than an address where he can leave his message or where to find some minor player who will take the news from there. Besides, it is not illegal to carry messages from one world to another."

Conn took a look around. The day had advanced well into the afternoon. The tired orange sun was sliding down the sky and causing shadows to lengthen. The sea was more gray than green, with flecks of white when the breeze stirred. He decided that the tales of Old Earth's blue waters must be misinformation. But the smell was interesting, like a too salty soup left to go sour in the pan.

Jenore said, "Beyond the terminus is a dock where water taxis are usually available. We can hire one to take us to the city, or call for an aircar."

"I have never been on the sea," Conn said, "except in simulations."

"I grew up with one foot in the water, as we say in Shorraff."

"Let us find a boat, then. It will be a new experience for me and a welcome home for you."

They went into the terminus. It was empty save for a machine polishing a corner of the waiting area. Conn had the impression that the device was malfunctioning: the corner was polished to a high gloss while the rest of the floor was dull and streaked with grime.

There were no formalities nor anyone to perform them. Beyond the terminus, a railed wooden walkway led out to a wharf where small boats were tied up. Jenore looked down into each craft while their owners affected airs of pleasant invitation or reserved disinterest as their natures moved them. She rejected one after another, finally giving a grudging nod to a yellow and red runabout with two hulls and a raked superstructure.

"The owner at least knows how to stow a line and polish the brightwork," she said. "He is therefore less likely than the others to overturn and drown us if the wind braces up."

The person referred to, a bald and grizzled man in a one-piece suit that had recently been cleaned without removing a spatter of grease stains, spat over the side and activated the motor. A moment later the lines were cast off and they were skating over the slight chop toward Olkney.

"Seen a boat before, have you?" said the boatman. He stared straight ahead but let the wind of their passage carry his words over his shoulder to the pair in the stern seats.

"I am of Shorraff."

This brought a nod and a silence, then, "Been away long?"

"Years."

The information brought a grunt and an even longer silence.

"You'll find there have been changes."

"What kind of changes?"

This time the boatman turned to look at her. One eye squinted as the breeze caught its corner. "Some say good. Some say not."

"Tell me," she said.

But his only answer was, "Best you see for yourself."

The water taxi let them off at a public wharf on the southern edge of the Olkney Peninsula. It was a district given over to docks, warehouses, chandlers and that breed of enterprises—the same on every sea-bearing world, Jenore said—that caters to sailors. It was not a place to attract aircars, but they soon found a three-wheeled motilator that was for hire.

"The Registry for Offworld Properties," Conn told the vehicle when they were seated in its compartment.

"No," said Jenore, "the Archonate Bureau of Scrutiny."

"Which of you is paying?" the taxi asked.

"I am," said Conn.

"Offworld property registry it is," was the response. Wheels hummed and they rolled forward.

"The scroots will not take it well if you engage in combat with whoever might be waiting for you at the registry," Jenore said.

"I am not planning any combat."

"But you are not ruling it out."

"True."

"If you hurt or kill anybody, the Bureau will charge you with an offense."

"Even though I act in self-defense?"

"That will be taken into consideration, but so will the degree of force you use versus that which is used against you, and whether or not you could have avoided confrontation altogether."

"If my blood is shed or my bones broken," Conn protested, "how is it anyone's business but my own?"

Jenore explained that the Bureau's role was to preserve the Archon's peace. All who disturbed it were taken up without regard for rank or role. Assessing the degree of individual guilt was a matter for another branch, the Bureau of Judiciars and Intercessors.

Conn signaled dissatisfaction with the concept. "I am an offworlder fearing attack from other offworlders over the ownership of an offworld property. How can I be assured that these 'scroots' will act in my best interests?"

"It is their duty."

"But who is their client, if they arrest everyone?"

"Their client is the public good."

"There is no such thing as 'the public good,'" Conn said. "All goods are private."

"The Bureau of Scrutiny has a different perspective. They also have the means to enforce it," Jenore said.

"She is correct," commented the vehicle. "All arguments with the scroots conclude with the click of a holdtight."

"Besides," Jenore said, "you agreed to deliver the message from Chief Constable Soof regarding Willifree."

They changed course and proceeded to the central headquarters of the Bureau of Scrutiny. It was in a district heavily favored by offices of several Archonate bureaus, all nestled against the lowest slopes of the Devenish Range whose black crags were Olkney's northern skyline, topped by the sprawling palace of the Archon himself.

Conn handed over Soof's message and told his story to a succession of green-on-black uniformed officers of ascending rank. Each telling was preceded by a period of waiting in a colorless anteroom on chairs not designed for comfort. The fourth iteration was to a hard-eyed woman of indeterminate age whose wide desk bore a plaque identifying her as Directing Agent Odell. No first name was specified and Conn wondered if that was because no one had ever had the temerity to ask what it might be.

The document conferring FRP auxiliary status on Conn had been proffered and returned, while Soof's missive regarding Granfer Willifree had been examined—for the fourth time—but this time retained. The woman consulted the Bureau's main integrator from her desk and entered the aristocrat's particulars.

"I do not have a positive identity for him," she said after perusing the data.

"The murdered woman's brother thought he might be an adherent of some cult called the Immersion," Conn said.

"Of Blue-Green Exemplar or Yellow Cynosure rank," Jenore added.

Odell asked them to describe in more detail the types and arrangements of Willifree's facial adornments. She referred the description to the integrator. When she had received its analysis she said, "His name is false, that of a character from a childhood fable."

She consulted the data again. "His arrangement of gems is now well out of fashion, suggesting that he has been off Old Earth for some time. We will pass the description to the major shipping lines so their security officers can watch for him, but if he travels by irregular vessels, or indeed if he simply stays put, the chances of finding him decrease daily. They do not call the planets of The Spray the Ten Thousand Worlds for nothing."

She then asked to hear about the other matter. Conn began to explain about the encrypted bearer deed.

"May I see it?" Odell said.

He handed it over. She scrutinized it with no great show of interest then pressed a stud on her desktop. A thin beam of purplish energy played across the bead. Odell looked at a readout on a screen Conn could not quite see. "It is seriously encrypted," she said.

"Can you decipher it?"

"Perhaps, but that is not my proper function. The Registry will do that for you tomorrow."

Conn recovered the bead and continued with his explanation of how he had come to possess it. Midway through the tale Odell raised a hand and said, "Is there a connection between any of this and Willifree?"

"Not that I know of," said Conn.

She looked at her timepiece. "Then you are wasting Bureau time. What do you require of us?"

"My companion recommended that I let you know that we propose to visit the Registry to discover what property the bearer deed pertains to."

"Why?"

"Because someone might try to take it from me."

Odell steepled her hands. "Because it may have been the cause of three murders on Thrais?"

"And an attempt on my life," Conn said.

"But you have no evidence to connect the bearer deed to these crimes?"

"The authorities on Thrais and Bashaw thought that a connection was probable."

The expression that passed over Directing Agent Odell's face might have been read in a number of ways, none of them complimentary to the police agencies of worlds she had scarcely heard of. "Are you requesting a protective escort?"

"I have no need of protection."

The wave of her hand was airy to the point of insouciance. "Then what?"

Conn took a deep breath. Although his training had made him capable of exercising great patience, he saw no reason to do so in this circumstance. But as he opened his mouth to offer the scroot the candid opinion that he was forming concerning her and her entire organization, Jenore cut in. "We thought it wise to advise you of the situation in case there are any difficulties when we visit the Registry," she said.

"Difficulties?"

"Breaches of the peace."

"I counsel you not to commit any," said Odell. "The Bureau does not endorse frontier-style brawling by wild-haired offworlders. This is Olkney."

Conn said, "We are aware of our location." He rose and added, "Now we will seek another."

"The Registry will be closed by now," the agent said, and for the first time since he had entered her office Conn saw something escape the control that Odell exercised over the microexpressions of her face: a flicker of satisfaction.

He said nothing as he and Jenore rode the descender to the lobby and went out into a street bustling with homeward-bound functionaries, some uniformed, some not. Their motilator had moved on, but Jenore displayed an ability to produce a piercing whistle which, along with a raised hand, brought a cruising aircar to the curb.

She gave the vehicle the name of a modest hotel on the edge of the Shambles district and it bore them aloft. Conn was interested to observe the city from a height; it was larger than Bay City and showed much more variety in its zones and architecture. One district seemed to be actually in ruins, another was all greenery and small lakes, while the structures ranged from tenements down by the river through every class of housing up to manses surrounded by formal gardens.

He wondered if Hallis Tharp had come from somewhere down there. The old man had spoken often of Old Earth and had even mentioned Olkney once or twice, he recalled. Then Jenore spoke.

"Are you angry? You looked ready to remove that woman's hide with your tongue."

He turned to her. "I do not permit myself anger, but I did begin to feel annoyed," he said. "Until I saw what she was doing. To her credit, she played me quite well, indeed well enough that it was only at the end that I realized I had been played."

"Played you how?"

"She kept us there until it was too late to go to the registry today."

He saw comprehension in her face. "So they will have time to investigate us and perhaps set up a surveillance on the place."

"That seems likely."

"So we need not worry about tomorrow."

"I was not worried," he said. "I have a good understanding of my own capabilities."

The Brzankh Hotel was at an intersection called Five Points just outside the Shambles. It was comfortable but small, its humble exterior embellished with stubby towers and ornamental cornices. On Thrais its obvious charm would not have saved it from being torn down and replaced with a vaster, more assertive edifice that would have trumpeted its identity through flashing, illuminated signs and uniformed personnel urging passersby to take a round at the gaming tables.

"Chabriz always stayed here when he was in Olkney," Jenore said. "The rates are reasonable and the guests are left undisturbed unless they inflict themselves upon the general peace."

After depositing their baggage in adjoining rooms on the third floor and refreshing themselves, they descended to the refectory and took an evening meal that Jenore said was typical of the season.

Conn found the food too mild to be interesting.

"Thraisian food is an assault upon the senses," Jenore said, "chilis that evacuate the sinuses and sauces that quell the palate with sheer violence. Here, the mix of textures and flavors is subtle and their enjoyment is an acquired art."

"I doubt I shall be here long enough to acquire it," Conn said.

"Where will you go, once you have solved your mystery?"

It was a question that had been circling in the back of Conn's mind, like a predatory bird seen high and at a distance. He had preferred to keep it there, but he knew that soon he must let it swoop and seize his attention.

"I do not know," he said. "I have tried traveling. It does not seem rewarding."

She made a dismissive noise. "You have seen only a couple of orbiting stations and Bashaw, The Spray's dullest corner. There are worlds scattered like seeds from here to the Back of Beyond, each one unique. Some are still rough frontier, some are well worn and cosmopolitan. In its own way, Old Earth is one of the most fascinating, replete with cultures that have been polishing themselves since the dawn time."

"And yet you left it."

"I was young and half-dreaming."

"So now you will return to Shorraff and find your true place?"

"If it will have me."

Conn said, "The boatman spoke of changes."

A pensive look came over Jenore. "If it had been frozen since I left it, like the magic land in the children's tale," she said, "it would still be different to me, because *I* have changed. That is the point of going and coming back."

"So Bay City will be transformed when I return?"

"Only if you have been. But do you truly intend to return to Thrais?"

Conn had not really thought about it. "I was at ease there," he said.

"But your place is gone. Surely you would not indenture yourself to another Horder?"

"No. I played all possible combinations of that game. Now it has no appeal."

The server brought them spicy punge and a tray of pastries. Jenore chose one. "You might be at ease somewhere else, once you found it."

Conn selected a flaked shell that surrounded pureed chestnuts. He let it dissolve then said, "I might never find it. I am, as you continue to remind me, unusual."

She formed her mouth into an expression that at least hinted at apology. "Yet you are not a monster. I'm sure there is a place that would receive you as comfortably as a well-tailored glove takes to its hand."

"That would be some glove," Conn said, selecting a fruit tart.

Later, a mummers troupe took over a small elevated stage at one end of the refectory and announced that they would perform selections from their repertoire. The first was the ancient tale of Fenoak, the statue brought to a kind of life by its sculptor's desire. The mummers presented the tragic version, in which Fenoak is unable to achieve full personhood and throws himself from the top of a tower, shattering himself into a myriad shards.

Conn did not remain to see the end. "They are persons pretending to be characters who never even existed," he said, when Jenore suggested that he stay. "What is the point of it?"

"They elucidate truths."

"What have lies to do with truth?" he said and would not stay to hear her answer.

The offworld property registry was in a narrow building of stone and dark wooden beams, between a fishmonger's and a depot for the recycling of used technology on Thrip Street. It was some distance from the hotel but they elected to walk, Conn wishing to be well warmed in case of trouble.

When they turned the corner onto Thrip from Wanless Way Conn scanned the street as if he were entering a scenario from one of Horder's seek-and-strike games. No vehicles moved on or above the pavement, although halfway down the block a velocitator was parked at the curb, its service hatch open and its operator bent over the components. On a porch across from the registry, another man was carefully polishing the lamp above the door. As Conn watched, he removed the lumen, inspected it at length, then replaced it in the holder.

An elderly woman was making a slow progress along the pedestrian way on Conn's side of the street, following the meanderings of a diminutive puff of feathery fur that demonstrated a close interest in whatever odors had been left on the bases of railings and signposts. At the mouth of an alley a heap of rags moved, revealing itself to be a dissolute man curled around a container of drink.

"Hmm," said Conn. Without pausing, he made his way to the registry. Jenore followed more tentatively.

"Any of these might be an assassin," she whispered.

"Yes," Conn said, "but not all of them. Therefore they are all police."

"How can you be sure of that 'all'?"

"Because any loiterer who was not of the police would already have been identified and arrested."

They had reached the steps of the registry. Conn took another look up and down the street and saw nothing to alarm him. He did notice, however, that the animal on a leash was actually a camouflaged surveillance instrument clad in fake fur and held by its operator, who was female but not actually aged, on a length of stiff wire.

Behind the registry's front door they found a bare office containing one battered and untenanted desk and a man in nondescript garb who was studying a yellowed notice affixed to an announcements board on the wall. The sheet of paper bore no more than twenty words in large type, but the man was studying it as if committing the text to permanent memory. He studiously ignored the entrance of Conn and Jenore.

Conn advanced to the desk and read what was written on a hand-sized card stuck to its top. *PRESS*, it said. The only other object on the desk was a stud connected to a wire that ran down the side of the desk and across the dusty floor to disappear into an inner wall next to a door marked *REGISTRAR*.

Conn pressed the stud and heard a faint buzzing from behind the door. He waited. Nothing occurred. He glanced over his shoulder at the man by the notice board and saw that the fellow was still rapt in contemplation of the twenty words. He pressed the stud once more, holding it down and hearing the buzzing continue unabated. After several seconds, he heard footsteps approaching loudly from beyond the door.

The portal was flung open and the doorway framed a short stub of a man with fiery red hair and a furious expression. "Can you not read?" he said. "We are closed!"

"Are you the Registrar?" Conn said.

"I said, can you not read?"

"I read quite well," said Conn. "The sign on that door says 'Registrar' while the one on the desk says 'press.' I assumed that doing the latter would summon the former, and here you are."

"I meant the sign on the door!"

"There is no sign on the door other than the plaque designating this as the Registry of Offworld Property."

Conn would not have thought it possible for the outrage on the Registrar's face to intensify, yet it now did. He stomped to the front door, yanked it open and glared at its unadorned outer face as if it had personally disparaged him.

He spun to face Conn and Jenore. "Return my sign!" he said.

"We do not have it," Conn said. "It was not there."

TEMPLATE

The official now seemed to become aware of the other occupant of the room: the student of the yellowed notice. "You!" he said. "Did you take my sign?"

The man at the notice board gave no answer. He studied the paper with renewed intensity. But the red-haired man had spotted something. He strode across the room on short legs and plunged his hand into a pocket of the other's drab overcoat. When he pulled it out it contained a crumpled sheet of paper.

While the notice board student feigned a complete lack of interest in the proceedings, the Registrar smoothed away the paper's wrinkles and held it up between two stub-fingered hands. In bold letters formed much like those on the card on the desktop, it read *CLOSED*.

He showed it first to Conn and Jenore, then to the man at the notice board. "This is theft and wanton destruction," he said. "I have a mind to summon the scroots."

"They are already here," said Conn. "If you rummage further in that man's pockets you should find some form of official identification."

At that the man at the notice board pulled his garments closer about himself and made for the door. The Registrar watched him go with a face that was struggling to maintain anger against a tide of bewilderment.

"We wish to identify something," Jenore said.

"Come back when we are open," snapped the red-haired man. He opened the outer door and sought to reattach the sheet of paper but could only swear and say, "The pin! He took the pin!"

"When are you open?" Jenore asked.

"We open when there is business to conduct," the Registrar said.

"We have business to conduct," said Conn.

The short man cocked his head as if Conn had spoken in a disused language. Then he signaled a negative with overtones of impossibility. "There is never any business to conduct," he said.

"This *is* the Registry for Offworld Properties?" said Jenore.

"Yes."

"And you *are* the Registrar?"

"For many years. Uttyer Hoplick is my name."

"Then we have business with you." She turned to Conn. "Show him the bearer deed."

Conn produced the figured bead. Hoplick's head moved forward on his shoulders as he peered at the object. Then he strode across the room and held out his hand.

"Three people have died, perhaps because of this," Conn said, "and an attempt was made on my life. I want to know what it is." He placed the bead in the Registrar's hand.

Hoplick examined it as if it were an arcane jewel. "I have not see one of these in decades," he said. "Not a real one, at least. There are some famous 'lost properties' for which there are lucrative standing offers to anyone who can provide the coordinates. Is this one such, I wonder?"

79

"All I know is that this is a deed to offworld property," Conn said. "I do not know what property it confers ownership of, but that is what I am here to learn."

The Registrar rubbed his hands together. "Then to business," he said. He waved his visitors toward the inner door. "Please come in."

Hoplick's office was clearly not just a place of business. It contained a sleeping mat, a comfortable chair, food storage and preparation facilities and the accouterments of a simple life. There were the smells of punge from a half-filled mug and of used socks from a pair left under the dresser.

The Registrar went to a corner where cartons were stacked and began to pull them aside; one tilted and fell, disgorging books and papers which were ignored as the search continued. Finally, he dug deep behind the rearmost box and emerged bearing a device not much larger than his fist. This he brought to a table by the window and set down before producing a square of cloth from his pocket and wiping away a film of dust.

He pressed a control on the object's top and it showed a light and made a noise. A circular piece of its upper surface receded, creating a hemisphere exactly sized to receive the bead. When Hoplick placed the bearer deed in the aperture, the machine hummed quietly to itself. After a moment a screen became visible in the air above the table then it filled with printed data.

Conn peered at the information but saw that it remained encrypted. Then Hoplick touched another control and the symbols on the top quarter of the screen resolved themselves into readable words and numbers.

"There you have it," said Hoplick.

Conn looked again. There were some archaic legalistic phrases involving stated rights and secure precedents. They referred to something called Forlor. Conn took this to be the name of the estate or house to which the deed conferred ownership. Then there was a long string of numerical coordinates; these he assumed to be surveyor's site descriptions setting out the bounds and borders of Forlor, wherever it might be. The rest of the screen revealed gibberish.

Hoplick regarded the information with an air of approbation. "Congratulations," he said.

"I am not sure congratulations are in order," he said. "It seems I now own something called Forlor, but have no idea where or what it may be."

Hoplick blinked. "The information is before you," he said. He pointed to the numbers. "Here are the spatial coordinates and the recommended route to take. Enter these into the navigation nexus of any space ship and it will take you unerringly there."

"But where is 'there'?" Conn asked.

Hoplick peered at the data. "Well beyond Gowdie's Last Reach, I can tell you that."

Everyone in The Spray knew of Gowdie's Last Reach. It was the ultimate world humans had settled during the Great Effloration. Past its blue white star hung the Back of Beyond, an empty gulf where a few lonely stars gleamed through rifts in vast clouds of obscuring hydrogen. "Forlor is on a planet in the Back of Beyond?" he said.

"No," said the Registrar. "Forlor *is* a planet in the Back of Beyond. You own a world."

Now it was Conn's turn to blink. He sat in Hoplick's comfortable chair. "I own a world," he said.

Jenore said, "What kind of a world is it?"

Hoplick rummaged through the stacks of cartons until he found a large book. Its cover identified it as *Hobey's Compleat Guide to the Settled Planets*. The Registrar set it on the table and riffled its pages then ran a finger down a column until he located the information he sought.

"Here we are," he said. "The planet was located millennia ago but registered under a blind. That means its coordinates were known only to whoever held the bearer deed." He scanned the information in the guide and went on. "Smallish place. White dwarf sun, orbital distance and axial tilt make for mainly bearable climates, rudimentary vegetation but no major fauna or intelligent species. Geologically inactive, mostly ocean, one continent, no moon but a couple of moonlets. No settlements noted." He closed the book. "Seems a reasonable sort of place. Probably some magnate's private retreat. If it had been acquired by a cult or some other fellowship, a settlement would almost certainly be listed. Of course, they might be of the kind that live in trees or caves, but such hermits usually eschew space travel."

"I own a world," Conn said again. "A reasonable sort of place." He was trying to come to terms with the notion of owning a planet but somehow it could not lodge securely in his mind.

Jenore pointed to the still encrypted part of the screen. "But what is all the rest of it?" she said.

Hoplick held up a finger. "Ah," he said. "That would be the security system to protect whatever's there. You place the bead into its lock, or perhaps into a communicator. It transmits the code to the facility's integrator which admits you. Without the code, other measures may ensue."

"What kind of measures?" Jenore asked.

The Registrar assumed a speculative air. "At the least, you would be apprehended and confined until someone in authority comes to legitimize your presence. Of course, if no such person is onworld, the confinement would be indefinite. But then, there may not be provisions for long-term prisoners . . ." He spread his hands in a gesture of inevitability. "Or the measures might be more forceful: noxious gases, irritating vibrations, direct fire. There is no police presence in the Back of Beyond so property owners can be as ruthless or as inventive as they see fit."

Conn had by now digested the change in his circumstances. His Thraisian upbringing asserted itself. "What is a world worth?" he said.

"What anything is worth," said Hoplick. "What someone will pay for it."

"Is there a market where they are bought and sold?"

"Not on Old Earth. Out among the Ten Thousand Worlds there is surely room for such an institution. But if it exists, news of it has not reached here.

The vogue for owning worlds came and went long since. If one wants solitude, one closes the door and bids the house integrator accept no contacts. Privacy is complete."

"What about people who wish to conduct themselves inappropriately?" Jenore said and Conn knew from the set of her face that she was thinking of Clariq Wallader.

"Fortunately, such are rarely able to afford their own private worlds," Hoplick said. "Even for the tiny few who would have the resources, it is still a long, long way to go."

At Conn's request, Hoplick printed out the bead's data. He folded the paper and put it away in his pocket then recovered the bearer deed. Somehow it now seemed heavier and more substantial than before.

On the street outside, the scroot surveillance team were as they had been, except for the man who had loitered inside the registry. He now leaned against a wall up the street, glancing frequently at his timepiece to give the impression of someone who waited impatiently for whatever had brought him to this spot. Conn approached him and said, "Please tell Directing Agent Odell that we are grateful for her concern but we do not require your services."

The scroot was a lanky fellow with prominent eyes and an even more prominent bulge in the front of his throat. The latter moved up and down as he swallowed nervously. He made a last effort to ignore them, consulting his timepiece again and tapping his foot impatiently.

"We are returning to our hotel now," Conn said. "Do you intend to shadow us to the lobby?"

"Go away," he whispered.

Conn shrugged. To Jenore he said, "I am glad I am not paying for this. They do not seem to offer good value."

They went to a call station on the corner and summoned an aircar. Within moments one had descended from the overhead flow. But when they were seated inside and Conn had proffered his credit instrument the vehicle refused to move.

"Your means of payment is unacceptable," it said.

Conn was puzzled. He reoffered the credit slip, but the result was the same. Neither he nor Jenore had any other form of payment and they were forced to leave the aircar, which flew away in search of custom.

"I do not understand," said Conn. "A Thraisian draft ought to be good on Old Earth."

"It was good enough at the hotel this morning," Jenore said. "Perhaps the vehicle was malfunctioning."

But when they summoned another aircar the credit instrument was again refused.

"It is not such a long walk back to the hotel," Conn said. "We will clear up the confusion once we are there."

But when they entered the lobby they found their baggage heaped on a cart and a tendentious manager waiting for them just inside the door. He handed them a list of fees and charges and informed them that they could not be paid from the draft Conn had produced the evening before. Unless some other form of payment was forthcoming forthwith, they would have to leave the establishment. The hotel would distrain their baggage.

"There has been a error," Conn said. He brought out his deposit book from Allguard Security. "My account on Thrais contains a substantial sum. My credit draft is secured by Allguard. Let us go to your office and we will rectify this."

But when they contacted the agency that handled affairs for Allguard in Olkney they were informed that Conn's account had been frozen and the draft therefore could not be honored. "Who has frozen my account?" Conn wanted to know.

"The Thraisian Arbitration," said the Allguard representative, a bland-faced woman whose taste in personal adornment ran to large wooden beads and filigreed eyebrow combs speckled with chips of precious stones. "There is a legal dispute concerning discharge of your indenture contract."

"Who has brought the suit?"

"Flagit Holdings of Trintrinobolis on Bashaw. They claim never to have received a payout of your obligation."

"The Arbitration received the payout on their behalf."

"That may well be, but they are disputing it. Since you are offworld, your account is frozen pending resolution of the suit."

"How long will that take?"

The eyebrow combs added a glitter to the woman's facial shrug. "Interworld legal disputes take time. The last that was heard, the Arbitration was waiting for a representative of Flagit to travel from Bashaw to Thrais."

"The amount needed to pay out my indenture was far less than what remains in the account. Can you not freeze only that portion and free the rest of my funds?"

"Perhaps, if we were on Thrais. From here I can do nothing."

"What can I do?" Conn said.

"Instruct counsel on Thrais to act for you."

"I know no intercessors on Thrais, and the funds needed to retain one are frozen. Even if I could, it would be a long time before the matter could be resolved."

Another glittering shrug. "Then your best course is to find some way to raise funds on Old Earth. They would not be encumbered by the dispute on Thrais."

They returned to the lobby, followed by the manager still waving his list of charges. The Bureau surveillance team had now disposed themselves around the open space. The vehicle repairer was seated on a circular bench, perusing a periodical, the allegedly old woman was in a far corner taking an apparent interest in a potted plant, the former lamp polisher was reading a brochure at the front desk while the pop-eyed student of notices was reprising his previous role by examining a wall-mounted list of organizations that used the hotel for meetings. The dissolute imbiber was across the street, still intent on his container of drink.

Conn took in the scene then focused more closely on one of the scroots. He crossed to the woman with the false pet and peered closely at her to confirm his surmise. "Directing Agent Odell," he said, "would the Bureau of Scrutiny advance me funds as a visiting auxiliary thrown upon hard times?"

From within the network of wrinkles that clouded her features, Odell's sharp eyes regarded him with a neutral stare. "The Bureau is not empowered to offer charity," she said. "Fortunately for you, vagrancy is not an offense in Olkney. Be thankful we're not in Zeel or you'd already be consigned to a work gang."

Conn left her and returned to the manager who was making fresh expostulations. Jenore dug a hand into a pocket and came up with the eardrops of Firenzian dark crystal. "Do you know what these are?" she asked the hotelier.

"I do," said the manager.

"They are worth what we owe you, are they not?"

"They are."

"Then will you hold them until we return with funds to redeem them?"

The man took the eardrops. He gave no commitment and Conn saw in his expression that the crystals were worth more than the debt and that he meant to keep them for himself.

Conn took from his pocket the figured bead. "Do you know what this is?" he said.

The hotelier did not.

"It is a bearer deed to a habitable planet in the Back of Beyond," he said. "We have just had it certified by the Registrar of Offworld Properties."

"What does this mean to me?" said the manager.

"At the moment," said Conn, "it is my intention to sell this planet. It ought to bring a good price somewhere along The Spray. When I have done so, I will have more than enough to purchase this hotel and relieve you of your position. I might even have enough wealth to have influence on any other establishment that would consider engaging you."

"Ah," said the manager.

"So I advise you to hold on to those crystals," Conn said, "because I will be back. Your behavior may have a direct bearing on the mood in which I return."

"Um," said the manager but Conn could see in the man's face that concern for his career far outweighed his desire for the eardrops.

The crystals were passed over. Conn and Jenore hoisted their baggage and went out onto Five Points. From the five possible directions she chose one that led into the Shambles and said, "This way."

They walked three blocks to a shopping precinct where the streets were lined with stores that appealed to those who were gratified by being able to spend large amounts on goods and services that flattered their sense of self worth. Odell and her scroots followed along, in ones and twos, at a discreet distance.

Jenore chose a sunny spot near a restaurant and indicated that they should place their baggage beneath a nearby bench. When Conn had done so, he said, "What do you plan to do?"

"The obvious," she said.

"Not to me."

"We cannot stay in Olkney," she said. "It costs too much to live here and there are few opportunities of employment for either gamers or dancers."

Conn had already had vague thoughts about seeking employment. Now he said, "I defer to your superior knowledge."

"So we will go to Shorraff. My family will provide resources to let you settle the Arbitration matter."

"Why would they do that?"

"Because I will ask them to."

"And why will you do that for me?"

"Because what are we here for if not to help each other?"

It did not seem to Conn to be a good occasion to contradict her supposition, but she must have seen the thought cross his face because she said, "Let us say that you have overpaid me for the assistance I have given you in getting here. Think of it as compensation." It was not an unreasonable point of view, Conn thought. "Very well," he said. "So what do we do here?"

"We earn funds to help us reach my father's house."

"How?"

She knelt and felt through her baggage until she retrieved a flat cap. "Remember the song you sang on the Firenz orbiter?"

"Yes."

"Sing it again, but louder this time." She placed the cap brim up on the pavement. "I will dance and passersby will give us money." She struck a preparatory pose.

"Wait," he said.

"For what?"

"We must establish the terms of the contract with the customers."

"No, we must not."

"But how will they know what to pay? How will we know when we have done enough?"

"They will pay what it pleases them to pay and we will perform until we are satisfied with our earnings."

He made a gesture of exasperation. "This is not an orderly way to do business."

She relaxed from her dancer's stance. "It is not business. It is busking, and it is commonly done this way."

"But it is . . ." he sought for the word, "indecent."

"Nonsense!"

"It is as if I asked you to dance naked."

"I have often danced naked. There are some worlds where it is expected."

"I am not getting through to you," Conn said.

"I understand you perfectly," Jenore said. "You want the philosophical template of Thrais to apply wherever you happen to be. I have seen enough of the varieties of human life to know that when one is on Haxxi one eats flonge and smiles."

"I do not know what that means."

"Be thankful you have never been on Haxxi. It is not easy to smile around a mouthful of flonge. Nor is it attractive."

Conn did not want the discussion to digress. He had found the flaw in her argument. "It is not that Thraisian standards should apply to other places. It is that they should apply to me."

"Why?"

"Because they are right and proper."

"For you."

"Certainly for me. Others may lack enlightenment but I must do what I know to be right."

"Wherever you happen to be?"

"Yes," he said, then, "perhaps, or at least I think so."

"Even if everybody else on the planet thinks in ways that are diametrically opposed to yours?"

"Yes."

She put a hand on top of her head as if she feared the lid of her skull needed to be held in place. "Would a Thraisian transactualist object if you simply stood on a street and sang for your own amusement?"

He thought about it and said, "No."

"Good," she said, "because I can assure you that your singing is not going to earn us a bent grimlet. If people put money into my hat it is because they will appreciate my dancing."

Despite her tone Conn realized that Jenore was trying to accommodate him even though she thought his philosophy was unuseful to their situation. He decided that if she could bend toward him, he could lean a little in her direction. "We will try it as you suggest," he said.

She made a face he had no difficulty in reading then again struck a pose. "Sing."

Conn sang the old lament and she stepped into the dance she had performed above Firenz.

The surveillance team filtered into the area and took up positions. Jenore executed a twirl and a dip and came up with the cap in her hand. She sashayed and glided from one scroot to another, refusing to move on until each had made a contribution.

"That's a good start," she said to Conn as she whirled back to where he stood singing. She put the cap down again and danced on. Soon people in search of lunch began to pass on their way to the restaurant. Some stopped to watch, a few hummed in accompaniment or let their heads sway to the rhythm. Grimlets and even a few hepts clinked into the hat.

Conn came to the end of the final verse. The crowd urged them to more. He thought of a song he had heard young men singing in the drinking areas of Horder's sporting house. It was about a fish and how it swam, ending with a repetitive chorus that was mostly the words *fishy-fishy, swishy-swishy, wishy-wishy*. It was supposed to be sexually suggestive, but Conn had never had much facility for deciphering metaphor. Nonetheless, it had a catchy rhythm. He launched into its opening line.

Jenore looked at him in surprise then adapted to the new beat. She twirled and leaped and gracefully strode about the pavement, arms swinging, hands stirring the air. More money clinked into the hat.

"Louder," she said.

Chapter 6

They alighted from the ferry at Round Bay across Mornedy Sound from Olkney, their baggage slung over their backs vagabond style. Near the ferry slip was a boat basin full of private craft large and small, from opulent pleasure yachts to one-person skimmers, moored at floating wooden walkways that went far out into the bay.

Jenore led the way toward an area where moderate-sized boats were tied up. She walked up and down the planked jetties, reading names and other identifying symbols painted on bows and transoms. She stopped at a dark-hulled ketch-rigged coaster that had the name *Omororo* in bright gilt across its stern. A thickly bearded man of middle years was taking his ease in sun-faded clothing in the conning pit, leaning back in a tiltable chair bolted to the deck, his feet on the gunwale and his hands wrapped around a mug of punge.

"Are you Grove Gallister?" Jenore said.

"Who is asking?"

"Jenore Mordene."

The man set the mug down on the deck and regarded her with an appraising eye. "Of the Grebe Isle Mordenes?"

"No, the Graysands branch."

The man stood up. "Then I am Grove Gallister. How may I help you?"

"Would you be going near Graysands any time soon?"

"I hadn't thought of it but anything is possible."

Jenore said, "It's just that I was hoping to get home and have no funds to hire a boat."

"You've been away?"

"Offworld."

"A long time?"

"It's been some years."

Gallister rubbed his jaw curls and considered the matter. Conn was watching the exchange between Jenore and the *Omororo*'s owner with interest. Although nothing was being put as bluntly as it would have been on Thrais, he had the strong impression that he was witnessing a contractual negotiation.

"Your father is . . . ?" Gallister waited for Jenore to supply the name.

"Eblon Mordene."

Conn saw a reaction flicker across the man's eyes: recognition followed by calculation. "I visited his workshop once," Gallister said. "There were some figurines of water spirits."

"He has made some very fine ones," Jenore said.

"They ranged from finger-sized to . . ." He put a hand to his chest, palm down, to indicate height.

"The hand-sized are among his best."

"But not to compare with some that I saw that were twice their height."

"You may well be right."

Gallister rubbed his hands. "Please step aboard. Who is your companion?"

Jenore introduced Conn. When Gallister heard the name of Conn's planet he indicated that its name was unknown to him. "But then the Ten Thousand Worlds are full of odd little places, pursuing their odd little destinies."

"I have heard the same said of Old Earth," Conn said then offered a wintry smile.

Gallister's eyes widened slightly. "And what do you do in your remote corner of the cosmos?" he said.

Conn could see that the Old Earther was only waiting for his occupation to be named so that he could disparage it. There were many terms to describe what Conn did for a living. He chose carefully. "I am a professional duelist," he said.

Gallister gave this information a brief consideration then said, "Make yourself comfortable below. I believe we can take advantage of the offshore breeze." He turned away to busy himself in casting off mooring lines and coaxing the boat's impeller into life.

The *Omororo*'s forward cabin was cramped but comfortable. Conn and Jenore stowed their baggage in compartments under the berths then sat facing each other across the narrow strait between the bunks.

Jenore said, "If the wind holds fair we could be at my father's house in the morning."

"Good," Conn said.

She picked at a nubbin of thread on the quilt that covered the bed. "It does not bother you that I shamelessly begged a ride?"

"I did not see you beg. I did see you haggle."

Her head came up sharply, her eyes locking with his. "I did no such thing!"

"You chaffered like any street corner mercantilist of Bay City."

"I recall no such exchange. There was an amiable conversation regarding my lineage and my father's artwork."

"I heard something more pointed," Conn said. "You wanted to hire this boat and its owner wanted a carved figurine in payment. You offered one the size of a hand and settled for one twice as big. I might have closed my eyes and imagined myself in a Bay City souk."

"Your imagination is as powerful as your views are rigid," Jenore said and returned to her inspection of the loose thread. "Shorraffis do not dicker. We do not know how."

The impeller was now throbbing beneath their feet and the boat was shifting. "Let us go on deck," Jenore said.

Long after the old orange sun had settled tiredly behind the rim of the world the glow of Olkney lit up the southern horizon as the *Omororo* glided out of Mornedy Sound and into the wide channel that led north to the New Shore. Above and ahead the black sky glittered with stars and orbitals and tiny chips of light that were inbound and outbound spacecraft.

Grove Gallister called them up to the cockpit, where he served a dinner of sea fruits and packaged bread, washed down with strong punge. After they had eaten, Conn and Jenore went forward. They sat on the narrow foredeck, shoulder to shoulder, their backs against the sloped wall of the forward cabin. For some time, they listened to the flap of the mainsail and the susurration of foam breaking on the *Omororo*'s bow and falling behind.

Jenore sat with her knees bent and her arms enfolding them. "It will be strange to be home," she said.

Conn made a noncommittal sound.

"Of course, I've changed," she went on, and he had the impression she was talking more to herself than to him. "But home is always home and family is always family."

Again he made no definite answer but her remark set him thinking. Horder's Unparalleled Gaming Emporium, its public rooms as well as its staff dormitories and retirement areas, were all that he could ever have called home—though he had never done so, that he could remember. Now, whether Horder's had been truly home or not, it was gone and the people he had known there were scattered. He asked himself if he had any strong desire to return to Thrais, if the lights and towers of Bay City held any nostalgic allure, and the answer came: *not really*.

"What will you do?" she asked him. "Once you're disentangled from the lawsuit?"

He had not yet given it much thought. "Perhaps I will charter a space yacht and go find this world I seem to own."

"You still have the mystery of who you are and where you came from."

That reminded him of something Hallis Tharp used to say. "What are you, where do you come from, where do you go?" he quoted then had to explain the reference.

She bit her lower lip pensively then said, "Those are questions that do not press many Old Earthers. And those who ask them find the answers obvious and jejune: 'I am what those around me are, what my forebears were and what my descendants will be. Thus I neither come nor go. I am simply here, as were the ten million generations before me and all those who will come after until the sun's belly swells and swallows this old world. In the meantime, I get along as best I can.'"

"Put that way, existence seems colorless," Conn said. "Is that why you went out there?" He gestured to the swath of light that blazed across the vault of black overhead.

"Perhaps," she said.

"And did you find much color?"

"I found Skrey," she said, "and almost found worse."

"But now you are coming home."

"That is because I also found you, strange though you are."

He made another noncommittal sound.

"Perhaps our destinies are entwined," she said.

"Destiny must be an Old Earth concept," he answered. "I am not aware of owning one."

She looked thoughtful. "I think there is a fourth question to add to the three that Hallis Tharp proposed. Perhaps it is the only one that matters."

"What is the fourth question?"

"Where do you belong?"

Graysands was a mid-sized island by the standards of the New Shore: a fit man could walk across it in a couple of hours or, if he was very fit, swim its circumference in a summer's day. Its north and center were filled by a broad, grassy hill decorated with copses of shade trees, but the land sloped south toward a shingle beach and a trim wharf on short pilings.

Here rested at anchor the Mordene family's foranq. Conn recognized the great barge from Jenore's description: its carved towers and minarets, painted arches and domes, most in white and gold, like a city from a children's tale but shrunk down to manageable dimensions and set upon a floating hull that was long and ample in beam. Just above the waterline was a repetition of red eyes painted on a blue field, the clash of colors making the eyes seem to stand out from the wood.

"Remarkable," Conn said as the *Omororo* warped in to the other side of the dock and he got a closer look at the intricacy of the carved embellishments and decorations. He saw columns twined with leaves from behind which the faces of humans and animals, and some forms that seemed a combination of the two, smiled or smirked or grimaced. There were walls entirely filled with dioramas in low or high relief: battle scenes, moments frozen from history or myth, landscapes populated by people or wild beasts. Other spaces were given over to individual portraitures so finely carved and painted that he half expected the eyes to move and the mouths to speak.

"How long has this been in the making?" he asked Jenore.

"The keel was laid in my great-great-great-great-grandfather's time," she said, "but many of the illuminations—that's what the carvings and paintings are called—were carried over from earlier versions."

The scope of the endeavor, generation after generation making their contributions then handing the work on, made an impression on Conn. *What must it be like*, he wondered, *to be embedded in a process that began long before one's birth and that would continue long after*? On Thrais, each worked for his own enrichment. Here was an artifact created by generations, even centuries, of effort, a distillation of artistry and artisanship. But for whom was it made?

"Who owns it?" he asked.

Jenore looked puzzled. "The question has never come up," she said after a moment. "My father is responsible for it at the moment, and I suppose my brother Iriess will take over when the time comes. In a sense it belongs to all of us, all the Mordenes, living, dead and yet to be."

They climbed onto the dock and Jenore pointed to a small face in a lower corner. "That is me," she said. "My grandfather did it when I was a young girl."

Conn studied the illuminated wooden face. The artist had caught the girl in a mood of wistful pensiveness, a child immersed in a child's wonderings. It was an endearing image.

Jenore also regarded the representation of her younger self. "He said he wanted to capture me before I spoiled," she said. "I didn't know what he meant, then."

Gallister had tied up the boat. "Come," he said, "let us wake up the house and give them the good news of your return."

At the foot of the wharf was a trail of wooden blocks set into crushed shell. It led to a rambling structure above the high-water line, a series of shingled walls that met at different angles to surround rooms of various sizes, from small chambers to a sizable hall. Gallister followed the blocks to a central door made of dark polished wood and pulled a rope hanging by the lintel. From within the house came a musical tinkling.

Conn followed but noted that Jenore hung back. He saw a kind of fear in her eyes washed over by guilt. "Do you not expect to be well received?" he asked her.

Now the look in her eyes fell away into sadness. "I do not know what to expect," she said.

Gallister rang the bell again and there came sounds of creaking floorboards and slow footsteps from within. A peephole opened in the upper center of the door, darkened as an eye filled it, then closed again. A lock snapped open and the door was pulled wide. A man, of senior years but still burly and vigorous, with sleep-disordered hair and clad in a knee-length bed robe, stood in the doorway.

"Gallister?" he said. "What brings you to my doorstep at dawn?"

"I have brought you a present." Gallister turned and directed Eblon Mordene's eyes toward his daughter.

The old man blinked then stared for several heartbeats while the young woman stood expectant. Then Eblon Mordene swept aside Grove Gallister as if he were an intervening stalk of grass and came down the pathway, house slippers slapping loosely against his heels. He gathered Jenore into a rib-straining hug, pulling her from her feet.

"Ha!" he cried as if he had been searching for something he had lost and now held it in his grasp. He swung the girl around and stood her down on her feet again but scarcely relaxed his embrace. He was saying things into her ear that Conn could not hear but the expression on Jenore's face left no doubt: she was home and all was well.

Finally, the old man held her out at arm's length and looked her up and down as if surprised to find her still possessed of all her pieces. Then he put an arm around her shoulders and drew her toward the house, saying, "Come in. We'll rouse your mother and set the pot to bubbling."

"Father," Jenore said, "this is Conn Labro."

Eblon Mordene registered Conn for the first time, taking him in in a single glance that ended with an expression in which the younger man read no great appreciation for offworlders or any person who might have some claim to the daughter's affections. "And he is . . . ?" the old man said.

Conn stepped forward and offered a formal greeting. "Your daughter's employer," he said. "I required a guide on Old Earth and engaged her for that purpose."

Jenore threw him an odd look. "I think of us as traveling companions," she said. "He is also in need of our help."

Eblon's inspection was now more penetrating. "Whatever we can do," he said.

"I do not wish to be a burden," Conn said. "I will repay any costs once my affairs are settled. Would you care to discuss a contractual framework?"

The old man cocked his head to one side and took another, longer look at Conn. Jenore said, "He is a transactualist, father. I wrote you about them."

"Ah," said her father. "So you did."

Grove Gallister re-entered the conversation at that point. "Breakfast sounds good," he said. "Also, I would be delighted to see your workshop again. Those figurines of water spirits are admirable."

The old man gave Gallister a dry look. "Let us go in," he said. He went ahead of them through the door, his arm around Jenore, crying, "Munn! Glad news! Everybody, come and see who has returned to us!"

Conn had never experienced a whirlwind but he had seen them depicted and what shortly ensued in the home of Eblon Mordene seemed a close equivalent. A round-faced woman came from the kitchen, flour on her hands and forearms, and threw herself at Jenore. There were tears and soft words. Then sleepy Mordenes of all ages appeared from all directions, rubbing eyes and stretching limbs then breaking into smiles and happy shouts as they competed with each other to enfold the returned daughter of the house in their embrace.

There were at least three generations present, Conn thought, considering the shifting eddy of men, women and children that ebbed and flowed around the kitchen. The noise of conversation and laughter formed a constant background as two tables were set, stove and boiler activated and pots and skillets were put to work. A clatter of cups and dishes soon followed as a sweet pulse porridge, fruited breads and pots of aromatic tea and punge were laid out.

"Sit," said Eblon Mordene and they did, adults and larger children on chairs, toddlers and infants on laps, midsized children standing in the gaps between seats. Conn was pressed to a place between a table and a wall. A mug of punge appeared before him, followed by a bowl of porridge with an oasis of cream in its center, delivered by the round-faced woman called Munn who he thought was likely Jenore's mother, although there were two other candidates of the appropriate age. She put a spoon in his hand and said, "Dig in."

Eyes asparkle and face flushed with pleasure, Jenore ended up across the table and down two places, surrounded by people roughly of her own generation, some of whom were surely siblings while the others he assumed were relations by marriage. A dark-haired girl with the same eyes must be Corali the younger sister, she who would someday have crystal eardrops from Firenz, though right now it seemed that her older sister's return was gift enough.

Conn dug his spoon into the porridge and found it excellent as was the punge with which he washed it down. He was taken back for a moment to scenes from his own youth, to the sporting house refectory with its scarred tables and rows of hardseat stools. He imagined what the indentor's reaction would have been if ever a breakfast had provoked such noise and ebullience: demerits and confinements all around.

He spooned up more of the porridge and suddenly it struck him that this was the first time in his life that he had sat down to a meal in someone's home. The realization brought up an emotion he could not name. After it came a realization that all of these people belonged here. They were at ease with themselves and with each other; even Jenore who had been for a long time far away appeared to have slipped seamlessly back into the fabric of her family. He looked at her, and it seemed that her face actually glowed with happiness. *That is how it feels to be where one is* supposed *to be*, he thought, and he felt something like envy when he considered that his face had never worn such a look of warm contentment.

Perhaps there is some place where I, too, could feel that way, he thought. *Some place where I belong.*

His thoughts were broken by a voice beside him asking, "So what would you rather do?"

Conn turned to find himself an object of interest to a man a few years older than himself who by the set of his eyes and shape of his nose was a brother or at least cousin to Jenore.

It was a puzzling question. At Horder's, one did what one was required to do. Likes or dislikes had no bearing. He sought for a reply, but was rescued by Jenore who obviously had heard the question even over the hubbub.

"Conn is from Bay City on Thrais," she called down the table. "They play games and sports there and everyone gambles. Conn was one of the best players, quite famous."

Her remark brought a strange cessation of noise, as if everyone around the table was suddenly drawn to an inner tension touched off by the mention of gambling. It seemed an odd response to Conn, but he would have put it down to another cultural dissonance if he had not seen the complete puzzlement on Jenore's face as she looked from one relative to another.

"What is it?" she said.

Her father cleared his throat, his face suddenly stiff. "We'll talk of it later."

The man who had questioned Conn spoke up. "There's no shame in it, father," he said.

"I said we will talk of it later, Iriess," Eblon Mordene responded, in a tone that would brook no argument. "In my house we do not wipe our feet on the traditions of Shorraff."

The man beside Conn put his chin out but after a glance at Jenore's uncertain and worried face he reluctantly subsided. Still tension around the table remained high and though the conversation resumed, the unfettered joy of only minutes ago was muted.

Into a conversational lull, Grove Gallister made another mention of the sea spirit figurines. That prompted Eblon Mordene to make a wry face but he rose and led the sailor to his workshop. When he was gone, Jenore spoke to Iriess. "What is wrong? Have you and father quarreled?"

Iriess looked at his hands and said nothing. Jenore turned to the round-faced woman. "Mother?" she said. "What is going on?"

But Munn gave her a smile steeped in sadness and said, "Time enough for all that folderol later. Tell us where you have been and what you have seen."

"Yes," said Jenore's sister, eyes wide, "do they really all do . . . you-know-what on Mizere?"

Jenore rolled her eyes. "Do they? They scarcely ever stop. One wonders how they can summon the energy to tend the foodbeasts. They say it's something in the water."

So you are a sportsman?" Iriess said. After breakfast, he had invited Conn to walk with him and some of the young men of the household along the Graysands shore. Jenore had been bustled away in a knot of women and girls and the children had been dispatched to their tutors.

"That was more usually a term for our customers," Conn said. "We simply called ourselves players."

"As do we," said Iriess. "Have you heard of the game of birl?"

Conn said he had not.

"It's a blaze," said one of boys tagging at their heels. Another said, "Blatantly ferocious."

Conn assumed the phrases were colloquial. "How is it played?" he said.

The young Shorraffis enthusiastically competed to describe the details and glories of the sport. Despite the overlapping voices and the tendency of one source to qualify or amplify what another was saying even before he had finished speaking, Conn thought he was developing a fairly clear image of what was essential to a lively game of birl.

It was a team sport, organized into a league of four divisions. Iriess played left forward on the Cresting Wave and every one of the men and boys escorting them was a fierce partisan of the team. "We are second in the Gold Division after a resounding victory over the Green Fins of Balakshi Cove last week."

"We blatantly submerged them!" said a boy. Conn was about to add the term to his vocabulary of Shorraff argot until he realized that the description was literal: a birl match was played on water and part of the strategy involved dunking the opposition.

The game was played on a roped-off rectangle of sea, three times as long as it was broad, in which large and small islets called "plats" were anchored. In some of the channels and gulfs between the firm footing of the plats were the "rolls"—floating logs which would turn under a player's foot and throw him into the water unless he exercised quick footwork to keep the wood spinning beneath him.

The players advanced and defended by leaping from plat to plat, while passing a fist-sized hollow ball from one to another, using a short-handled racket with a netted basket at one end. The passing was hedged about with rules about being off-side or zoned-out. At either end of the pool was an undefended circular goal not much larger than the ball which had to pass through it.

The game was designed to minimize direct physical contact between opposing players although the referees tolerated a certain amount of jostling that inevitably led to dunkings. But one-on-one log-rolling duels were a crucial element of the contest, the most nimble-footed players competing to stay on top and earn a free shot on goal.

It sounded like a simple game that could become complex in the hands of skilled, experienced players. The play moved fast and there was scope for both team strategy and individual excellence. Particularly prized by aficionados were instances when the opposing teams' finest players landed simultaneously on the same roll and dueled to see who would be pitched into the water. The techniques of "variance" and "saltation"—the former an alternation between slow and fast footwork to throw an opponent off his rhythm, the latter a sudden daring leap straight up into the air, causing the other end of the log to sink— afforded delightful suspense to those who knew how to gauge a first-rate match.

"Would you like to see a game?" Iriess asked.

"Why not?" Conn said. "I am likely to be here for some time until I can engage an intercessor to act for me on Bashaw and free my assets."

A play-off match was scheduled for the next day. It would decide which of a pair of Red Division teams, the highly rated Incomparables and the upstart Jaunty Crabs, would advance to the championships. Iriess was particularly interested to judge the style and quality of the Crabs' forward line, since he and his fellow Waves might have to face them if the Crabs won tomorrow and the Wave triumphed over the Deep in the upcoming Gold Division final. It was decided that Conn would accompany a group of Mordenes to the contest on Five Fingers Key.

"But your father seemed displeased by the mention of gaming," he said. "I would not want to transgress against the morals of my host."

Iriess waved away the concern. "My father does not condemn birl. Indeed, he was a handy player in his youth and even captained the Wave of his time to a championship."

"Then what is the conflict?"

"He opposes the Tote," Iriess said, "as do many of the older folk. We of the younger crowd see no harm in it."

"Load of fackle," said the opinionated boy.

"Blatant," agreed another.

"What is the Tote?" Conn said.

Another multi-voiced explanation ensued from which Conn understood that the Tote was some form of mutual betting pool that handled wagers on birl matches and individual results, such as whether a particular player would score or win more encounters than he lost in rolling against a top-ranked rival.

"Alwan Foulaine conceived the concept," Iriess said. "It adds to the interest in matches. The setting of odds for and against this or that team or player can liven up a discussion over at Oplah's Grotto."

"Oplah's Grotto?" Conn said.

Iriess described it as a congenial tavern on Darsh Strand, a short distance from Five Fingers Key across a shallow strait called the Ripple. Birlers and their supporters often went there for ale and fritters after a match.

One issue puzzled Conn. "I was told that Shorraffis use no currency. With what do you wager?"

Iriess said, "Alwan devised a system of tokens."

"Redeemable for goods and services?"

Jenore's brother looked shocked. "Of course not! The tokens are just a way of keeping score. He who best analyzes the many factors involved in predicting the outcome of a particular match or roll-off amasses the most tokens. It is an infallible method for deciding who is most handy at understanding the game of birl."

Their progress along the shore had brought them to a place where a cliff rose on the landward side of the beach. They followed its rising contours until they stood high over a narrow stretch of sand that was covered by a jumble of logs, snags and other storm-wrack.

Offshore, across a narrow strait, was a rocky islet on which a remarkable structure had been built of the same kind of debris that littered the beach at their feet. It was low and rambling, for the most part, although a precarious second story had been constructed in the center of the sprawl, buttressed by driftwood logs whose butts were anchored in heaps of boulders.

The place was still under construction. Conn could see a few men and boys splitting short lengths of fine-grained timber to make shingles for the roof. Another crew were spreading the shakes on a roof made of rough-sawn boards. The sound of hammers came faintly over the suffle of the wind.

"What is that place?" Conn asked.

"It is Alwan Foulaine's," said Iriess. "His family has split over the Tote. He was asked to leave."

The way Iriess hushed his voice to pronounce his last words signaled to Conn that behind the simple phrasing stood a fearsome concept. Clearly it was no small thing for a Shorraffi to be asked to leave his family steading.

"If he has gone into exile, he has not gone far," said Conn. "Nor has he gone alone."

"It was blatantly unfair," said the opinionated youth. "Lots of us are helping him."

"And thereby making a bad situation worse," said Iriess. "No good comes from division, especially when it splits a family."

The boy stood his ground. "Right's right, though the world crack," he said. A couple of the others spoke up in support of the young iconoclast but Conn saw discomfort on a number of faces.

Iriess held up a hand. "It is a discourtesy to squabble so in front of a guest, especially a guest who has done us the kindness of bringing home our Jenore. Let us go back."

The group reversed its steps and headed back to the Mordene family compound.

"I regret bringing up a painful issue," said Conn.

"You meant no ill," Iriess said. "I am sorry you are not seeing us at our best."

He turned the conversation to other matters and Conn found himself being asked to relate some of his experiences in the arenas and game rooms at Horder's. The younger Mordenes, hearing of his duels to the point of blood or breakage, forgot their differences over Foulaine. They pressed for details. Their eyes widened and they greeted Conn's recounting of some of his experiences with exclamations of "Blatant!" and "Ferocious!" and "Mythical!"

"Did you kill people?" one boy asked, and Conn read in his eyes that he both craved and dreaded the answer.

"In virtual encounters, I slew hundreds."

"And in—what did you call it?—full flesh?"

"Very few sportsmen require that level of risk."

"But some do?" said the boy.

"It is a serious matter, not to be lightly spoken of," said Conn and though they pressed him he would say no more.

When they returned to the rambling house, Jenore and her father were on the dock. Grove Gallister was aboard his ketch, a parcel wrapped in brown paper and twine under his arm and a happy expression on his face. He waved brusquely and let the impellor back the ship out into open water then turned her and raised the sail. As the wind took him away, Conn saw him unwrap the parcel to gaze at what it contained.

The old man sent the young men and boys off to their occupations then led Conn to a circular wooden bench built around a dark-leaved tree with a widespread crown that stood beside the house. They sat and Eblon Mordene gave the young man another close inspection. Conn saw nothing in the old man's eyes to trouble him.

"Jenore has told me of your situation," Eblon said. "I am happy to help."

Conn started to speak but the old man cut him off. "I understand," he said. "You are a transactualist. You wish to establish terms and so forth. Such concerns are meaningless to me."

"They are essential to me," Conn said.

"Very well. If you require a framework of this-for-that, consider this: anything I do for you is payment, though insufficient, for restoring my daughter to my house."

When on Haxxi, Conn thought. He said, "If it does not offend, I will consider that our contract."

"Then we are agreed," said Eblon. "Now, I have had no dealings with intercessors for longer than I can remember, but Rietlief Bublick over on Filberg built a houseboat for one some years back. We will go to Bublick. He will help."

Conn let his face show his discomfort.

"Consider Bublick a subcontractor of mine," Eblon said. "Then his relations with me do not concern you."

"That is true," Conn said.

Filberg Island was on the far side of Graysands, beyond a broad shallow channel and a salt marsh. They crossed Graysands by foot, the distance being inconsequential, then borrowed a stilt-hack from the family that farmed the southern half of the island. The craft carried them across the strait and marsh, its six segmented legs lengthening or shortening as the sea bottom rose or fell. Although at first sight of the vehicle Conn expected a bumpy ride he found the passage remarkably smooth, each leg moving in perfect synchronization with all the others.

The stilt-hack's leisurely pace brought them to their destination just as Rietlief Bublick and his crew were sitting down to a sumptuous lunch in the boatyard. A broad-beamed craft with high peaks fore and aft was in the ways, its keel well laid and half its overlapping strakes already adhered to the ribs by a strong smelling glue. "Keeps the sea worms away," the boat builder said when Conn reacted as did all first-time visitors to the odor.

Bublick was a small, neat man with bright blue eyes and oversized hands and forearms covered in fine sandy hairs flecked with sawdust. He beamed at Eblon Mordene and welcomed Jenore home from offworld as if she were a daughter of his own house. Conn was waved graciously to a seat at the long common table, fortunately at a distance and upwind from the bubbling glue pot. Fried breads, batter-dipped fish and pressed seaweed cake, washed down with a pale ale, made a good lunch.

After their mission was explained, Bublick took them into his office and had his integrator contact an intercessor named Lok Gievel in Olkney. The face that appeared on the screen was that of a subtle and experienced man beneath a crown of pink skin surrounded by snowy hair. After introductions were made, Gievel invited Conn to relate his situation, asked several pertinent questions then said he would contact the agency that handled business for the Thrais Arbitration in Olkney and make inquiries. It was agreed that he would report his findings through Eblon Mordene's integrator within a day or so.

The business settled, Bublick and Mordene fell into a meandering discussion involving events that had concerned them both in the past. The former mentioned the construction of a skiff as well as some minor repairs to the stern of the Mordene foranq. The latter recalled an ornate rack carved from bone and designed to accommodate the exact number and dimensions of certain pipes in Bublick's possession.

A silence fell and both men fell into contemplation. After a while Bublick said that he had been wondering if his formal dining table might be enhanced by a new centerpiece, perhaps something with dolphins. Eblon's face took on a reflective cast. He recalled that he had carved a number of such pieces over the past year, some of them still in his workshop. If Bublick were to visit, he might examine them to see if one took his fancy.

"I might be inclined to pay a visit," Bublick said.

"Come around lunch time. The berries have been exceptional this year and Munn's pies are the best they've ever been."

It was agreed that Bublick would wander over to Graysands when he had a day to spare.

On the return trip Conn and Jenore sat in the rear of the stilt-hack while the old man operated the controls up front. When they had traversed the salt marsh and were crossing the channel, Conn said, "The conversation between your father and Bublick concerning the centerpiece—my impression was that they were negotiating a price for Bublick's engaging the intercessor."

"No," said Jenore, "you measure everything to a transactualist template. I heard only a discussion of matters of interest to them both."

"Yet there was a transaction."

"There was not. Did my father say, 'Give me thus and I will repay you so'?"

"He did not. Yet one gave and the other repaid."

"That is only how you see it."

"No. It was how it was though you refuse to see it."

She set her jaw. "It is you who refuses to see. Bublick did as he wished. So did my father. No one said, 'If this then that. If not this, then nothing,' as they would have done on Thrais."

Conn knew he was right. At the same time he recognized that the woman was equally sure of her interpretation. Both had seen the same event; each had viewed it through a lens shaped by culture. He remembered the Hauserian Farbuck and his inexplicable outrage over the mundane practice of selling superfluous children. Conn had thought the pastoralist mad. Now he wondered if on Hauser Conn Labro would seem the loon. The thought brought a vague discomfort.

"You may be right," he said to Jenore, more to end a fruitless dispute than to concede his position. Perhaps when his affairs were settled he would undertake a study of representative cultures of The Spray. Narrowness of focus could be useful in some endeavors, but a wise man was able to call on a diversity of perspectives. Someone had said as much to him somewhere back in his past, though he could not remember the occasion.

Dinner was served on long trestle tables out in the yard, the news that an interesting offworlder was staying with the Mordenes having motivated neighbors from several islands to drop in unannounced. But Conn noted that no one came without a steaming pot or well-filled basket to add to the bill of fare.

After they ate, he was importuned to tell more tales from his years in the gaming rooms and again deflected inquiries about full-flesh contests that had gone to the ultimate outcome. After a while, he steered the conversation to a discussion of birl and tomorrow's match but soon saw the discussion grow too technical for his grasp of the sport.

When the eating was done and the arguments had finally worn down to trivialities, Eblon stood and announced that the company should now move to the family foranq for an evening of music and conviviality. Several Mordenes and a number of their guests retrieved musical instruments and rhythmics that had been left under the great tree then the patriarch led the way aboard the barge. He stepped aboard at the landward end of the vessel and threw wide a pair of doors carved in close detail, a scene that depicted an epic battle between fish and other sea creatures, some of them real sharks and tentacled decabrachs, others fanciful images of gilled men from maritime myth.

Beyond the doors was a spacious hall. The old man waved a hand and hundreds of lumens set in a half a dozen ornate chandeliers threw a warm glow onto walls half-paneled in dark wood so deeply polished that they resembled somber mirrors. Above the wainscoting was a painted frieze of men and women visible from the shoulders up, their faces representationally rendered, though in a variety of disparate styles and clearly by many different hands. The effect was such that the panels seemed to be a barrier behind which a crowd stood to watch the goings-on on the wide dance floor of sprung wood. Conn examined some of the painted faces and saw resemblances between them and Jenore's family.

"Yes," she said, when he asked the obvious question, "they are all Mordenes, all painted from life. My father is already there." She pointed to a portrait of Eblon Mordene which looked to have been captured when the patriarch was decades younger.

"Will your face be up there someday?" Conn asked.

"If my handedness as a dancer is ever judged good enough," she said, "though that's not likely."

The musicians had grouped themselves on seats at one end of the hall. The family and guests brought chairs and benches in from the walls and became an audience, leaving a broad open space between them and the players—"Some will want to dance," Jenore said—while the children sat on the floor or in their parents' laps. She led Conn to a seat in the front row, next to her parents.

A period of tuning and tentative exchanges of riffs and passages ensued, then the ensemble settled on a rolling rhythm that soon evolved into a rousing song about an energetic folk dance. Everyone joined in on the chorus, then a young man among the musicians stood and sang a verse that sounded to Conn as if it was made up on the spot. It concerned a young woman who had many suitors and kept them all uncertain of her intentions. When he had finished there was laughter. The musicians vamped until the merriment subsided then there followed another round of the chorus. Now a sharp-eyed girl rose from the audience and sang a verse about young men who were so full of themselves that they thought young women should abandon their own concerns to focus entirely on the vain fantasizings of idle fellows.

It seemed to Conn that all of the verses referred to the faults and foibles of persons who were never named outright but adverted to by nicknames and references to incidents familiar to all except Conn Labro. Still, he enjoyed the witty turns of phrase and clever puns even if he could not recognize the targets.

Next came a selection of ballads, each offered by a different soloist or duet. Eblon Mordene sang a lament in a rich baritone, an old man's look back at lost youth that brought wry grimaces to the faces of the young and tears to the eyes of their elders. A pair of sisters from Bider's Pool harmonized sweetly over the tale of a diver who went deep into the green sea to win a pearl for his true love and never came up.

A cry went up for Jenore to dance. "Show us what you learned offworld," called someone from amongst a knot of young men.

"The Mizere Divestiture!" The suggestion came from someone who took care to remain anonymous and was met with expressions of disapproval from the older folks, though it drew a smattering of whistles and wordless hoots from the young bucks.

Jenore's composure was unshaken. "I will dance the third movement from Rimble's Seventh," she said.

The musicians retuned to a minor key then went into a simple, elegiac melody. Jenore stood still with head bowed through the opening bars, waiting until the woodwinds came in behind the strings before lifting an arm then following its motion in a slow turn. She had put on a loose dress for the evening, sleeveless and knee-length. It swirled and flowed about her as she glided across the floor, stopping and turning as the music evolved into a complex counterpoint between the woodwinds and muted brass, the strings rising above their duet like wind sweeping across a darkening landscape.

The music voiced a final statement of regret and ended on a diminuendo of departing spirits. Jenore executed a final pirouette, deliberately faltering as she sank to the floor. The hall was hushed. Then came a soft sound as the crowd exhaled a collective breath, followed by a burst of hand clapping and cries of approbation.

Jenore rose and executed a formal posture of gratitude but her face was aglow with pleasure. When the applause died, she beamed at the assemblage, her eyes moving from face to face, and said, "Thank you. It is as if I had never left."

A single pair of hands resumed clapping. Conn saw Jenore's face change as her regard came to rest at a point beyond the rear of the crowd. He turned to follow her gaze, hearing a scrape of chairs and a rustle of clothing as the rest of the room did likewise. Standing in the open doorway, a fleshy man, balding and jowly, slowly clapped. He wore an ankle-length robe of dark stuff with a starburst of gold and silver spangles on the breast and a supercilious expression on his face. Behind and to one side skulked a wiry, thin-shouldered fellow with his hair oiled straight back and his lips set in a practiced smirk.

The balding one waited until all eyes were upon him before he said, in an unctuous tone, "Welcome home, Jenore Mordene."

Eblon rose from the front rank of the crowd. "I do not recall inviting any of your crowd onto this foranq, Alwan Foulaine, least of all you."

The man dismissed the inhospitable remark with a flexing of his eyebrows and a slight widening of his eyes. "When I heard that my betrothed was returned from the stars it never occurred to me that I would be denied an opportunity to call upon her." He turned an incisive gaze upon Jenore. "Well, at least you haven't run to fat," he said.

"No," said Jenore, looking him up and down, "but it seems I unknowingly ran from it."

A laugh rippled through the crowd and Foulaine's face went rigid. Eblon gave his daughter a look of approval before turning back to the man in the doorway to say, "The traditions of Mordene hospitality are rigid but wide of extent. You have appeared, therefore you must be allowed in. Join us, if you will."

Foulaine assumed an air of unconcern and strode into the hall, his auxiliary at his heels. They seated themselves on an empty bench that had remained against the wall. The young man who had sung the verse about his fickle inamorata rose and crossed to sit with him. A few of the other boys and young men followed. Conn saw one of them open the collar of his shirt to reveal what looked to be a necklace of colored disks.

Eblon Mordene was still standing where he had risen. Conn saw his face harden as he saw the boy reveal the necklace. But before the old man could take a step toward the group around Alwan Foulaine, Munn reached up from where she was sitting and stayed him with a hand on his arm and a motion of her head that said, *Not here, not now.*

The patriarch acquiesced and gestured to the musicians to play. "Something all can dance to," he said.

The players gave him a sprightly tune that spiraled away and back through two octaves. Munn rose and Eblon led her out onto the floor where they performed what struck Conn as an unlikely combination of high-spirited rompery and dignified bearing. Whatever it was, they had clearly pushed Alwan

Foulaine beyond their notice, leaving themselves free to enjoy the music, the motion and each other.

"Dance with me," said Jenore, pressing her warm palm against Conn's.

"I know no steps," he said. "Certainly nothing like what you just did."

She shrugged. "When you were slaying opponents with falchions and epiniards, you must have been light on your feet, surely?"

"There was a certain amount of stamping involved," he said, "but, yes, there was lightfootedness as well."

She showed him how to hold her. "Follow me and let the rhythm do the rest."

He did as she bid and was surprised to find that within a few moments they were moving in tandem. The process grew even more smooth when he stopped thinking about where his feet should go and thought instead of how pleasant it felt to enclose Jenore Mordene in his arms.

The song ended but a new one began almost immediately, this time slower and with a different time signature. The change at first disconcerted Conn but within a few moments Jenore had him adapted to the new rhythm. He found it was even more engrossing to be dancing slowly with her, especially when she rested her head upon his shoulder.

The intrusive sound of a throat being cleared caused him to reluctantly shift his attention. Alwan Foulaine had come to find them on the dance floor.

"Might I have the pleasure?" he asked, in a tone that on Thrais would have told Conn that a personage of highly elevated status was addressing someone he considered unworthy to scrape ordure from his footwear. But perhaps things were different here.

Conn made allowances. "I do not understand," he said. "What pleasure?"

"He wishes to dance with me," said Jenore.

"Do you wish to dance with him?"

"No."

"Then the matter is settled," Conn said to Foulaine. He stepped and glided as Jenore had shown him and they moved away from the former suitor.

But Foulaine followed, plodding straight lines while they executed arcs. His heavy face had reddened well up into the region at which it could more properly be called scalp. Foulaine's look of condescension became a glower of angry resentment. "I heard that you had descended into poverty or worse on some barbaric hole," he said. "So you have come crawling back."

"No, we came by space liner and sailboat," said Jenore.

Foulaine made a face that said he found her remark a poor riposte. "I have done well," he said. "I am spoken of from one end of the New Shore to the other."

"Indeed," Jenore said, "I heard my father speak of you at some length."

Foulaine's plump hand flicked her comment away. "The old mud-sticks will maunder on. We of the modern age set our own standards."

Conn was finding that he disliked this man. "I am sure that makes it easier to live up to them," he said.

He was rewarded with a contemptuous glance, then Foulaine addressed himself again to Jenore. "I am building my own manse on Griff Island."

Jenore said, "I heard that a pile of driftwood and sea wrack had appeared there. You have burrowed into it?"

Foulaine's face was rigid. "Young people from all over Shorraff are joining me in a common effort. We will create a new community, with new standards. Our goals are noble. Our achievement will be astounding."

"I will certainly be astounded," Jenore said.

Foulaine looked Conn up and down. "What is this that you have brought back from the ragtaggle end of The Spray?" Foulaine asked Jenore.

Jenore's tone was airy as she drew closer to Conn. "This is Conn Labro. We met on Thrais, the gaming world."

"A gambler, is it?" Foulaine's condescension showed in a meager motion of his brows and a half lowering of his eyelids. "Many such pitter about my feet."

"Not a gambler," said Jenore, "but such as gamblers win fortunes on. Conn is a renowned duelist. How many men is it that you have killed, my dear?"

Conn watched the flush drain from Foulaine's face. "I prefer not to speak of it," he said.

"That is probably for the best," she said.

"You two," Foulaine said, "are you affianced?"

Conn let Jenore answer. "We have an understanding."

Conn saw rage and fear contend in the man's heavy face. He watched until the outcome was apparent: Foulaine would not precipitate a violent confrontation here, breast to breast. But if circumstances should ever deliver Conn and Jenore into his hands the outcome would be unpleasant.

Foulaine retook possession of himself by a visible effort. He appeared to notice someone elsewhere in the room whom he desired to greet and walked away without a parting word.

"I thought that went well," Jenore said.

Conn watched the man go. "Too much of him would tempt me to anger," he said.

Jenore gave her head a dismissive shake. "He was always a puffed up fool."

"Even fools can be dangerous. I would not care to be chained to a wall in *his* basement," Conn said.

"I have occasionally thought about how it would be to encounter Alwan again," Jenore said. "That was as enjoyable a scenario as many I imagined."

"So you do not feel that you are here to help him?"

"There are limits to every philosophy," she quoted. "It's a wise rule that admits the possibility of exceptions."

The music they were dancing to came to an end. They stood together on the dance floor, she still in his arms.

"He is of the past. What does it matter?" Conn said.

"The past is inextricably woven into the present. Any separation between what was, what is and what will be is merely a matter of perception."

"You truly believe that?"

She indicated the faces painted on the walls. "Look about you."

"I do not see it that way," Conn said. "Each moment is distinct, in and of itself, one in a succession of uniquenesses, to be appreciated while it lasts."

"On the contrary," she said, "all existence is a continuum. Yesterday, the substance of our dinners swam in the sea and grew in the sunlight. Today, they have become part of our flesh. Tomorrow, they will be on their way again. We fade into each other, from one to the next, leaving behind memories and mementos to mark our passage. This foranq is such a reminder. There are rooms whose walls are tiled with the milk teeth of hundreds of generations of infants, others tapestried in the woven hair of women who have been dust for centuries. Not all the bone my father carves is from fish or animal."

He lifted her hand and regarded the bone ring on her finger. "When you said this was your grandfather's, I took it to mean that he had owned it."

"Well, it was definitely his," she said, "for a while. And perhaps it will be his again when it passes to one of my descendants."

"You believe in transmigration from one life to another?"

"How else could it be? Where else could we have come from, where else could we go? We know that this *here* exists and we know that we are in it. Any other realms of existence are nebulous and speculative, mere possibilities set against this inarguable reality."

"I have no sense that I have lived before, nor that I will do so hereafter."

"Truly?" Her tone was reflective. "You are unusual," she said. "I sometimes sense that there are more differences between us than our cultures can account for."

"Perhaps," Conn said. "While I was experiencing the effects of the whimsy I felt a strong sense that I had spent much time in a kind of limbo. I could not account for it."

"A womb memory?" she said. "It is not unheard of. The unborn often bring with them an awareness of the timelessness of the life between lives."

While they spoke, the musicians had agreed on another number. The drums set up a solid rhythm for the other instruments to ride on.

"I am who I am," Conn said, "whether I probe and prod my inner mysteries or leave them unmolested. But right now I have discovered that dancing is a pleasure. Or perhaps it is just because I am dancing with you. Either way, I wish to do more of it."

He spun her around and away they went.

Later, when the lights on the last guests' boats and skimmers were winking away across the still waters, the house's integrator summoned Eblon and Conn. It was receiving a call from the intercessor Gievel.

"An interesting result," the face on the screen said. "I filed a preliminary notice of dispute this afternoon, a mere formality. Yet just now I received a message from the other side."

"What was the message?" Conn said.

"They wish to make an offer of settlement."

Conn's voice echoed the surprise in Gievel's. "Is it not unusual that those who bring an action should offer to settle before we've even argued our side of the dispute?"

"Highly," said Gievel. "Indeed, unheard of in my practice."

"What is their offer?"

"They wish to present it in person. They will come to wherever you are tomorrow."

"I will be at a sporting event."

"The birl?" Gievel said. "I envy you."

Eblon Mordene said, "He will be with my household and their friends on Five Fingers Key."

"I will come with the other side's representative," Gievel said, "both to protect your interest and to see the match."

"Who is the Other side? Is it Flagit Holdings on Bashaw?"

"Another surprise. He is from here. Flagit is now controlled by Lord Vullamir, head of one of the oldest of the old families."

Conn felt a twinge of coincidence. "Does he have jewels embedded in his face?"

Gievel looked puzzled. "That style passed on years ago. These days, the vogue among the aristocracy is life masks."

"I have not seen one," said Conn.

"Then you will tomorrow."

Chapter 7

Five Fingers Key was a long, low tongue of land that barely missed being a peninsula of Graysands Island, and would have been such for half of each day if Old Earth had not long ago lost its moon, and therefore its tides, as an unintended outcome of the hubris that can grip even the most gifted scientific minds. The island and the key were connected by a floating footbridge.

One end of Five Fingers Key was dedicated to birl. An oblong playing area had been dug to connect with the sea then ringed with tall, transparent panels to protect spectators on the surrounding bleachers from flying balls and splashes of water. Most of the Mordene household attended the match, only the smallest children remaining at the house with some of the young parents to oversee them.

Eblon led the way to a section of the steeply tiered seats that Conn deduced must have been reserved for Mordenes. Jenore discovered some old girlfriends in an adjacent section and went to sit with them, leaving Conn in the care of her brother Iriess. Conn looked about as the seats filled. Like the Mordenes, other clans occupied their own sections. Even a casual inspection of the crowd showed Conn similarities in facial feature and coloring in the different sections. There also seemed to be some connection between family and team. Every Mordene, he noticed, wore something—scarf, hat, tabard—of sea green accented by white, the colors of the Cresting Wave.

He asked Iriess, "Are teams formed from members of individual families?"

"Not quite," Iriess said. "Theoretically, anyone can try out for any team and, if possessed of the requisite skills and élan, be enlisted. But over the generations, some families have built up relationships with certain teams. The Wave's roster is mostly drawn from Mordenes, Folliocks from Flatstone Cove, Rabbaths from over by Mud Bay and a few Grubbers from Boddle.

"Now, the Crabs are interesting because they were formed only a few years back from the remnants of two longstanding teams that broke up—the Terns and the Periwinkles—after neither had come within hailing distance of a championship in decades. They have merged the best of two mediocre teams into a surprisingly potent distillation. Last year they came second in Red Division; this year they may go all the way to the finals."

Iriess proceeded to discuss individual Crab players and their attributes in detail while Conn strove to form images of a game he had not yet seen played. After a few minutes the Wave forward's voice was summarily drowned out by a blaring fanfare of trumpets, brassoons and stagehorns from a small orchestra seated on the flat roof of a single-story structure built of coral blocks at the landward end of the pool. The music signaled the emergence of the Jaunty Crabs and Incomparables from their respective preparation rooms at either end of the building.

The Crabs wore electric blue singlets and harness—the latter useful when being hauled out of the water—while the Incomparables favored deep purple slashed with silver. They marched to either side of the playing area and positioned themselves in front of benches between the water and the transparent partitions. The horns blew a different sequence of notes and everyone in the bleachers stood to hear a young woman dressed in flowing white sing an anthem that Conn later learned was called *We Strive*. Her last notes were buried beneath a rising roar of cheers, handclaps and whistles and the players advanced into the field.

The team captains met on the broad center plat, their forwards arranging themselves as strategy dictated. The arbiter threw the bone-colored ball into the air between and above them and the contest began. Conn watched the play with growing interest, Iriess providing a running commentary broken by shouts of approbation or condemnation as players conducted themselves in manners he approved or disapproved of.

The field was divided into several segments laterally and longitudinally. Passes could not be completed across more than two contiguous zones. Nor could a far forward player legally catch a pass unless there was a member of the opposing team between the receiver and the opposition's goal. The rules made for a fast-moving game of strategic maneuver, the ball passing back and forth as a team advanced into enemy territory, with plenty of jostling and blocking when opponents met.

Direct checking, whether from behind or head-on, was penalized by the offending player's removal from the game for two minutes, but players could brush past each other with vigor, and if one happened to end up in the water it was considered fair play. But the real skill was in skipping from the solid footing of the substantial plats onto the smaller floating spots which sank beneath a player's weight or, even more difficult, onto the rolls which both sank and spun. Each landing must be perfectly executed.

Conn soon saw that any aggressive play required the players to leave the security of the plats and skip from one rolling, sinking footfall to another. He watched as the Incomparables' first advance carried their left forward into a leap from a plat onto a roll in Crab territory. The man deftly caught a pass in his scoop-shaped basket while spinning the roll beneath his footwear. But as he made to leap to a plat from which he could have taken a shot on goal, a young woman in Crab blue joined him on the roll.

The ensuing contest was brief but full of energy. The Crab defender spun the floating cylinder in the same direction as the Incomparable forward had set it rolling, but faster, the roughened soles of her tightly laced boots seeming scarcely to touch the log's surface. The Incomparable first matched the pace then edged sidewise down the log toward the Crab, forcing her end deeper into the water. But she countered with a saltation, bending her knees to spring into the air and land back on the spinning roll with enough shock to throw the man off his rhythm. Now he was backpedaling while the soles of her boots controlled the speed of the log.

Conn saw the Incomparable's back curve while his head went forward in an attempt to counterbalance and thought, *That can't be good*. A moment later, the Crab abruptly used her feet to slow the speed of the roll's spin and her purple-clad opponent tried a desperate lateral pass to an Incomparable on another roll. The attempt came to nothing. The ball went wide and the Incomparable went into the water, to hoots and shouts from the section of the seating where electric blue scarves and berets waved, and groans from where the purple sat.

At the end of the first of four periods, with the score at three to two for the Crabs, the teams exchanged ends. By halftime the Incomparables had added two more goals to their total. But in a lighting-fast, last-moment rush the Crabs leapfrogged up the right side of the pool then executed a brilliant series of lateral leaps and passages that put their left forward in position to hurl the ball through the Incomparables' goal just before the bell rang.

"This is an enjoyable game to watch," Conn said as the players retired to the preparation rooms for the halftime rest.

"Even more enjoyable to play," said Iriess, unpacking a basket of filled buns and cold fish pies. "You look to be well coordinated, and I can teach you the strategy if you would like to try out for the reserves."

"I cannot swim."

Iriess blinked in surprise. "You may be the first adult I have ever met who could make that statement."

"My employer on Thrais saw no need for me to learn. In any case, I lived all of my life in a single large building. It did not contain a pool."

Jenore had left her friends to join them and heard the exchange. "Conn is not like us," she said. "The Spray is strewn with worlds based on profoundly different strategies for organizing lives."

"You were a slave, were you not?" Iriess said.

"No," said Conn. "I was not owned as a chattel. I had obligations to my employer. I met them honorably, as he met his obligations to me."

"Yet he decided all things."

"Many decisions were mine to make. Others were negotiable. It was a complex relationship."

Iriess gave a small shudder. "I prefer our way," he said, passing Conn a seeded bun and a smoked eel pastie. "All is simple and above board. Each sets his course as he sees fit and we all get along."

As they had been speaking, the crowd around them had been generating a buzz of conversation punctuated by shouts and laughs from its younger members who sought to impress each other and especially those who were of the same age but of different family and gender. Now Conn heard a new note under the general hubbub: a darker grumble pierced by growls of disapproval.

His eyes were drawn to the landward end of the playing pool where a knot of older boys and young men were gathered around the portly figure of Alwan Foulaine, highly visible in a robe of yellow and green at the foot of one of the tiers of seats. He stood on a box that raised him head and shoulders above the crowd. He held a clipboard to which he continually affixed small slips of paper passed to him by the men and boys surrounding him. He would consider each slip in turn, compare it with information on the board, then speak to the skulker of the night before who waited at his elbow.

The assistant—Conn had learned that his name was Whitlow—wore an apron faced with several bulging pouches. Upon each instruction he would reach into a pouch and count out a number of colored disks—red, yellow and green—placing them in the hand of whoever had passed a slip to the balding man above him. Some recipients would take the tokens and string them onto a cord worn about the neck; others could be seen immediately passing the tokens back to the wiry man and, after a brief exchange, receiving a new slip of paper from Foulaine.

Conn noted that some of the crowd wore complete necklaces of tokens, some with two or three strands. Others boasted only a few disks on a string. Those who had more generally looked happier than those who had few, but Conn could see that the distribution of smiles and frowns depended on whether an individual was proffering a slip to collect a reward or tearing one up and throwing away the pieces.

"That is the Tote," he said.

"Indeed," said Iriess. "You have already met Alwan Foulaine, its originator."

Now it was Jenore's turn to shudder slightly. "He not only grew the paunch but acquired the face of a truculent dog," she said. "I remember now why I was so glad to join Chabriz's show."

"Shame," said a deep voice nearby, not as loud as a shout but well above a mutter. Conn looked up to see Eblon Mordene glowering at the swirl around Alwan Foulaine and especially at its centerpiece. Other growls and rumbles could be heard from the spectators and the faces of many older members of the crowd showed the same grim censure that darkened Conn's host.

The troop of men and boys around Foulaine and Whitlow was shrinking as people collected winnings and made fresh bets. Some of them did so with defiant glances at their grumbling elders, others filing back to their seats with careful faces, as if they heard nothing. Foulaine himself turned a bland face to the bleachers then went back to business.

"What is the problem?" Conn asked.

"It is the tokens," Iriess said. "For some, they seem too much like money."

"But they cannot be spent for anything, so they are no more significant than colored pebbles from the beach."

"I tend to agree. My father has different views. It is a generational divide."

Jenore stepped into the conversation. "I agree with our father. No coin has been passed between Shorraffis since time out of mind. This is not good."

"They are not coins," said her brother. "What can they buy?"

"Respect," she said. "Those who have strings of tokens about their necks are judged to be more handed at predicting outcomes of birl matches."

Iriess waved dismissively. "They do not purchase their handedness with tokens. The strings are mere symbols of their ability."

"Perhaps because I have been among coin-passers I see dangers that are not apparent to you."

"Or perhaps you disapprove because it was Alwan Foulaine who originated the Tote."

"What is Foulaine's handedness?" Conn asked.

Jenore made a rude noise with lips and tongue. Her brother ignored the sound and answered the question. "He was very good at throwing knives and hand-axes, though it's not a skill that commands much respect. But he has an amazing facility with numbers. He can multiply one four-digit number by another in less time than it takes to state the integers."

"Impressive," Conn said.

"Give him a date and he can tell you what day of the week it fell on, though it be a thousand years ago."

"Remarkable."

"But useless," said Jenore. "If I need an arithmetical result, I ask an integrator. If I need to know the day of a date, I consult a calendar."

Iriess had to agree that Foulaine's gift was of little practical purpose. "It is a shame, in a way," he said. "If he'd been able to do anything that would win him praise he might not have become such a . . ."

His assessment of Alwan Foulaine was drowned in a blare of horns from the roof above the preparation rooms. Now the players marched back onto the field to the strains of *Yet Again to The Fray*. It was an ancient paean, one Conn had heard often during his own contests on Thrais and it raised an unfamiliar feeling in him to hear it here. But he shook off the sentiment and concentrated on the Crabs and Incomparables.

Play was even more brisk as the second half opened, the players in blue clearly energized by their success in holding the highly regarded purple-silvers to a first-half draw. The Crab forwards seemed almost to walk on water as they skipped from plat to roll while the Incomparables quickly lost whatever élan they had summoned up between halves. Within minutes, the score was five to four for the upstarts and the Crabs were pressing hard for an insurance goal.

"The Incomparables needed a come-uppance," Iriess said. "Their playbook has not changed since I was a first-year reservist."

"But do you look forward to facing the Crabs?" Conn asked. "I sense an aura of ensuance about them."

At Iriess's blank look he explained that he had used a Thraisian term for a competitor's sense of being attuned to victory, when every stroke and motion achieves exactly its intended effect and the body seems guided toward perfection by some irresistible outside force.

"We shall see," said Iriess. "They won't be playing those lumberers if they come to our pool. They'll be . . ."

He broke off to shade his eyes against the sun. Something bright and flashing was in the air above Five Fingers Key and as Conn followed Iriess's gaze the object resolved itself into a long and luxurious air yacht, yellow and black with crimson sponsons and fairings and the coat of arms of a noble house prominent on the tail fin. It swooped gracefully toward the open field behind the preparation building and even the birlers watched it come down. Then it passed out of their sight behind the building and the game went on.

Conn shaded his eyes. He saw a portal open and a ramp descend. Four figures descended. "That, I believe, is the intercessor Gievel," he said.

"Yes," Jenore said. "Along with two lords and, probably, their own intercessor."

"Well." Conn stood up. "I will go and see what there is to see."

Jenore also rose and said to her brother, "Are you coming?"

At that moment the crowd erupted in mingled cheers and groans as a Crab forward was dunked. Iriess tore his gaze away from the action to look up at Conn and Jenore but could not keep his eyes from sliding back toward the pool.

"Never mind," she said.

"You do not need to accompany me either," Conn told her.

"When we were on Thrais I contracted to guide you in encounters with some of Old Earth's peculiarities. You are about to meet some of them." She linked an arm in his and drew him down the steps between rows of seats. "Besides, I have another motive. We will pass within close range of Alwan Foulaine. I wish him to see me in your company again."

"You should forget him."

"I do not forget as easily as you," she said. "There, we have caught his eye. Try to appear serene and dangerous."

They passed behind the bench where the Incomparables' reserves sat. Conn noted a forlornness in the set of the players' shoulders and the degree of elevation at which they held their heads. If he were interested in collecting Tote tokens, he would have bet against the purples. He was familiar with the aura of impending defeat.

During his brief inspection of the losing team his peripheral vision caught a motion of yellow and green. "Foulaine is following us," he said.

Jenore tossed her head and made a wordless sound that paradoxically conveyed both victory and indifference. They made their way around the robing room and saw the air yacht hovering just above a stretch of lawn. Gievel and the three others were waiting at the bottom of the ramp.

"A quick lesson," said Jenore as they approached. "When we meet them you must make the motions I do."

"On Thrais, we greet each other thus and so," Conn said, demonstrating the chest-tap and knuckle-brush that constituted a formal greeting.

"I know," she said, "but these are more sensitive circumstances. Old Earth aristocrats are trained from infancy to respond to forms and procedures. If you do not make the right gestures they may not be able even to see you."

"I am capable of drawing myself to their attention," Conn said.

"There is a difference between seeing and recognizing," Jenore said. "As well, they will know that you were recently indentured, therefore your present rank puts you beneath their normal threshold of perception. They will have difficulty seeing you in the best of circumstances and will not address you at all. They will speak to their intercessor who will speak to Gievel. It would be best if you replied through him."

"I am accustomed to negotiate for myself," Conn said.

"They are not accustomed to negotiate at all. To let Gievel be the buffer will avert unnecessary lapses in communication. Remember, when on Haxxi . . ."

Conn acceded to her greater experience. "They certainly are remarkable in their appearance."

The aristocrats wore loose upper garments of shimmering fabric which constantly changed color as the breeze altered the angle at which it encountered sunlight. The sleeves were slashed to reveal the contrasting buff fabric of their linings and the shoulders, which extended well beyond the width of the rest of the garments, were augmented by long quills ending in feathery tassels. The blouses were gathered at the hips by broad belts of supple leather; beneath was pastel-shaded, limb-hugging hose that hardened to become boots. The lords' hands and wrists were encased in metallic gauntlets that each sported one finger more than should have been necessary.

But what captured Conn's attention were the spherical masks that fully covered the visitors' heads. Fashioned from a translucent material, each made it appear as if its wearer had replaced his own head with a transparent helmet in which someone else's head floated. Above the shoulders of the taller of the two aristocrats was the head of a mature man wearing an expression of studied inattention. The shorter wore the curls and features of a little girl.

As Conn and Jenore approached, the tall one's mask turned briefly toward them, though its eyes did not quite focus, then redirected its attention to the intercessor, a man in understated clothing who stood with Gievel. Jenore stopped a short distance before reaching the group and executed a series of formal gestures which Conn copied. Then she took a step closer, repeated two of the motions and adopted an attitude of decorous expectation. Again Conn did as she did.

The taller lord inclined his floating head toward the other intercessor and spoke softly. The man turned to Conn and said, "I am Ezrail Opteram. I have the honor to name Lord Vullamir and Lord Magratte. They decline a statement of lineages and exquisitries, these being without meaning to you."

"I am Conn Labro, an unencumbered consumer . . . " Conn began, but Gievel indicated that there was no need to identify himself. The intercessor said to Opteram, "My client is present and desires to hear your offer."

Opteram said something to Lord Vullamir, the taller of the two aristocrats. Words passed from the lord to his intercessor.

Opteram said, "Your client has come into possession of an object that was stolen from its rightful owners many years ago. My clients are interested in . . ."

Gievel listened attentively, his face neutral, but Conn interrupted the other intercessor. "Am I accused of theft? Is that why my assets have been distrained?"

Again, Gievel gestured for calm and quiet. "Let me counsel that we hear the other side in full before we make a response." To Opteram he said, "Please continue."

"I will address the point," the other man said. "No accusation of theft is leveled against your client. The object was stolen by one Cooblor Tonn, who it turned out also went by the name Hallis Tharp. It was taken from his employers and carried away."

At the mention of the old man's name, it seemed to Conn that the sun's warmth grew weaker and the air took on a chill. "Who were his employers?" he said.

"Please," said Gievel, an edge creeping into his tone, "let me handle this."

"The identity of Tonn's employers is not germane to the issue at hand," Opteram said. "We are here to discuss the object and its disposition."

"Just so," said Gievel. "Pray continue."

"No," said Conn. "The matter of Hallis Tharp is of relevance to me. I believe he was killed by someone who wished to obtain the 'object,' and there was an attempt on my life. I will not discuss the matter unless my questions are answered."

Gievel and Opteram put their heads together and spoke quietly, then the latter spoke in turn to Lord Vullamir. The lordly head on the aristocrat's shoulders rotated until its eyes focused on Conn. The young man found the gaze disconcerting because he was unable to read any expression in it. Although the head appeared to be fully realized it conveyed no more sense of an inner life than if it had been carved from stone. Meanwhile, the little girl's head on the second lord's shoulders peered at him with a peevish expression.

Vullamir turned back to Opteram and said something. The intercessor bowed and turned to Gievel. "I will relate what I know of the matter."

He said that Cooblor Tonn, as he had then been known, had been employed for several years by the Flagit brothers, Ermin and Blathe, as a developer of entertainments and amusements. He had designed and overseen the construction of a play area on their vast estate at the landward end of the Olkney peninsula as well as some offworld retreats.

"What sorts of entertainments and amusements?" Conn interrupted. "Who are these Flagits?"

The Flagits turned out to have been the inheritors of an immense fortune built up by generations of entrepreneurial ancestors who seemed to have reliably passed down the gene for turning opportunity into profit. They entered adulthood with a greater net worth than any other residents of Old Earth, indeed greater than the fortunes of the next three wealthiest families combined.

However, unlike the long succession of Flagits that preceded them, the brothers did not use their mind-staggering riches to generate even greater heaps of plenty. Instead, they devoted their lives to amusing themselves on grander and grander scales.

"They liked to play games," Opteram said, "against each other. Very large games, so large that eventually their scale grew too great for their estate. They acquired a small, private planet named Forlor and there they conducted wars using robot armies and fleets."

The armies and fleets grew bigger and the fighting ever more ferocious, but with each iteration the Flagits would experience the same cycle of initial excitement and a growing absorption that ultimately led to satiation and ennui.

"Then, it is said, they decided that the robots were the problem, that they were too predictable. The brothers wanted to fight their wars with armies of men and so they put out calls for recruits. At that point, a number of governments became concerned as they often do when private armies begin to blossom in their areas of jurisdiction.

"The Flagits encountered active discouragement, of both the official and unofficial varieties. When they tried to use their wealth to overcome the authorities' resistance they found that they had spent so much of what they had inherited that they no longer commanded the influence their ancestors had enjoyed."

Piqued, Ermin and Blathe had dropped out of sight for a long while—perhaps a dozen years—and when they next appeared on Old Earth they had developed new interests, largely centered around growing vicious unnatural creatures and setting them against each other. Each brother maintained his own array of recombinative vats from which he produced ever more repugnant and fearsome monstrosities. Though they varied imaginatively in the numbers of their limbs and the arrangement of their claws, pincers and poison sacs, Ermin's products always bore the face of Blathe, and vice versa.

"In the end," Opteram said, "they arranged a duel between two of their most lethal and loathsome creations in a sealed arena on the estate. Matters got out of hand, however. The brothers seemed to have gotten too close to the combatants, whether in an attempt to separate them or in their enthusiasm to egg them on—the recordings were inconclusive. What was clear was that the four-armed, sting-tailed brute that bore Ermin's face tore Blathe into increasingly smaller pieces, while the thick-necked behemoth with Blathe's features stomped Ermin into an inseparable mixture of sand and gore."

"Where does Hallis Tharp come into this picture?" Conn said, when the intercessor had concluded.

"Oh," said Opteram, "I have digressed. He was mentioned in a memorandum that turned up in Flagit Holding's corporate records when the estate was being evaluated. The bearer deed to a property was found to be missing and since it was last known to be in the possession of Cooblor Tonn, who was nowhere to be found, it was deduced that he had absconded with it."

"Did no one pursue him?" Gievel asked.

"Apparently not. The brothers had long ago lost interest in the property, having abandoned it when they returned to Old Earth to take up breeding their monsters. They had given no orders so nothing was done."

"Where do your clients' interests and those of the Flagit brothers intersect?" said Conn.

"My clients are members of a consortium that has come into control of some of the Flagit assets. Therefore the bearer deed belongs to them."

"Allegedly," said Lok Gievel. "It is quite possible that the brothers gave the deed to this Tonn or Tharp and failed to make note of it. They were remarkably cavalier as to their possessions."

Opteram dismissed the objection as irrelevant. "What matters," he said, "is that your client possesses the object and my clients wish to acquire it."

"So it is a haggle?" said Gievel.

"In so many words, yes."

"Then state your offer."

"My clients will drop the action against your client concerning the indenture contract, thus unfreezing his assets. They will also pay a reasonable price for the bearer deed."

Gievel tugged at his nose. "One person's 'reasonable' is another's ludicrous folly," he said. "What price?"

Opteram named a figure. Gievel snorted. The chaffering began and continued for some time. At times, Opteram placed a palm to his breast and looked up at the sky as if to call down judgment on Gievel. Gievel, for his part held his head in both hands, staring at the ground as if dumbfounded to encounter such irrationality in a brother intercessor. At times, each walked sadly away from the other only to turn after a few paces and come back with an air of compromise. The voices ranged a gamut of emotions from gentle entreaty to justified outrage and back again.

At no time during all of this did Opteram refer to his clients for fresh instruction, nor did Gievel find it necessary to involve Conn in the discussion. The two lords gave the matter no attention. They conversed together quietly as if they were the only two persons present. For his part, Conn watched the aristocrats. It disturbed him not to be able to read their thoughts or feelings in their eyes, and their garments so disguised their natural forms that he was almost equally unable to deduce anything from their stance.

He cleared his throat, more loudly than he had need to. Vullamir made no response but Magratte slightly turned toward the sound. Conn could read nothing in the face above the ruffled collar—it was now no longer an insect's but that of a noble youth—yet thought he saw even through the exaggerated line of the man's shoulders an indication of hostility. He coughed again, even more loudly, and now he was sure from the way Magratte's gloved hands reflexively moved that the aristocrat disliked having Conn's existence brought to his notice.

Whether the animosity was personal or merely the irritation that the nobly born often feel when thrust into the presence of the lower orders, Conn could not say. But it gratified him to know that he was having an effect on at least one of the two aristocrats, though why he should want to affect them at all he also could not say.

The negotiations reached a crescendo, each intercessor appealing to unseen forces to save him from the impossible rapacity of the other. But the climax was muted: they put their hands together in a complicated way, with some odd motions of individual fingers, and the business was done. Each turned to speak with his clients.

Gievel lowered his voice to include only Conn and Jenore in his remarks and said, "We have agreed upon a price of fourteen million hepts. If you concur, it will be transferred to whatever account you wish this afternoon."

Conn mentally changed the Olkney currency into Thraisian worths. The sum represented a substantial fortune and was certainly agreeable. But he said, "There is another matter. Who killed Hallis Tharp and tried to kill me?"

"Do you wish to deal with the property matter first then raise these ancillary matters after?" Gievel said.

"I have a presentiment that once the property matter is resolved, no attention will be paid to any question I might put."

"Very well," said the intercessor. He took Opteram off to one side and a whispered discussion ensued. Then Opteram approached the lords and there was more whispering, followed by another conclave between the intercessors.

Gievel came back. "Here is what they say: the consortium posted a substantial standing offer for the return of the bearer deed. Many licensed freelance discriminators and a number of unabashed adventurers were motivated to search for it. A while ago a man named Chask Daitoo advised the consortium that he had located Tonn and would soon have the deed. He was able to convince them of the truth of his assertions. Expenses were advanced, he went offworld, and has not been seen since.

"Then you turned up at the Flagit office on Bashaw, flourishing a bearer bead and talking about coming to Old Earth. When the consortium were advised that you had arrived, they launched a legal action against you to make sure they had your attention. And so we are where we are today."

Conn had listened closely. He said, "At certain points this explanation does not entirely coincide with the facts."

"Do you wish me to say as much to Master Opteram?" Gievel said.

Conn thought for a moment then said, "No. But tell them I wish to think about their offer. I will contact them through you tomorrow and deliver my response. In the meantime, I wish them to withdraw the action against me so that my assets are unfrozen. I will not be coerced."

"Very well."

Gievel relayed Conn's response to Opteram who took it to the lords. Again, Vullamir remained impassive but Conn saw a reflexive reaction from Magratte. Still, the aristocrats agreed to the terms. It was decided that Conn would contact Gievel in the morning through Eblon Mordene's integrator.

Conn had expected that some more formal folderol would be required before he could take himself out of the aristocrats' presence, but such was not the case. The lords turned their backs on him and withdrew to their air yacht. The two intercessors followed, chatting collegially.

Jenore took Conn's arm again but her earlier carefree air was gone. "They lied about Hallis Tharp and the attempt on your life," she said.

"Yes. There is something they do not want me to know."

"Will you pursue the matter?"

"I do not know."

She stopped and he must do likewise. "Hallis Tharp was your friend," she said.

"No, he was *your* friend. To me he was a partner in a game of paduay."

Her face had darkened. "He died protecting you and left you everything he owned, money he had saved when he could have spent it on a better life for himself."

"Yes," Conn said. After a moment he added, "That puzzles me."

"It shouldn't. It is what a good friend would do."

"All right," Conn said. "Suppose we were friends. How did we come to be so? He was a mature man and I only an infant when he opened the account for me."

"Perhaps he was more than a friend," Jenore said. "Perhaps he was of your family."

Conn summoned a mental image of the old man. There was perhaps a faint resemblance. Still, he found it hard to imagine that Tharp would have sold his own kin into indenture; he had spent enough time off Thrais to understand that other worlds frowned upon the custom of selling surplus children, and Tharp had been no Thraisian.

"I cannot make the pieces fit," he said. "I cannot see Tharp as a thief, yet I also cannot see him as having the kind of wealth that allows a man to acquire a private world."

"Perhaps it was as Gievel said, the Flagit brothers gave him the bearer deed when they lost interest in the planet."

"Then why did he not just sell it? Why did he hide himself in poverty on Thrais? Why did he sell me to Horder?"

Jenore had no answers.

"I am faced with a choice," Conn said. "I can take the consortium's money and leave those questions unanswered. The funds would let me return to Thrais and establish my own sporting house, or go and do where and what I please. Or I can withhold the bearer deed until my curiosity is satisfied."

"If you do the latter, the consortium will surely try to pressure you into relinquishing the deed."

"Yes, surely. But if I continue to investigate the mystery of Hallis Tharp I may well discover the answers to his questions and yours: where do I come from, and where do I belong?"

She took his arm again and they walked on, the sounds of the birl match growing louder as they approached the building that contained the robing rooms. As they rounded the corner they saw that Alwan Foulaine was back in his seat. He stared at them a long moment, then turned to say something to Whitlow that intensified the sneer on the thin man's face.

"He was eavesdropping on us," Conn said.

"Perhaps," Jenore said, "but I believe I will adopt your attitude and let him fall behind me, to be lost in the shadows."

They headed back to where the Mordenes were sitting, skirting the playing area, Conn keeping one eye on the progress of the birl match. The Crabs were romping toward victory, the Incomparables bogged down in hopelessness. He saw a pair of the blues pull off a magnificent pass but the resulting roar from the crowd suddenly changed in mid voice and took on a new note. Conn heard angry shouts and hoots of derision.

In the pool, the birl match abruptly came to a halt, the players standing on the plats or sitting astraddle the rolls. Up in the bleachers, many of the spectators had risen to their feet. They formed knots and clumps of arguing folk. In the middle of one of these was Eblon Mordene. He held one hand raised above his head, and from his fingers hung a cord on which dozens of tokens were strung. One of the young Mordenes—Conn thought it was the boy who considered so many things blatant—was fruitlessly trying to retrieve the necklace while Eblon's other hand held him at a distance.

Now the old man took his hand from the boy's chest and brought it up to join the one that held the tokens aloft. With one sharp jerk he snapped the cord. Then he flung the necklace toward the pool, colored tokens flying free of the string and spinning brightly in the sunlight.

A shout of approval rose from some of the crowd. Others sent up a loud protest, not the least of which came from the boy whose tokens had been scattered. In another section of the seating a man with a grizzled beard grabbed for the tokens around a nearby youngster's neck. The boy dodged but the motion tumbled him back into the arms of a woman who pushed him free. Now everyone around the disputants was on his feet, and a number of tussles ensued.

Most of the spectators had by now taken sides, divided roughly but not exclusively by age. Among the men there were few neutrals, and even among the women there were several who were making their views known. In places, the altercations brimmed on violence.

Alwan Foulaine had risen from his place at the foot of the bleachers in the landward end zone. Conn could not tell from the motions he was making whether he was trying to calm the crowd or urge on the supporters of the Tote.

The brawl now became general. Fists and feet flew where a group of younger men—and a few women—who disdained the Tote had met a crowd of its adherents in one of the lower bleachers. Other objects also began to fly: seat cushions at first, then more substantial missiles—a couple of heavy mugs from box lunches, then someone's boots.

Conn turned to speak to Jenore. As he did so, something brushed Conn's shoulder and he heard the sound of solid metal striking wood. He looked down and saw a ferric rod almost as long as his forearm and thick as two fingers rolling out of sight under one of the benches. He stooped and picked it up. It seemed to be a core from which tokens were sliced. He hefted it in his hand, a solid weight of metal. If it had struck his head he would not have avoided injury. If it had struck him end on he might have been killed.

He looked to where Alwan Foulaine stood. A cluster of brawny young men had gathered around the Toteman and Whitlow, protecting them from elements of the crowd who saw in the riot an opportunity to make their opinions forcibly felt. Foulaine regarded Conn with a mildly regretful mien, Whitlow with his habitual smirk. Conn remembered what Iriess had said about the man's proficiency at throwing knives and hand-axes. There was no doubt about where the rod had come from, nor the intent behind its throwing.

Chapter 8

Oplah's Grotto was less congenial than usual, Conn suspected, although the ale was good and the fritters—various sea creatures unrecognizable under thick coats of deep-fried batter—offered novel and rewarding flavors. Iriess and Jenore and a few others from the Mordene clan had led him across the Ripple, a shelf of rock only a finger's width beneath the surface of the sea. They had walked barefoot, carrying their shoes in their hands or around their necks.

The birl match had eventually been resumed and completed, although not before most of the older Shorraffis had left the stadium, taking the smallest of the children with them. The Jaunty Crabs had triumphed, the Incomparables simply collapsing in the final frames, but the talk around the Grotto was not of the game or the effects on league standings.

Alwan Foulaine's adherents pulled together some small tables to form a single large board. They sat around it on chairs and benches, muttering and occasionally raising their voices. Thin-faced Whitlow led the conversation—Conn could hear his high-pitched tone rising above the others—while Foulaine sat erect with arms folded, his heavy features set in an arrangement that bespoke smugness and triumph. But when he glanced toward Conn and Jenore, an emotion that was both hotter and colder glinted in his eyes.

After a while, Iriess left to walk home with friends from another table and Conn and Jenore sat mostly in silence. Others were rising and calling it an early night. Conn had brought with him the rod of metal that had so narrowly missed him during the riot. He rolled it back and forth across the wooden table top, evoking a soft but ominous rumble. "I should return this to Alwan Foulaine," he said after a while.

Jenore put her hand atop his, stopping the motion of the bar. "No."

"Would it breach some custom?" he asked.

"No. It would just not be . . . good."

Again, he was tempted to ask her to define what she meant by the word, but he could sense that she would not welcome the discussion.

"The trouble at the birl match has upset you," he said.

She looked around the room. "I suppose," she said, then, "no, it's more than that. When I was out among the Ten Thousand Worlds, encountering strangeness or nastiness, I would always remind myself that there was a place called Graysands, a place where I belonged. I had a home to go to."

She gestured to the angry faces and abrupt motions of the young people around Alwan Foulaine. "Now I come back and it's like this."

Conn saw Foulaine glaring at them. He had caught her gesture and doubtless concluded that she was disparaging him, that being what the Tote's creator would have done if their situations had been reversed.

"I believe I should settle matters with that man," Conn said. "He looks the type to let an injury fester."

"Please take me home," she said, then repeated the last word and added a sound that indicated an ironic perspective.

They went. The tavern had largely emptied. Most of those who had wished for a Jaunty Crab victory had already left, their boats and stilt-hacks leaving faint phosphorescent wakes on the dark sea. Conn and Jenore walked in the direction of her home, first across the shallow strait to Five Fingers Key then down the shingle beach to the bridge that led to Graysands. Conn carried the metal rod in one hand, and as they splashed through the shallows he found Jenore's fingers stealing into the clasp of the other.

They gained the far shore then turned and followed the narrow beach that led to the bridge. They walked in silence for a while. Conn's eyes adjusted to the darkness and he found there was just enough light from the stars and orbitals overhead, augmented by the natural glow of tiny sea creatures in the water rippling along the shore, to find his way.

He was thinking of what Jenore had said, about having a home to go to. For a moment he wondered if he would like to be back again on his narrow cot in his narrow room in Ovam Horder's gaming house, a day's tasks completed behind him and another day's agenda awaiting him at the sound of the first morning buzzer.

He decided he would not, even if it were possible for him to reverse time's flow. The universe had turned out to be more complex than he had realized, back when he had fitted the routine at Horder's like a precisely machined cog in a well-tuned mechanism. The initial stages of discovering that greater complexity had been discomfiting, he would admit. But now he was beginning to see the course of events as if he were playing a game that first presented as straightforward but evolved into arabesques and mazes as one progressed beyond its early stages. *Much like paduay*, he thought, which again brought him back to the puzzle that was Hallis Tharp.

He was beginning to pick at that conundrum once more when his ears caught a distant rattle of stones. Almost immediately, he heard the sound again, but closer and from multiple sources. Footsteps. Running. Coming this way.

He released Jenore's hand and said, "Run. Run home now," even as he turned to meet the rush from the darkness. *Clear noncombatants from the killing zone* said his training. *Turn toward the attack and engage the enemy.*

The light was too dim to see them clearly. There were six or seven young men, Alwan Foulaine's followers almost certainly, closing rapidly, running down the beach toward them. He could make out straight lines, lengths of wood possibly, or more of the metal bars.

He heard Jenore say something and said again, over his shoulder, "I am fine. Run!"

Then he was in action. They would expect him to run or perhaps to stand his ground. But he had not won a thousand fights by doing what the opponents expected. He ran toward them, as silently as he could manage on the shingle but counting on the noise of their own passage to disguise his. He held the rod in both hands, arms extended before him at head height, aiming for the middle of the dark knot of attackers.

He hit one of them hard. Bone cracked, blood splattered Conn's face and he heard a sob of surprise and pain. *Nose broken,* he thought. His momentum carried him past the injured man, whose knees had folded under him, and into the path of another who was coming close on the first one's heels.

Conn kept the rod extended, letting it ride up and over the first target so that it struck the next man in the forehead. The impact was less but the second man went down without a sound except for the clatter of his cudgel on the stones. Now Conn was through the pack and turning to follow them.

His stratagem was working. Those still on their feet would have thought that those who were down had stumbled. They could hear Jenore ahead of them, running for home as fast as she could without any attempt to silence her steps. They continued after her. One of them slowed and looked back into the darkness, calling in a forced whisper, "Jeege, are you all right?"

The words were scarcely out of the man's mouth when he received his answer. Conn's rod came arcing out of the darkness and struck the side of his head above the ear. *Blood or breakage,* Conn thought. He was unsure how the Shorraffis would react if he killed the attackers—he was learning not to take common sense for granted among strangers—but the chances were good that merely disabling them temporarily would bring fewer consequences. He did not want his options limited.

Three down and, by the sounds of their footsteps, four more to deal with. He ran after them, finding them now beginning to string themselves out as each pursuer put on his best speed, hearing their quarry just ahead. They were no match for Conn's swiftness. He caught them up and took them down, one after another, with precisely judged blows to each man's head. He closed with the last one just as the fellow reached out to seize Jenore's collar. "Got you," the man said, but his prediction was revealed as premature when Conn's weapon sent him sprawling unconscious on the beach.

Jenore did not look back. Conn loped after her, hearing her breath coming hard. "It is finished," he said, close to her ear, his wind scarcely affected by the exercise. "They are all taken care of."

He had to repeat himself and even so she ran several more steps before she stopped and bent over, hands on knees, sucking air into her lungs. After several seconds, when she could talk again, she said between gasps, "Are you . . . all right?"

"I am fine."

"Are they . . . you didn't . . ."

"They will all have sore heads, perhaps some slight concussions. One has a broken nose."

"This should . . . be reported."

"I would prefer to avoid complications."

She stood straight, her breathing coming under control. "Thank you," she said.

"I am not sure they were after you, as such. Foulaine would like to see me dead, though."

"I do not think you understand how deep the sin of pride can go," she said.

"Perhaps not." He broke off and turned his head. "Listen," he said.

From out in the water came the soft susurration of water over a boat's bow and the burbling whisper of an impellor. Conn could make out the outline of the dark-hulled craft against the stars that crowded the horizon. A whisper came across the water, "Wengh? Jeege? Did you get them?"

Conn said softly to Jenore, "I think you were right. He wanted to harm both of us."

"And me more than you," she whispered back.

"Shall I pretend to be Jeege or Wengh, lure him in?"

"I never want him any closer than he is now," Jenore said. She stood and called out across the water, "Your bully boys are all stretched out senseless on the shore, Alwan. If you were not such a pasty-faced coward, you would be with them, and tomorrow your head would have harsh things to say to you."

There was silence from the sea, then they heard the sound of the boat's passage fading as it turned and sped away. At last, Foulaine's voice came faintly on the wind, a snatch of words: ". . . not over."

"We had best not speak of this to anyone," Jenore said as they walked on. "There has been trouble enough today, and this can only make things worse."

"As you wish," Conn said. "This trouble, at least, I understand. The other business still mystifies me."

It is filthy stuff," the patriarch of the Mordenes was saying as Conn and Jenore entered the big common room. "Money has never fouled this house. It will not do so in my time." The boy whose tokens had been thrown into the pool opened his mouth to make an angry reply but Iriess restrained him with an admonitory hand and spoke in his place.

"Father, it is not money. It cannot be used to buy or sell."

The old man's eyes flashed. "It buys handedness—in itself a monstrous idea—at predicting the outcome of birl matches. It is wagered and those who win or lose it value the outcome."

"No," Iriess said, "it does no more than symbolize success or failure. There is no transaction."

The argument had been going on since the return from the birl match. Now Eblon turned to Conn who had taken a seat beside Jenore, on a carved bench against the wall of the big family room. "We will ask an expert. Conn Labro, what do you say?"

"I prefer not to take sides," Conn said. "I have nothing to gain by inserting myself into this dispute."

But the old man insisted and the younger ones also clamored for his verdict, each side sure it would support its point of view. Conn looked to Jenore who sat near him and saw that her father's request made her deeply uncomfortable yet she moved her eyes and mouth in a way that urged him to answer it.

"All dealings between human beings are transactions," he quoted. "The goal of the reasoning person is to ensure that there is equity between buyer and seller, that the price is fair, the goods or services delivered as advertised so that the contract is justly consummated. Thus does the market retain the perfection that is its essence."

From the looks on the faces around the room Conn realized that something prevented the Mordenes from grasping the elementary concept. It was as if he had spoken to them in an incomprehensible language. After a moment, Eblon Mordene shook his head as if to throw off something that might be clinging to his scalp and said, "But you have not answered the specific question: is the wagering of tokens a transaction?"

"It must be. It can be nothing else. All human interactions are transactions."

"Then you believe the tokens are money?" Iriess said.

"No," Conn said. "Money is a general medium of exchange that facilitates transactions involving goods or services of differing types. These tokens can purchase only one specific commodity."

"Prestige," Eblon said.

"Yes."

"But they do not buy that 'commodity,'" Iriess said. "The prestige of being handed at predicting birl outcomes—which takes knowledge and analytical skill—comes from success in the endeavor."

"A pointless endeavor," said Eblon, "like Foulaine's tricks with numbers. Who benefits?"

"That is another issue," Iriess said. "For some, it increases the enjoyment of the game."

"Because they have wagered and stand to win or lose money!" his father said.

"No. Only to win or lose prestige!"

"Say what you like. I see members of my household getting and spending, their pelf dangling from their necks. It is obscene. It is a corruption of the young. I will not have it."

Jenore sought to intervene. "Father . . ." she said.

Eblon folded his arms. "I have said what I have said."

Jenore turned to her mother, but Munn gestured in a manner that meant she could do nothing.

The old man's mind had closed. "Those who wish to traffic in money may do so," he said. "But they may not stay under this family's roof."

"This is not fair, father," Iriess said. "Where can the young ones go?"

"To Alwan Foulaine's rat heap, for all I care," said Eblon. "Let him take care of them. Let him prepare them for their ratherings. And a fine preparation that would be." He would hear no more.

The oldest and youngest Mordenes went to bed. Those of the inbetween generations argued in clumps. The token bearers formed into a knot of angry protest and went outside to offer each other mutual support, or at least shared resentment.

Conn sat alone on his bench and observed the aftermath of the argument. He could not help contrasting the caustic mood of the evening's gathering with the warmth and solidarity that had prevailed the morning he had arrived. It brought him a sadness that he had not known was within him, an emotion made deeper by his certainty that the bitter dispute was entirely pointless.

The tokens were not money. In any case, money itself was an innocent concept, not to mention an indispensable factor in the operation of markets, which were themselves the arena of free action. Everyone on Thrais knew this. How could anyone fix on money as an instrument of corruption?

The arguments around him were less vociferous than the earlier set-to had been, but the emotions with which they were freighted caused Conn discomfort. He went outside and walked down to the jetty. The night was clear, the sky strewn with the cold winks of stars and the scintillations of transiting orbitals. He looked up at the glitter and thought about the world he owned.

He heard Jenore's footsteps on the path before her arm linked into his. "Are you all right?" she said. "The arguing seemed to upset you."

"I was not at ease," he said. "Your father took a strong stance."

"He'll have softened by morning. He's just frustrated."

"That much was clear."

"What do you really think?" she said. "About the tokens."

"I said what I think. All I can add is that I do not understand why there is an argument in the first place."

"It's because of how we feel about money. You would not understand."

"You are right," Conn said. "I do not understand. If you used money, you would not have to go through all that rigmarole where you trade one thing for another while pretending that no such transaction is taking place."

She raised a finger and opened her mouth as if to refute his observation but instead she said, "Never mind. These things are complex and not germane to you and me at this moment."

They walked toward the Mordene foranq. The great barge sat at the dock, its paintwork glowing dimly in the light from the house. When Conn had first seen it he had been struck by the strangeness of the concept that generations would labor to create a priceless artifact that not one of the Mordenes actually possessed—as if, instead of the foranq belonging to the family, they belonged to the foranq.

His first impression had evoked a sense of wonder that people so like him in form and movement could be so different in their inner noöscapes. Now the foranq was just one more alien object, a reminder that while every other being he encountered was well fitted to some corner of the universe, strange though that corner might seem, Conn Labro had no such place. Unlike the bearer deed and its reader, there was no precisely shaped impression into which he could settle.

They reached the end of the jetty and sat on the wide bollard to which the foranq was tied. The silence between them lengthened until Jenore said, "Where are your thoughts taking you?"

"I am wondering about several things," he said. "Hallis Tharp is alleged to have stolen the deed to Forlor. Might he also have stolen me? Do I have parents somewhere, siblings, aunts and uncles like yours? Are they perhaps stranded on that far distant world, abandoned when Tharp took their child and absconded?"

"I cannot conceive of Hallis performing an evil act," Jenore said. "He had a gentle and unassuming nature."

"Perhaps he became so in remorse for having committed a great misdeed."

He saw her turn the concept over in her mind. "It is possible," she said. "I prefer to think that Hallis was a good man who rescued you from danger or at least from neglect."

"But only to sell me into servitude. How was that a kindness?"

"You have said, yourself, that you were at ease in the sporting house," she said. "You had the necessities of life and an opportunity to become skilled at a profession that seems to have suited you."

"True, but that might be only because I had been raised by Ovam Horder to know nothing else."

"Perhaps Hallis lacked options," she said. "In truth, I do not know and nor do you."

"No, I do not know," Conn said. "But it is becoming clear to me that I should. I should know where I belong."

Jenore placed her hands on her knees and looked down at them. Without raising her head, she said, "When I was wandering The Spray, especially when I was stranded on Thrais, I thought that I belonged here—this island, these waters. Now I come home and I find it a hard fit, as if it were an old garment that has grown too tight in the shoulders."

Conn often had trouble with metaphors. He asked her, "What are you saying?"

"That where you come from may be just where you come from. Where you belong may be somewhere else."

"I thought I came from Thrais," he said. "Now I am not sure that I ever belonged there. That is why I want to see Forlor."

She laid her head on his shoulder. "I have been wondering if you might ever come to feel that you belong with me," she said. "And that I belong right here."

She put her hand on his chest so that he felt its heat through his shirt. She looked at him and the expression in her eyes opened an unexpected door inside him. The opening was no more than a crack, but beyond it there beckoned to him a soft light and a sweet warmth. Still, he hesitated on the threshold. "Perhaps I do," he said, "but what if there are others, my kinfolk, on Forlor?"

"What if there are not? What if there is just an empty house, filling with dust?"

"Then I will know I do not belong there," he said.

"And I know how to find out if you belong here," she said, taking his hand and carrying it to her breast. He could feel her heart beating within.

She stood up and said, "There is a place along there . . ." she pointed to a patch of darkness under some trees, "where the moss grows exceptionally deep and soft."

He rose and she led him into the secluded bower. By the time the first light of day touched the tops of the trees above them, Conn Labro was willing to admit that he had engaged in a transaction on which he would have had great difficulty setting a price. They walked out into the morning, the sun like a tarnished coin on the mainland hills across the eastern water, and sat again on the bollard at the end of the dock. Jenore put her head on his shoulder and encouraged him to place an arm around her.

"I've been thinking," she said. "You have skills that could bring you a good living on many of the Ten Thousand Worlds."

"I believe most women don't care to pay for that sort of thing," he said, "and I might find it difficult to accommodate those who do."

She looked up at him. "Was that humor?"

"Yes," he said, "I think it was."

"You're changing."

"I suppose. I am forced to recognize that Thrais is but one world among many. It is statistically unlikely that the great majority of humankind is mad and that the fragment on Thrais is sane. Although common sense argues that it is so."

"Common sense as it is defined on Thrais?" she said.

"That is so. Apparently the view is different depending on where one stands."

They were silent for a few moments, Jenore snuggling in close as the cool early morning breeze wrapped around them. "I was thinking," she began again, "that you might open a school to teach fighting techniques."

Conn envisioned himself surrounded by persons half his size. "I have no affinity for children," he said.

"I was thinking more of adults, young men and women who believe they might someday find themselves in desperate situations. Or the young and socially prominent who might wish to defend their honor."

"It is not an appealing concept. I am not used to dealing with incompetence."

She shifted against him. "You could deal only with competents who wish to refine their technique."

He made a noncommittal noise.

"Or you could be a police agent. You have a sharp eye for details and you can tell when people are attempting to deceive."

"True," Conn said, "but apparently I am almost completely innocent of human nature. Also, I think my standards of morality only apply on Thrais."

"You could learn new standards. I believe you are at heart a good man."

He made the neutral noise again. In Jenore's mind, the simple word "good" covered a great complexity of meanings.

"Well," she said, "we'll think of something."

There was a world of assumptions in that assertion, he was sure. But he thought it best not to challenge or explore them at the moment because with her last remark she stood and stretched and announced that she was in the mood for breakfast.

Contrary to Jenore's prediction of the night before, morning had not produced a softened Eblon Mordene. When the family gathered for breakfast in the great room the generational division soon revealed itself to be deeper than when the disputants had gone to bed.

"It is like the tale of the fish coaxer who let the lutroid sun itself on his foredeck," the old man said.

"What is a lutroid?" Conn whispered to Jenore and learned that it was an aquatic mammal with webbed hands and almost human intelligence and sometimes more than human cunning.

"When his boat had become a floating playground for lutroids and he was swimming home the man regretted his initial leniency," the patriarch concluded. "I do not mean to make that mistake. I have drawn a line. Those who would choose money over family must do so now."

The older men of the family, Eblon's brothers by blood or law, stood with him, as did most of the older women. Munn argued that they should all seek a middle ground. Her words were seconded by Jenore and Iriess and some of the 'tween generation. But the tokeners did not offer any compromise, and the traditionalists would not have accepted one if it had been offered. So it was a cold breakfast no matter how much steam rose from the pots of porridge and punge.

Eblon said, "I have been in touch with some of the other family heads. I can tell you that what is happening here is also happening in other houses. We are resolved to end this evil before it takes full root."

"Father," said Iriess, from his place across the table from the old man, "'evil' is too strong a word. It is but a harmless pastime."

"Then it should not be a hardship to give it up."

"A forced acquiescence endures only while the fist is raised," quoted Munn.

"Enough!" said Eblon. "We have waited patiently for this scurrilous fad to run its foul course. Instead, its claws sink ever deeper into the young. The elders are resolute. Those who wish to sail in Alwan Foulaine's wake may do so. But the doors of their family's houses will be closed to them." He paused and looked around the room. "As will the chambers of their foranqs."

This last declaration brought a hiss of astonishment and anger from several quarters. "Father," Iriess said, "you cannot deny access to the foranq. It is every Mordene's right by birth. You are saying that no one who disagrees with you can marry or name a child or even commune with the gone-bys."

Eblon's face was set hard. "The foranq is in my keeping. I will say how it is used."

"In your keeping on behalf of all of us," said Iriess. "And on behalf of those gone by and those yet to come. It is not yours to offer or withhold. Father, this is revolution."

"Foulaine's money is also revolution," said the old man, "yet you find it easy enough to swallow."

Some of the older Mordenes looked uncomfortable, but none of them broke ranks. The young, especially the older boys and the men newly come to adulthood, glowered and grumbled darkly. Last night's breach had become a chasm. The unhappy rebels stalked off to pack their possessions and depart. Their equally unhappy elders went to work, leaving the common room to Conn and Jenore, Eblon and Munn.

Jenore said, "Mother, ask him to reconsider."

Munn folded her hands and sighed. "I have done so," she said. She looked at her husband. "I do so again."

"No," said Eblon Mordene. "A stand must be taken."

Jenore stood. "I am sorry that I have come home to this," she said. "When I was far out in The Spray, lost among strangers who treated each other in beastly ways, I used to dream of this room and these people. Every night it was my last thought before sleep.

"Now I am here and it is all wrong. What has happened to us?" She sat down and ostentatiously took Conn's hand in hers.

Her father peered at her from beneath lowered brows then turned to Conn. "That brings us to another matter," he said. "Conn Labro, we are grateful to you for bringing Jenore back to us. If this were another time, the hospitality of our house would be yours for as long as you cared to partake of it."

The old man cleared his throat and looked uncomfortable as he continued, "But this is a difficult time for us. Thus it would be better for all if we were left to ourselves to resolve it. Without the complicating presence of strangers."

Conn's first reaction was to note that this was an arbitrary alteration to the contract he and the patriarch had struck when they had talked beneath the tree outside. But the pressure that Jenore's fingers exerted on his hand caused him to look at her. She had gone pale and he saw the distress in her face. She did not want him to confront her father.

"I have no wish to remain where I am unwanted," he said. "In any case, I have decided that I ought to be seeking the place, if it exists, where I belong. I will go to Forlor."

"This is the first I have heard of any decision," Jenore said. He saw a hurt in her eyes that he could not account for.

"I have just come to it," he said.

Her face reddened. "And this seemed the best time to tell me? Is there no one I can rely on?"

She did not wait for an answer to either question but fled to an inner room.

It seemed to Conn that he ought to go after her and explain but Munn let him know by quiet signs that that was not a good strategy. Instead, he asked the old man for the use of his integrator so that he could contact Lok Gievel and arrange matters.

He was shown into Eblon's study where he sat at the patriarch's massive desk and bid the integrator contact the intercessor. When Gievel's face appeared on the display Conn said, "Please advise Opteram that I agree in principle to the sale of Forlor, but that I wish to visit the planet first to ascertain if there is anything there that may help me discover my origins."

"I will convey the message to them," Gievel said. "Judging by the speed with which they have responded so far, we may have an answer very soon."

"I will wait here."

As the intercessor had expected, an answer was not long in coming. Within minutes, Gievel was back to say that not only was Conn's condition accepted but that he was welcome to travel to Forlor on Lord Vullamir's space yacht, as the aristocrat was desirous of seeing the place as soon as possible.

"He is eager," Conn said. "Is there any indication as to the reasons behind his hurry?"

Gievel's image in the integrator's display showed an expression somewhere between an appreciation of the ineffable and the comic. "Among Vullamir's ilk," he said, "reasons are often utterly idiosyncratic. They see mountains where we apprehend anthills, and vice versa. In any case, he will send an aircar to collect you whenever you say."

"I am ready now," Conn said. Then he remembered to ask to have his and Jenore's luggage collected from the Brzankh Hotel in Olkney, the bill paid and the crystal ear drops recovered. Gievel said it would be done.

Conn went looking for Jenore but found her mother instead.

"She has gone over to her cousins' place on Longstrand," Munn said.

"How do I get there? I would speak with her before I leave."

"To say what? That you are going? That you will return?" Munn said. "She already knows the first and no one knows the second."

"To ask her to come with me."

"She is all done with going far away. She is of a mind to stand still for a while, perhaps a long while, in the hope that life will stop rushing past her."

"I have to go," Conn said. "I have to know where I came from. Where I belong."

"The two may not be the same."

"Yet I will not know that until I know more."

Munn sighed. "Then go. It may be more important to Jenore that you come back."

"I will," Conn said.

Munn's mouth made no reply, but her face said that she hoped so, yet she had lived long enough to know that hopes can go unrewarded.

Vullamir's spaceship made his air yacht, parked beside it at a private terminal on the outskirts of Olkney, seem a trifle. The *Martichor* was almost as large as the *Dan* and far more lovingly maintained. Her forward component was a wide oval of burnished alloy, her rearworks an intimidating array of thrusters, obviators and drive housings, broadly striped in the Vullamir colors of black and yellow. An antique gonfalon flew from a gantry above the webbed cradle in which the ship nestled, the family's arms popping in and out of view as a brisk wind snapped the fabric.

When the aircar delivered Conn he found Lok Gievel and Ezrail Opteram standing at the foot of a gangway that led to a small port toward the ship's stern. There were documents to sign and initial, establishing the agreement in principle and ending the lawsuit. Gievel announced that all of Conn's encumbrances had been cleared. His luggage had been retrieved from the hotel and was already aboard. Jenore's had been sent to her home.

Conn gave Gievel the coordinates of Forlor. The intercessor passed them to Opteram who said he would convey them to the *Martichor*'s captain. Opteram said, "You should go aboard. My lord plans an immediate departure."

"Vullamir has already arrived?" Conn said.

"Some time since." He made a complex gesture to Gievel signifying that their business was done and went into the ship.

Gievel brought out a small package from a pocket in his robe. "Here are the crystal eardrops," he said. "The manager of the Brzankh seemed glad to be relieved of them."

"Please send them to Jenore," Conn said. "She is staying with cousins on an island named Longstrand. There have been difficulties among the Mordenes." He explained briefly about the Tote, then said, "Perhaps we can do business again. I have been satisfied with your assistance."

Gievel made his farewells and departed. Conn turned toward the spaceship and saw a man in yellow and black livery appear in the rear port. The fellow stood within the ship and struck an expectant pose.

Conn went to the open port. As he made to enter he almost collided with a man who was coming out. He had the look of a veteran spacer, a stocky man moderately advanced in years, fair of skin and pale of eye. He wore an officer's uniform of light blue with the yellow and black of Vullamir's house in a badge on his chest.

"Who are you?" he said and when Conn had identified himself, the man made a polite gesture and said that he was Yalum Erkatchian, captain of the *Martichor*. "You are the one who provided the coordinates?"

"I am," said Conn.

"And you are coming with us?"

"Yes," said Conn. "Did Lord Vullamir not inform you that I would be his guest?"

"My lord Vullamir does not deal with a mere captain," Erkatchian said. "His major domo informs me of the numbers of passengers to be accommodated, and the proportions by which they are divided into those who serve and those who are served. They even load their own provisions."

"I see," said Conn. "Well, I had better come aboard."

The captain looked surprised. He glanced at the waiting servant whose eyes were fixed on a point in the air somewhere out on the landing field.

"One grows tired of this," the spacer said to no one in particular. Then he addressed Conn. "Do not enter through this port. It is for servants. You travel as the Lord Vullamir's guest and should board the ship through the forward port."

"It makes small difference to me," Conn said.

"It will," said Erkatchian. He beckoned peremptorily to the liveried servant and said, "You are in error. Conduct your master's guest to the appropriate entry." To Conn he said, "Do I detect the accents of Thrais?"

"I was raised there."

"Have you spent much time on Old Earth?"

"Only a few days."

The captain gave himself a confirmatory nod. "There is not time to acquaint you with the myriad peculiarities of Old Earth aristocrats," he said. "But let me say this: their first perceptions are not of persons, but of ranks, and if they ever have second thoughts I am not aware of them. Unless you overcome that first hurdle you will have difficulty even in being seen and heard."

"The person with whom I traveled to Old Earth spoke of this," Conn said.

"The servants do not suffer from their masters' perceptual flaw, but they act as if they do. Without a clear establishing of rank they might feed you on scraps and scrapings all the way to Forlor."

"I thank you again," Conn said. He turned to the footman, who waited with an air of condescension and an elevation of nose that Conn thought would be painful to the man's neck if it were not such a patently practiced posture.

"You understand that I am Lord Vullamir's guest," he said.

The servant's eyes flicked toward Conn then again regarded the upper air. "His lordship may have mentioned something. He was not specific."

"Did he specify anything to the contrary?"

The man's lips drew in briefly. "No."

"Shall we seek him out and ask him to state his wishes in detail?"

Conn saw a flicker of alarm in the liveryman's eyes. "No," was the answer.

"Sir," said the captain.

"No, sir," said the footman.

"Well, then," said Conn.

The servant made an obeisance. Erkatchian moved one hand in a way that indicated the servant's gesture had been appropriate if not fully sincere. "I must conclude some formalities with the space port authorities, then we will lift off," he said and departed.

Conn motioned the footman to lead the way to the forward port. Here access was by a moving ramp. As they ascended toward the hull a circular portion cycled open to admit them then sealed itself.

Conn followed the servant into an antechamber that led to a corridor paneled in dark wood with embellishments of crystal set in precious metals. The servant stopped and languidly inquired as to which part of the ship the master's guest preferred to visit.

"What is your name?" Conn asked.

"Umlat," was the answer.

"Well, Umlat, I am innocent of the ship's layout as well as of the etiquette appropriate to my situation," Conn said. "How would you advise me?"

In the footman's eyes he saw hints of cruelty and an appetite for domination so he added, "You will bear in mind that on the planet we are bound for, until I transfer ownership to your master, I will quite likely be an unquestioned autocrat. If it pleases me to have you offered as dinner to whatever beasts we might find there, no one will deter me."

He saw that a new series of emotions had arisen behind Umlat's gaze and he repeated his question, "How would you advise me?"

"It would be proper to go to your quarters and refresh yourself."

"Lord Vullamir would not expect me to pay my respects?"

"It is now the Hour of Contemplating Essences," Umlat said. "My lord and his other guests will each be in their separate quarters, mulling or meditating as their temperaments incline."

"Should I do the same?"

Now Conn saw a blink of amusement in the man's face, quickly subdued. "If you wish," Umlat said.

When on Haxxi, Conn thought, and said, "I will consider it. Lead on."

The footman led him to a spacious cabin, luxuriously appointed. "Where is my luggage?" Conn said.

A tinge of anxiety accompanied the answer. "It appears to have been erroneously placed in another cabin, towards the stern."

"Probably smaller than this," Conn suggested, "and in close proximity to a communal privy."

"I will bring it at once."

"I will also want you to advise me on what to wear," Conn said. "Perhaps even to furnish suitable clothing if my own garments are not proper to an occasion."

Umlat showed another tinge of anxiety. "Those would be the duties of an undervalet."

"Has such a functionary been assigned to me?"

"I believe so."

"Any others?"

"One of the cooks has been detailed to learn your requirements. Also, a skivvy will maintain your quarters."

"And when would I have learned of all this?"

The man looked abashed.

"Send them to me now," Conn said, "and bring my luggage. I will forgo contemplating essences."

"Yes, sir." Umlat turned to leave.

"And have the goodness to mention the matter of beasts and their dinners."

"Yes, sir."

Conn's interview with the staff went well. It was followed by a flurry of activity in which his luggage was brought and unpacked, his dietary preferences noted and the cabin's various amenities were displayed to him. The skivvy, a gaunt woman of more than middle years with a rosaceous nose and a disinclination to meet Conn's eyes, concluded the proceedings by turning down the bed.

"The Hour of Contemplating Essences having passed," Umlat said, "my lord and his companions will be resting from their exertions, if you would care to do the same."

"I have undertaken no exertions," Conn said. "What else might I do?"

The servant looked apprehensive. "There are no restrictions on your activities," he said, "but my lord prefers a quiet ship when he is resting."

"Is there a library?" Conn said.

Umlat indicated a desk against one wall. He opened it to reveal an integrator console. "Do you require assistance?"

"I think I should acquire some information on the aristocracy before I encounter them."

Umlat touched a few controls and information appeared on the integrator's display. "Will there be anything else, sir?"

"No."

"I will be outside if you should need anything."

As Conn seated himself at the console he felt a slight vibration; the *Martichor* was lifting off. His experience of space flight was limited, but the unobtrusive way that Lord Vullamir's craft rejected the planet's gravity argued for a well-run ship and an experienced crew.

He turned his attention back to the integrator and for the next hour immersed himself in a consideration of Old Earth's topmost social segment. His investigations touched upon history, philosophy, theories of social organization and political relationships, genealogy and inheritance customs. He also took side trips into fashion, architecture, furniture design and symbolic languages, but at the end of the hour he was left with the realization that he had ventured no more than toe-deep into an ocean of subtleties. Understanding the ways and purposes of aristocrats would be the work of a lifetime, and he could think of better goals on which to expend the effort. He would rely on advice from Vullamir's servants.

He folded the integrator back into the desk and poured himself a restorative glass from a carafe of improved water. The substances dissolved in the liquid clarified his mind while rebalancing his metabolism. He drank another glass then stretched himself upon the bed. It attempted to ease him into sleep but he notified it that he intended instead to think. It rearranged itself then generated a purr of white noise that obliterated all other sounds that might distract him.

He clasped his hands behind his neck and crossed his ankles, staring up at the ceiling and allowing his inner eye to present him with images. He replayed many of the incidents in which he had been involved since the moment he had gone to seek out Hallis Tharp: the old man's broken body, Jenore's face as she understood who he was, Daitoo's grim concentration as he had brought his weapon up, Hilfdan Klepht's skeptical speculating mien, Willifree's appetite for the Divorgian woman, the Hauserian Farbuck's revulsion against innocent transactions. There was more: the clerk at Flagit Holdings and the Registrar of Offworld Properties, Odell and the scroot team, Eblon Mordene and Alwan Foulaine.

It was a wide array of emotions, some of which he understood, most of which he did not share. It appeared that the world outside his head was full of deeply held sentiments and raging storms of passion. Men and women suffered and made each other suffer for the most trivial of causes, striving violently and even desperately for gains that were to Conn Labro no gain at all, or to avoid losses that had no practical value.

From recent experience, it was reasonable to believe that most of the human species were as mad as Stigs. But then, he reflected, the different madnesses were so widely shared. Could it be insanity to believe what every other person around one believed? Did distraction vary according to location and circumstance, so that Conn Labro was quite sane on Thrais yet became a muddlewit the moment he set down on the plains of Hauser or ran his boat up onto a Shorraffi beach?

Jenore Mordene had clearly been out of her element on Thrais. When she had expected to be helped just because Hallis Tharp had requested it, Hilfdan Klepht had been just as puzzled as Conn, or as any Thraisian would have been. So Jenore had been operating on false premises, no less than if she had seen specters that were invisible to all but her. Yet when she had returned to Graysands she had become just another Shorraffi, perfectly fitted to her surroundings. Then it was Conn who was the misfit. It was he who, when he spoke his mind, left others scratching their heads and puzzling their brows.

So, life on Thrais was right for him, though he had no urge to go back there and spend his years gaming and dueling. Yet that life was right only because it was the one he knew. With effort, he might become a Hauserian, offering his shoulder to the blunt point of the hassenge and counting each pang of its slow passage through him as a coin that bought satisfaction. Or a Shorraffi, chaffering for this or that without acknowledging that any transaction was taking place.

He questioned himself and found that he did not wish to return to the world of his upbringing, nor to the sporting houses—even if he came to own one. Shorraff, though strange, was not unpleasant. Then he thought of Shorraff

TEMPLATE

with Jenore Mordene added, thought of the way her parents were with each other, and he had to admit that the vision called to him.

Still, somewhere beyond The Spray was the world he had been taken from in infancy. Perhaps it was a place to which he was perfectly suited, where he could open his mouth and speak his mind and see every head nod in agreement—or if not agreement, at least understanding.

In the course of his review it occurred to him that these past few moments, spent lying on his back in Lord Vullamir's spaceship, were the first occasion in quite some time when he was not closely engaged with some other person or persons, usually in an unstructured conflict. He had had little time for reflection. It was as if the death of Ovam Horder had tipped Conn Labro off a high platform where he had always known solid footing. Ever since, he had been in free fall, colliding with other persons who all seemed to be well grounded where they were, having to deal with them by tactics improvised to suit the occasion.

But it had been all tactics, with no strategy. First it had been about survival, finding out who had wanted to kill him and why. Then it had become about unraveling a mystery involving his origins. From there, as his perspective widened, it had become a matter of finding where he belonged.

Now, as he thought about where he had come from and to, he saw that the motif he had identified in his recent life—that it was all tactics, no strategy—had governed his existence since well before the death of Horder. It was the basic structure of his whole life. He had never had a goal that was not essentially confined to the short or middle term. He had accepted the circumstances of his place and role at Horder's without question. His life had been centered on matters of who and where and when, of how and with what; he had never touched upon the most fundamental question of all: *why?*

Now he found that he had come upon one of those questions that, once asked, could not be ignored. He was astonished that it had never occurred to him before. He had never gone into a bout without preparing a strategy, never entered a struggle expecting to improvise from a grab bag of tactics. To do so was to guarantee eventual defeat. The combatant who had a clear strategic goal was always a step ahead of an opponent whose only recourse was to react and survive.

It was a chilling realization. Conn Labro's life, that had seemed so well ordered, executed with such seeming brilliance, was nothing more than a pastiche of techniques and acquired skills. In his infancy, he had been pointed in a certain direction. Since then he had plodded forward, head down, climbing over each obstacle as it presented itself. He had never looked up, to see where his steps would ultimately take him. He had never questioned the route or the destination, never even asked if there was a destination, let alone whether he wanted to reach it.

And who had set him on this course? Who had placed him on the track and pushed him forward?

Hallis Tharp.

And why? He wished now that the universe still contained a Hallis Tharp so that Conn could put that question to him. Still, it did contain the place where he had been brought from, a world named Forlor that waited for him at a set of coordinates far out past the Back of Beyond.

He reflected on the irony of his situation. For a few moments, he had had the beginnings of a strategy for his life: the companionship of Jenore, a place for them in a big household, some kind of useful work for him to do, perhaps even a spot on a birl team and a chance to win renown. A life marked by friendships, children and the adventure of aging. But here he was, flying away from all of that, toward an unknown world that probably offered him no more than an answer to the mystery of his past, when what he truly needed, as Jenore had said, was a reason to get up in the morning.

No, he doubted that he would find what he needed on Forlor. Yet, though he did not know how it would happen, he was confident that he was traveling toward a point where his life would somehow come into focus. Like a visual puzzle that cannot be solved until it is viewed from just the right vantage, when he came to the world of his origin he felt that the true shape of his existence would be revealed.

What are you, where do you come from, where do you go? On Forlor he would find answers to all three of Hallis Tharp's questions. But he suspected he already knew where he belonged: with a woman who waited for him on the New Shore.

Chapter 9

Conn's musings were interrupted by a tapping on the cabin door and the entry of Po, the undervalet. This was a short and portly man with lacquered hair, close-set eyes and a soft mouth. He moved with bustling speed into the room, bringing with him a tall portmanteau which he opened to reveal several sets of garments, each with matching footwear and accouterments.

"You will be expected for dinner," he said. "I have brought suitable attire. Would you care to choose?"

Conn rose from the bed. "Perhaps you should make suggestions," he said.

Po tugged his lower lip, then thrust a hand into the trunk and brought out a short-sleeved, floor-length gown, deep red with a luxurious pile that shimmered its surface. He laid it upon the bed then placed atop it a shirt of some lightweight fabric, white figured in pale blue rectangles, and a pair of breeches of the same scarlet as the gown. He completed the ensemble with hose that were equipped with thickened soles to make slippers.

The man then helped Conn into the garments, the first time for as long as Conn could remember that anyone had assisted him in such a private undertaking. But it soon became clear that the breeches closed by a complicated system of strings and tapes, with the shirt connected to the breeches by yet more dangling appendages. The hose had to be embellished by bows at the knee, the tying of which Po asserted was an abstruse art, even though no one would see them: they would be under the gown when Conn was standing and under the table when he was seated.

With Conn standing, the servant circled him, giving gentle tugs and twists to the clothing. The intelligence imbued into its fibers responded by fitting the garments more perfectly to his shape. Then Po stepped back and surveyed the result.

"Forgive me if the question seems impertinent," he said, "but on your own world, what is your rank?"

"On Thrais," Conn said, "my wealth would place me in the upper two percentiles. My accomplishments as a competitor would add a strong aura of distinction. I was considered superb in several difficult arts."

The undervalet digested the information then his plump hands rapidly sought through a selection of drawers and compartments to produce a chain of thick links, a heavy bracelet of worked metal, three ornate rings and a demilune of wire filigree, spotted with blue and green gems, meant to be hung about the neck from a finger-thick cable of plaited gold.

Conn resisted. "I do not wear jewelry," he said.

"These are not idle decorations," Po said, "but precise indicators of social rank. If you do not wear them, my lord and his companions will have difficulty perceiving you. To be blunt, you will tend to slip from their notice unless they make an effort to keep you in view. They are unaccustomed to make such an effort."

"I do not understand," Conn said.

The servant pinched his lower lip together again. He appeared to be gathering his thoughts, then he said, "Among the aristocracy, there are degrees and gradations. Much depends on the age of the lineage."

Conn indicated the integrator console. "I saw something about that in my reading."

"There are seven tiers of nobility. My lord Vullamir and his circle are members of the Original caste. They trace their ancestry back to the dawn-time of the Young Earth."

"That seems unlikely," Conn said. "Before it was Old Earth, this planet was largely depopulated for eons. Its only inhabitants were the brutish and the eccentric."

"Nonetheless," said Po. "And if I may advise, that is not a good supposition to put before my lord. But to return to our discussion, Originals have achieved an exquisite refinement of perception. They are scarcely aware of their surroundings, almost completely unaware of persons. Rather, they recognize place and station, largely through symbolic indicators."

"That seems a self-imposed handicap," Conn said.

"Not at all," said Po. "With myriads of servants attending to their every want and need, our masters' environment is always entirely congenial. Among ourselves we who provide that environment refer to it as 'The Cushion.' The Cushion allows the Originals to focus their attention on matters that truly concern them: rank, privilege, precedence, and the constant process by which those standards are subject to tiny but crucial adjustments."

"What process? What prompts these 'adjustments'?"

"Achievements and advances in their pastimes and diversions."

"And what might those be?"

At Conn's question a distance suddenly grew between him and the undervalet. He examined the man's eyes and saw a reluctance to carry the discussion further, tinged with a faint undercurrent of fear.

"Those are matters that do not concern us," Po said.

"They may concern me," Conn said. "I am engaged in a significant transaction with Lord Vullamir. Yet his motives are opaque to me. Where I come from, a place that offered me no cushions, I learned to take good account of other peoples' agendas."

The servant set his lips in a small, prim line and indicated that he did not wish to say any more. Conn resolved to press him. "Did Umlat mention the peculiar status I will assume once we touch down on Forlor?" he said.

Po nodded a very small nod.

"Would you be much missed in Lord Vullamir's household? Would anyone throw himself between you and some fanged and clawed appetite?"

Po's smooth head trembled. Conn took the movement for a negative. "Well, then," he said.

The servant's voice dropped to a whisper and he leaned closer. "We are not supposed to know about these things, and indeed we know little enough. We open doors to admit certain 'visitors.' We do not see what goes on once we close the doors, nor do we wish to. We clean the premises afterwards. We are instructed to compensate the visitors with items of value. Sometimes the visitors need assistance before they can depart. But no one speaks of it."

"Your masters engage in illicit activities and you are their accomplices," Conn suggested.

"The encounters are voluntary. How can they be illicit?"

"Hmm," said Conn. On Thrais, the logic of the man's view would have carried the argument. Yet he wondered how Jenore Mordene or Ren Farbuck might answer.

"How does rank change as a result of these 'pastimes and diversions'?" he asked.

"Those who have encompassed more esoteric experiences and sensations are accorded higher stature. There are agreed-upon gradations."

A connection closed in Conn's brain. To confirm it, he asked, "Is Yellow Cynosure one of those gradations? Or Blue Green Exemplar?"

A mingling of relief and puzzlement showed in Po's face. "Ah," he said. "You are acquainted with the Immersion?"

Conn made a noncommittal motion. "Tangentially," he said.

"If I may ask, is the transaction that you and my lord are engaged in related to his rank therein?"

Conn's initial response would have been to say no. But it was clear from his reading of Po's face that such an answer would not admit him further into the servant's confidence. He adopted a careful tone. "I do not say yes, but I also do not say no."

Po looked thoughtful. He laced the digits of his plump hands together, all but the index fingers. These he steepled together then touched them briefly to his nose and lips. Conn was sure he was seeing a signal of some kind, perhaps a gesture by which members of a clandestine organization revealed themselves to each other.

He mimicked the gesture and saw sly calculation appear behind Po's gaze. "Ah," he said again. "Allow me to guess: your own rank is Sky Blue Epitome."

Conn said nothing, his face immobile.

"Crimson Acme?"

Conn again said nothing but allowed one eyebrow a moment's dip.

"Say no more," said Po.

A soft chime sounded from somewhere. "Dinner is imminent," Po said. "I will summon Umlat to conduct you."

"Wait," said Conn. "Will the others be wearing life masks?"

"Certainly."

"Then should I not wear one also?"

Po made a dismissive gesture. "No one will expect you to do so."

"I do not wish to seem outlandish."

"But you do not own one, surely?"

Conn looked down at his attire. "Nor do I own these garments."

Now the undervalet seemed at a loss how to respond. Finally, he said, "If you wish to borrow a mask, I suppose there must be a number of them in my lord's quarters. I could ask the junior keeper of the wardrobe to inquire of the senior keeper if one could be made available. Perhaps some misremembered third cousin, but . . ."

Conn was beginning to think he had traveled one step too far into unmapped territory, but he did not want to show indecisiveness in front of this man. He smiled and said, "At least let us see how it fits," he said.

The servant was plainly discomfited but he left Conn's cabin. In his absence, Conn practiced walking and sitting in the unfamiliar garments, finding that short steps worked better than his customary long stride—he assumed that the gown was not supposed to gape and expose the knees. He was midway through a room crossing when Po returned.

"If you clasp your hands at your waist, you will achieve the desired effect of unruffled nonchalance," the servant said, then added, "Very good," when Conn followed his advice.

Po's plump hands held a cylindrical box made of material that captured the room's lights in a metallic sheen. He placed the container on a table and pressed a stud that caused its top and sides to unfold, revealing a translucent globe much like a giant pearl, but with a flattened bottom.

The undervalet turned to Conn and assumed an air of one who does as he is bid, regardless of his own opinions. "This was left by Lord Faurenel and never collected. It is, the senior keeper of the wardrobe believes, a distaff cousin of the Faurenels' cadet branch, though with several removes." He lifted the object in two hands. "If you would sit."

Conn sat on a chair at the dressing table. In the reflector he saw the servant approach from behind, holding the globe before him as if officiating at a coronation, his face set in a wry look that abruptly disappeared when his eyes met Conn's reflected gaze. Then the mask was lowered over Conn's head and he saw only gray light. He heard a click.

"It will take a few moments to establish itself," Po said.

Even as he spoke, Conn felt a tickling and tingling at several points on his skull. Something brushed across his brow. There was a wriggling sensation in his nostrils and a brief but unbearable itching in his ears. Then the sensations stopped.

Vision abruptly returned. He was looking at himself in the reflector, but instead of the globe's opaque surface he now saw the face of a woman of middle years. She was plain of feature, heavy of brow and chin, with dull, dark eyes that somehow seemed to express an expectation that no particularly pleasant sights would pass before them.

Conn looked up; the mask's eyes looked up. He turned his head to one side and regarded the reflector from the corners of his eyes; the face in the mask mimicked him. He turned and regarded the room. Everything looked as it had before, although the colors seemed slightly different, the blues a little deeper. Before he had seen three shades of green in the wall coverings; now there were clearly four.

There came yet another new perception—not in what he saw, but in what he recognized. There was a familiarity to the cabin that he had not felt before, a vague sense that he had been here in the past. The impression was not strong, just a mild recognition of having spent time in these same surroundings, the comfort of knowing where he was. He probed at the sensation and realized with a shock that the faint memory was not his.

"Remove this!" he said to the undervalet and had the unsettling experience of hearing his words spoken in another voice. It was a female voice—*hers*, the woman whose face regarded him with alarm as he turned back to the reflector. Behind him, he saw Po jump, startled, and immediately reach for the globe.

No, wait! Please, not yet! said the same voice. But Po's hands did not stop and Conn realized that the woman had spoken only in his own mind. Now he heard again the click that had activated the mask, though this time the action of the control was reversed. He was blind in soft gray light and felt once more the touches and ticklings as the device withdrew from his senses. Then the mask was lifted away and Conn saw his own features in the reflector, his cheeks pale and his eyes troubled, with the undervalet's anxious face behind and above him.

"That was . . . unpleasant," Conn said.

Po was profuse in his apologies. "I thought you knew what to expect," he said, a trembling lower lip adding a stammer to his words. "I did not think it my place to offer advice."

Conn looked at the pearly globe. "Put it away," he said. "The fault was mine. I thought it merely a simulacrum. I did not know about the . . . intimacy."

In memory, he could still hear the voice inside his head. Worse, he could still feel the emotions that had accompanied the plea not to remove the mask—the loneliness, the desperate longing to live—behind which he had sensed the darkness out of which the speaker had come and to which she was about to return, having had only seconds of existence.

"There is cruelty in it," he told Po. "Explain."

Po was putting the mask back in its container. "It was a custom among the aristocracy, quite some time ago. When death was unavoidable they would preserve the animating essence by artificial means."

He went on to explain that the essences were stored in devices that accompanied the funerary containers. When the calendar indicated that it was time to bring out the ashes of a great-grandparent or favorite uncle for veneration and to reflect on life's transitory nature, the device was also activated. The descendants could then commune with a simulated persona generated out of the deceased's essence, evoking a mood of fatalism and romantic melancholy.

"The custom eventually fell out of favor, as all customs do," Po said. "The essences were left on back shelves and in storage rooms. Then someone thought it might be diverting to incorporate them into systems that allowed them to interact with the senses and consciousness of the living."

The masks allowed an integration of the living and dead minds, putting the perceptions and memories of the latter at the behest of the former. The wearer derived novelty and sometimes insight; the worn regained a kind of life, which their essences had not experienced when they had been confined to the funerary devices.

"But they became like ghosts in old stories," the servant said, "poor, sad wraiths hungry for a simulation of life, however brief."

"Your masters must be hard indeed if they can do that to their own kin," Conn said.

Po dropped his voice conspiratorially. "Sometimes, when we are supposed to be cleaning the masks, we don them and reactivate the essences. The ghosts do not like to find their minds coupled with those of underlings, but they prefer it to being adrift in an echoless darkness. We servants find it stimulating to experience our world through the perceptions of our betters."

The chime sounded again. Conn stood up. "I will go to dinner without the mask," he said.

Po looked relieved. "It might have caused confusion. Perhaps even dissension."

Con's brows contracted. "Yet you did not think to warn me."

Po's relief evaporated. "I did not think it my place. I am, frankly, not entirely sure how to serve you. You seem to be, at one and the same time, helpless and menacing. I thought it best to tread lightly."

"I will not bridle at any advice sincerely intended to aid me," Conn said. "Indeed, I will reward it amply. You might pass that information to the other staff."

"I shall."

"Now, will you conduct me to dinner?"

"May I advise that we have Umlat do so? It is his function. It would appear odd if you were preceded by your dresser."

"Assuming," Conn said, "that the others would notice."

"They notice anything out of the ordinary. Again, if I may advise you, eat the dinner, say as little as possible, and do not ask questions." He dropped his voice to a whisper. "They may seem distant, even comically effete. But they are dangerous."

Conn bid Po to summon Umlat. While the man was out of the room, he opened a concealed inner compartment of his suitcase. From it he took out one of the weapons he had received from Hilfdan Klepht: a short-range shocker, an appropriate weapon for personal defense on a space ship. He tucked it into the waist of his breeches beneath the robe.

Conn found the *Martichor*'s dining room oppressive. Its dimensions were wide, leaving ample space for a table that could comfortably seat a dozen, as well as sideboards, cupboards and assorted paraphernalia involved in the final preparation and serving of foods. But the walls were invisible behind hangings of thick fabric: brocaded swag drapes and a tapestry depicting what Conn assumed to be Vullamir's ancestors at their pleasures. The furniture was dark and massive, projecting a brooding sense of immobility, as if the chairs themselves were saying, "Here I am; move me if you can."

The persons seated around the table conveyed the same aura. They were dressed in a fashion similar to what Po had conjured up for Conn, though the insignia and jewelry varied widely from his. Fingers, wrists, upper arms and throats flashed and glittered with adornment, and Conn recognized that if their ornaments constituted a symbolic language it would be a lifetime's work to master it.

There was nothing to be learned from an inspection of the aristocrats' faces. All wore life masks, a collection of projected faces in whose eyes Conn could read nothing. He assumed that the figure at the head of the table was Vullamir, but only because the others subtly deferred to him. The face he projected tonight was different from the magisterial visage Conn had seen when they had met behind the birl field—this one was old and lean, with the look of a predator.

To the lord's left and right six other personages regarded each other with borrowed faces. They spoke in undertones, their words accompanied by subtle gestures of their hands and small movements of their projected eyes and mouths. Their attention was all for each other; after one small glance toward Conn as his entrance was minimally acknowledged by their host they ignored him completely.

Umlat led Conn to a seat at the other end of the table. He sat across from the only other non-aristocratic diner: Yalum Erkatchian, the *Martichor*'s captain. The spacer smiled and told Conn, "Don't worry about which knife to use. Just do as I do."

Conn had been wondering about the uses of the various implements with which his place was set: besides the ones he recognized, there were things with hooks and spikes and some whose functions he could not begin to guess at. He thanked the captain.

"This is the only occasion when all of the ship's complement will be required to dine together," Erkatchian said. "You may take your other meals in your cabin, or you are welcome to join me."

"Why?" Conn asked.

"To which of my statements are you asking 'Why?'" the captain said.

"Why is it required that we all dine together?"

"It is the custom." The captain used his head to indicate the others around the table. "Over these people custom reigns with a rule of iron."

"Though, from all I hear, nothing else restrains them," Conn said.

"I have heard it argued that irony is the unifying principle of the cosmos."

"It may be so," Conn said. "I have seen little to contradict the argument."

The captain declared that he found Conn a congenial table mate and renewed the invitation to dine in his cabin, adding, "I am not just observing the custom. Please join me for breakfast. There is something I'd like to discuss with you."

"What?"

But the spacer indicated that the moment was not appropriate and digressed into their previous area of discussion. Conn learned that among the Old Earth aristocracy an invitation to dine was hedged about with a complexity of inviolable rules and procedures: the first invitation was always ignored; the second must provoke a protestation of unworthiness; the third raised concerns as to unavailability and a mutual checking of diaries; the fourth brought renewed expressions that it would all be far too much trouble for the prospective host; finally, the inviter informed the invitee that unless the latter would come to the table, the former risked death from mortification, and time and place were agreed upon.

"It seems a great deal of trouble just to arrange a meal," Conn said. "Where I come from, it is much simpler: a contract is proposed, details are negotiated. The whole matter is concluded in under a minute."

Erkatchian nodded. "What is it they say about your world? That the Thraisians built an admirable civilization, then tore it down and put up a marketplace instead."

"The two are not mutually exclusive," said Conn.

But the captain only made a comic face. A footman set a dish of soup before him and he turned his attention to it. Umlat served Conn who watched the captain select a spoon of middling size from the phalanx of silverware before doing likewise. He dipped into the liquid, tasted it and found it cold and bland.

"I expected better fare at a lord's table," Conn whispered to Erkatchian.

"Another tradition," was the response. "Watch."

No sooner had the dish been tasted than it was whisked away by the servants and replaced with steaming bowls of a more toothsome broth. Conn chose another spoon and began to eat.

"What is the meaning of the cold soup tradition?" he asked the captain.

"No one remembers anymore."

"Then why is it still observed?"

"Because that is what traditions are for."

There seemed no point in pursuing the matter. Conn returned to their earlier discussion. "You have been to Thrais?"

"I have been up and down The Spray, first as a commercial spacer and in my present capacity—up, down and well beyond."

"You have been where we are going? To Forlor?"

"How could I? Until you delivered the coordinates, no one but you knew where it was. The secret died with the Flagit brothers." Erkatchian spooned up the last of the soup and dabbed his lips with fabric. "This craft is rarely in use. My lord Vullamir allowed me to go out and search for your hidden planet. Nor was I the only searcher. My lord offered a financial inducement that drew the avaricious and adventurous."

Erkatchian's eyes looked into a distance beyond the walls of the saloon. "Had I been the lucky one, I would have had enough to buy a decent yacht of my own. Then I would run charters among the wealthier worlds. It would be my ideal life."

"Was one of the searchers named Chask Daitoo?"

The name meant nothing to Erkatchian. "There must have been dozens. Some came back empty handed. Others were never heard of again."

"What about the name Willifree?"

The captain laughed. "That would be a masking name. It is a name from a children's story. Willifree is a secret kingdom hidden beneath a magical stone. Its inhabitants have unusual powers and pursuits. The tale was not read to you when you were a child, to engage your imagination?"

"My childhood was centered on other priorities."

They were served something in pastry. A delicate waft of herbs and vapor greeted Conn when he broke the crust. He chewed thoughtfully and watched the aristocrats at the end of the table. They were able to eat through the mouths of their life masks; the translucent material could apparently admit solids and liquids just as it allowed air to pass back and forth. The lords were conversing in tones too low for him to hear.

"What use will Lord Vullamir make of Forlor once he acquires it?"

Erkatchian looked away. "I have decided not to ask that question," he said. "The answer may trouble me."

"A man who called himself Willifree, an aristocrat, killed a woman on the ship that brought me to Old Earth. His motives were unsavory," Conn said. "One who seemed knowledgeable about these things connected him with the Immersion."

The captain's gaze sharpened. "You know about that?"

"Perhaps not as much as I should."

"You are a peculiar Thraisian," Erkatchian said. "Does not your credo counsel you to let others alone if they accord you the same liberty?"

"Perhaps I am not as Thraisian as I thought I was. Certainly I am not the same as I was before I left the planet," Conn said.

"I believe that is why few Thraisians have a yen to travel off their own world," the captain observed. "They are satisfied with their perspectives and do not enjoy having them contradicted. The visiting foreigners they encounter at home are merely peculiar and quaintly misguided, objects of behind-the-hand mockery. Offworld, the strangers are encountered in strength and on their own ground. It must be sorely abrasive to Thraisian sensibilities."

"I think I am coming to believe that some sensibilities are all the better for an occasional abrading," Conn said.

"That is as may be," said the captain, "though I would not advise you to apply the rough side of anything to the sentiments of your present host and my employer. These Old Earth nobles affect a languid ease, but poke them in a sensitive spot and they can make the most tightly wound Thraisian look all happity-slappity-pull-it-again."

They were now eating some kind of fish paste spread on thin rounds of dried vegetable that had to be conveyed to the lips by a pair of small tongs. The maneuver took more practice than Conn would have anticipated and he was too occupied to talk until the next course—chopped meats, vegetables and cubes of an unidentifiable substance—was placed before him. He used the time to consider his situation and the directions in which it might evolve.

By the standards of his upbringing, it should concern him not a whit what Vullamir intended to do on Forlor. Both the lord and Conn were free individuals, neither of them in any way responsible for whatever the other might get up to. It was an elegantly simple philosophy, all sharp edges and precise shapes. A Thraisian school child could have demonstrated, by geometric logic, that Conn was exempt from any consideration of events that might transpire on Forlor once it was Vullamir's.

Yet Conn had seen something more of the universe than was revealed to Thraisian schoolchildren. He believed he could summon up a sense of how Ren Farbuck would respond to the idea of a world made safe for Willifrees, a hidden world to which other Clariq Walladers might be transported and not heard from again. Conn certainly knew how Jenore Mordene would view his role in bringing about such an eventuality.

It came down to the meaning that Jenore would give to the word "good." It was a concept that had great meaning to her. She had called him "a good man." If he wished to go back to her and resume the relationship that they had begun he could not turn what she would call a morally blind eye to the question of what Vullamir would do on Forlor. He found that he did indeed wish to return to the woman who had placed his hand upon her heart. In all the Ten Thousand Worlds, she was the only person who had taken his side; he knew he must take hers.

This might be his only opportunity to confront his host before they arrived at Forlor. He put down the four-tined fork he had been using to eat the stew. He stared straight ahead for a few moments, his eyes unfocused, his breathing regulated, as he concentrated his energies. It was a technique he had known since boyhood, appropriate before any confrontation. Then he rose and faced Lord Vullamir.

It was a few seconds before he was noticed by the group at the head of the table. The life masks turned toward him, one face angular and female, a couple of others jowly and florid, three ancient and seamed, and Vullamir's magisterial visage. There was silence.

"My lord Vullamir," Conn said, "I must ask you what you mean to do with Forlor once I have made it over to you."

The face in the mask assumed an expression of amused surprise, as if Conn were a precocious child who had made an outré request. Then the lord's long fingers rippled in a gesture of dismissal and mild contempt.

"Lad," said the captain, placing a hand on Conn's arm, "best you should sit down."

Conn did not glance in the man's direction but kept his gaze locked on Vullamir as he gently but firmly broke the captain's light grip. Erkatchian sighed and returned to his stew.

"Lord Vullamir," Conn said, "I apologize if I am contravening any laws of hospitality, but I must have an answer."

Now the mask's expression lost all indulgence. Conn could not read the dead man's eyes as he could those of the living, but there was no way to misinterpret what was looking back at him: pride and power, both of them challenged and both entirely unused to being opposed.

"You are impertinent," said a voice that exactly matched the imperious aspect of the mask. "Sit."

"I cannot," said Conn.

There was a hiss from one of the other aristocrats. The eyes of Vullamir's mask narrowed. His hand motioned to the servants who stood against the wall, their faces impassive, their eyes averted. But two of them caught the lord's gesture and they stepped toward Conn.

"Whatever it is, lad," the captain said. "Let it go."

But Conn drew his shocker and aimed it at the approaching footmen. They froze. He stepped back from the table and spoke over his shoulder to Umlat who stood behind him. "Umlat, you and the captain's server will go to the head of the table. You, too, captain."

When they were all grouped where he could see them, Conn said, "Lord Vullamir, if you will not answer my question I must revoke my agreement in principle. The sale is off. I intend to accompany the captain to the bridge. We will turn the ship around and return to Old Earth."

Vullamir said nothing. Magratte spoke instead. "The punishments for piracy are several and highly inventive."

"As I am sure they are for kidnapping," Conn answered. "Or for murder."

"There has been no murder," the aristocrat said.

"We will see. All of you will remove your masks."

"Why?"

"Because it will be more comfortable for you if you do so, rather than if I remove the masks after I have shocked their wearers unconscious." Conn gestured with the weapon.

"It is difficult to remove a mask that has been worn for several hours," Magratte said.

"The footmen may assist."

No one at the head of the table moved. Conn raised the shocker, ostentatiously adjusted its output setting and aimed at the nearest of the nobles.

For a long moment there was absolute stillness in the room. Conn's arm did not waver. His finger slid into the control aperture.

Magratte spoke quietly to Vullamir. The latter's hand lifted, flicked once. The footmen stepped forward and laid their hands on the guests' masks. A sequence of soft clicks deactivated the devices. The displayed faces disappeared, taking with them looks of fury and outrage. One of the servants made to lift a mask free of its wearer's head, evoking a muffled grunt of pain and a stream of indistinct profanity.

"Wait," said Magratte. "They must detach."

Time passed, then one of the lords put his beringed hands to the neck of his mask. A footman reached and gently lifted it free, revealing a narrow, balding pate to which wisps of thin white hair were glued by sweat. A pair of dark eyes peered at Conn from either side of a knifeblade nose, and he could have read their hatred in the dark.

"Another," Conn said.

One by one, the masks were removed. Though Conn had not asked for it, Vullamir had his removed as well. The face he revealed was not much different from his saturnine ancestor's, and as full of cold rage as the simulacrum had been.

Magratte was the last to dispense with his disguise. When the gray globe was lifted free, Conn recognized the face it had concealed. The jewels were gone from the skin and the formerly long hair was close cropped.

"Willifree," Conn said.

The aristocrat sneered as he offered a correction. "Lord Magratte, though I will not say, 'at your service.'"

"I suspected you were one of the party," Conn said. "I am arresting you for the killing of Clariq Wallader."

Magratte snorted and said, "By what authority?"

"I am an auxiliary of First Response Protection Corporation of Thrais, also empowered to act for the security department of the Gunter Line. This is a legal apprehension and all are required to offer me any aid I request."

"I believe I will nonetheless decline," said Magratte. He returned his attention to the dish in front of him. "Even cooled, this is very good," he told Vullamir.

"Captain," Conn said. "Is there a secure room on this ship?"

"There is," Erkatchian said.

"Please lead my prisoner and me to it. Magratte, stand and come with me."

But the margrave only lifted another forkful of stew and chewed it with satisfaction, looking straight ahead. Then he swallowed and turned his head toward Conn. The message of his eyes bespoke only cruel amusement. "I think not," he said.

"It makes no difference to me whether you arrive there conscious or not," Conn said. He aimed the shocker.

"Enough," said Vullamir. "You are no longer entertaining."

TEMPLATE

Conn squeezed the weapon's grip. His last awareness was of a flash of light and a shock that passed from his hand, up his arm and into his head. Then blackness descended.

He regained consciousness in his darkened cabin, awakening to find himself lying on his side on his bed. His arms were pinioned behind him and when he strained against whatever gripped his wrists he felt the subtle response of a holdtight, the device increasing its pressure to match his attempts to pull free. He relaxed and the mechanism eased to a looser grip. Another set of fetters bound his ankles.

He considered his situation. He had been foolish to give in to the impulse to act against Magratte. Clearly, he had let his relationship with Jenore Mordene cloud his judgment, had substituted her frame of reference for his own, had let self-indulgent emotion trump rational self-interest. If he had ever shown such an inclination during his days as a house player, Ovam Horder would have sent him for reevaluation forthwith.

Conn sighed and immediately recognized the response as yet another infiltration of his inner tranquility by alien emotion. Hadn't Hallis Tharp also inveighed against vain regrets: *Do not sigh over the morning's reverses; breathe life into the afternoon's advances.*

Somewhere a bell chimed discreetly. They were nearing the first whimsy that would carry them toward Forlor. The sac of chemicals that would shield Conn from its effect was in a dispenser set into the bed's ornate headboard. He had no means of reaching it. Instead, he performed the exercises that calmed the surface of his mind, yet even as stillness reasserted itself he noted a fading echo of regret that he had not been able to bring Magratte to book. He pushed it into the back reaches of his mind.

Over the bell's soft reminder he heard the latch of his cabin door disengage. A figure appeared briefly against the light from the corridor before entering and closing the door. A moment later, the cabin's lumens came up casting a soft and shadowless light over its furnishings and adornments, and Conn recognized Erkatchian.

When he saw that the prisoner was capable of discourse the spacer said, "I wanted to make sure you did not enter the whimsy unmedicated. Also, I would like us to come to some kind of arrangement."

"What have you in mind?" Conn said.

Chapter 10

"You cannot commandeer the ship," Erkatchian said. "No captain would allow it."

"I take it you have seized my weapons," Conn said.

The spacer signaled that that was true. "But even if we hadn't, they were useless. Each had already been put out of commission."

Conn was puzzled. "Not by you?"

"No. It seems someone else wanted you harmless."

The information raised several questions but Conn put them aside to concentrate on more immediate concerns. "You were saying?"

"When we have passed through the first whimsy we will be well down The Spray in the direction of the Breen Cluster. In less than a day we will enter another whimsy that will throw us far out into the Beyond. Apparently, if we take the right heading, after another three days we will encounter a third whimsy that will bring us to the edge of a gas cloud, beyond which lies Forlor."

Conn's face showed Erkatchian an expression that was noncommittal but invited him to continue.

"If I have your parole that you will not interfere with the passengers or the operations of the ship, I will release you from your bonds and allow you limited freedom to move about."

"How limited?"

"I will move you to a cabin in crew quarters and you will stay away from the owner and his guests."

Conn thought about it. The conditions were reasonable. "Agreed," he said. "Until we arrive at Forlor."

"And then?"

"And then we will see."

The spacer's face showed relief. He produced the holdtight's key and directed it at Conn's pinioned limbs. Two *clicks* sounded and the young man was free.

The chime sounded again. Conn reached for the medicine sac dispenser at the head of his bed. A moment later he squeezed oblivion into his palm.

Conn awoke to find a steward seated in a chair beside the bed. "The Captain asks that you refresh yourself then change into nondescript clothing and accompany me to his quarters."

Conn did so then followed the crewman through unobtrusive passages to Erkatchian's accommodations. The captain rated a spacious sitting room, sleeping chamber and private ablutory, equipped and furnished to a degree just short of luxurious. Erkatchian waved Conn toward one of the comfortable chairs then went to a sideboard and filled two glasses from a decanter of rose Phalum. When they had sat and completed the brief formalities that preceded the first sip, the spacer leaned toward the younger man and said, "I wish to discuss a transaction—in fact, more than that, a business partnership."

"On Thrais this would be an improper conversation," Conn said. Prospective partners were expected to begin their courtship by discussing topics of little importance, gradually leading to amiable talks about each other's goals and interests and only coming around to even the first hint of an interest in forming a serious business relationship after weeks of polite preliminaries. "However, I am reminded that you are from Old Earth, where I have seen that standards are lax." In truth, however, Thraisian insistence on such a roundabout approach now seemed arbitrary. Besides, *When in Haxxi* . . . .

"No offense is intended," Erkatchian said. "Indeed, I seek your good will."

"Very well." Conn sipped the wine and waited.

"I will be direct," the captain said. "My lord Vullamir will pay you a fortune for Forlor. That has been agreed."

"The situation has undergone a material change," Conn said. "He may also have to pay me a bonus."

"Oh?"

"In the form of Magratte."

"That is an unusual way for a Thraisian to transact business," Erkatchian said.

"Perhaps I am an unusual Thraisian."

"Ah," said the spacer, but he formed his lips in a way that said the idea was not unthinkable. "The margrave is of a significantly lower tier, and well without Vullamir's first three circles of consanguinity. They can work closely together only because they are of comparable rank in the Immersion. But, ultimately, that association is not as important as breeding. If Vullamir can come to the issue without any appearance of having been coerced, it might be possible."

"How could I bring him to that position?" Conn asked.

"There are specific words to be spoken, gestures to be made. You would require the guidance of one accustomed to dealing with the high aristocracy."

"And where might I find such a guide?"

"By sheerest chance, you are drinking wine with one. Would you care for some more?"

"It is very good," Conn said and allowed Erkatchian to refill his glass.

When the captain was once more settled in his chair he said, "So now we know what I can do for you. Let us cross the road to view matters from the other side."

"Very well, what would you have me do for you?"

"I mentioned the fortune you may—I think, will—receive for tendering Forlor to my lord. Have you given any thought as to how you might use it?"

In fact, Conn had not but saw no reason to say as much to the spacer. He shrugged. "I have thought about this and that. My plans have not yet solidified."

"You are not intending to return to Thrais?"

"Nothing calls me there."

"Is it possible that you might wish to view some of the worlds of The Spray with a view to settling on one of the more congenial?"

"It is possible," said Conn.

"Travel by commercial ships can be tedious," Erkatchian said. "They are bound by schedules, and all the waiting around while they take on and discharge cargoes. The traveler lacks a true sense of independence."

"I have noticed that," Conn said.

The captain leaned forward. "But if one owns one's own ship, one travels in comfort and in complete freedom."

"Indeed." Conn assumed a thoughtful air. "But there are other concerns: safe operation of the ship, maintenance and upkeep, not flying into the wrong whimsy and ending up as a trinket on some transdimensional being's equivalent of a bracelet."

Erkatchian conceded the validity of Conn's view. "But if the traveler shares ownership with an experienced spacefarer, these concerns fade to negligibility. The co-owner says, 'Let us go here or perhaps there, see the sunsets, taste the local brews, consort with agreeable companions, some of them winsomely female,' and zippety-zip, he is where he chooses to be."

"It all sounds enticingly simple," Conn said, "but surely there are some prickles and stickles amidst all this tasting and dallying."

"One or two," said Erkatchian, and so they fell to serious discussions. The gist of the spacer's proposition was that Conn should combine part of his coming fortune with Erkatchian's savings so that they could together purchase a well-founded yacht, new or of recent manufacture, suitable for the private charter trade. The craft would be at Conn's disposal a certain portion of the time, so that he might visit places that took his interest; the rest of the time it would be given over to profitable charters. The partners would share in the proceeds each according to his investment in the common venture and after an agreed-upon date, Erkatchian would have the option to buy out Conn's share of the vessel by returning his capital plus a percentage profit, also to be agreed upon.

"It is an interesting proposition," Conn said, when the full shape of Erkatchian's proposal was revealed, "but there is one consideration it leaves unaddressed."

The spacer invited him to name it.

"My origins are a mystery. It is possible that I will discover more on Forlor than a means to acquire a fortune. I may find the place I was meant to be, the place where I belong. If so, I will not be rambling about The Spray like Betherin in search of his perambulating pizzle. I will be staying put."

Erkatchian snorted, then said, "Forgive me. From what I've heard of Forlor under the Flagit brothers, it is not a place in which any one ever wanted to sink roots."

"What have you heard?"

"Spacers' tales, with widely varying details but tending toward a common theme: that the Flagits made the place a battlefield for their playtime wars. Any stretch of territory may contain still live ordinance, unsprung traps or self-actuating defenses. A casual stroll might turn suddenly into a scene from Shaifen's *Flesh and Fire*."

"I am not familiar with that work," Conn said.

"You are all the better for it," Erkatchian said. "It disturbs one's nights."

"If the tales distill to a basis of truth, I wonder that the Immersion wants the place."

The captain made a gesture that expressed his refusal to consider his employer's motives. "There will be a lodge or some such, probably of fortress strength surrounding unstinting comfort. The Flagits preferred to keep their mayhems at a safe distance."

"Still," said Conn, "I cannot make a commitment without first seeing what there is to see."

"But you do not reject my proposition out of hand?"

Conn let his mind conjure up images: walking along glittering promenades, surveying magnificent landscapes, sampling cuisines and cultures of a thousand worlds. The prospect had a faint appeal. He was not surprised to discover that its attractiveness increased markedly when he added to each scene the presence of Jenore Mordene—Jenore laughing, Jenore dancing, Jenore close beside him as she had been the last night at Graysands. "No, I do not reject it," he told Erkatchian.

"Good," said the captain, "because there is one other element that makes the idea of our partnership attractive."

Conn waited to hear it.

"The way you added an ethical condition to your bargain with my lord Vullamir. It bespeaks a moral depth that is unusual in a Thraisian."

The captain's choice of words, coupled with the images of Jenore still fresh in Conn's mind, caused a pang of emotion to pass through the younger man's being. "I am coming to see myself as only an accidental Thraisian," he said.

When he left the captain a crewman led Conn along another passageway to a small cabin with walls of painted metal and utilitarian furbishings. His belongings had been moved to his new quarters and stowed while he had been in discussion with Erkatchian. A meal waited for him on a warming tray. He supposed that it was the plainer fare that the crew ate rather than the overwrought delicacies that were served to the owner and his guests, and found it suited his palate well enough. When he had eaten he placed the tray outside his door and reposed himself on the narrow bunk to consider what he had come to and where it might lead him.

. . . a moral depth that is unusual in a Thraisian, the captain had said. The first time he had been called "unusual"—by Jenore Mordene—he had bridled as if the term had been meant to insult. He had thought himself typical of his world, albeit his view of things had been constrained by his status as an indentured house player, however much he had been favored by his indentor. Then had come his first encounters with other world views, those of the disparate company on the *Dan*: Jenore's peculiar definition of "good," the pride of the pastoralist Ren Farbuck, the overweening lust of the Immersionist lord, the gluttonous appetite for experience of the Divorgians. He had thought them all addle-pates, persons who had been denied the perfected simplicity of Transactualism and had been forced to build for themselves airy castles of supposition and superstition in which to live out their confused lives.

Now he was no longer so sanguine. He had to face the fact that Thrais was an anomaly among the Ten Thousand Worlds, one slightly off-key note in the great symphony of philosophies and perspectives that had flowered along with the human settlement of The Spray. And the farther Conn Labro roamed from the getters and spenders of Bay City, the more he encountered systems based on entirely different principles, systems that nonetheless had worked very well for their adherents through millennia.

Perhaps it is because I am not bred to Transactualism, he thought as he lay on the bunk's rough cover and regarded the blank page that was the gray painted ceiling. *I am not, after all, a true Thraisian. I was merely brought there to be raised as one*. That led back to the central mystery of his existence: who was he? *Whose* was he? Was he stolen from a family? If so, why? Had he come to Thrais, as the ship's doctor on the *Grayling* had indicated, in the womb of his mother? Then where was she, and why had he not known her?

Between Conn and the answers to these questions rose the specter of Hallis Tharp, who could have answered all of Conn's wonderings but had instead departed with all his motivations to a place where Conn could not follow. And now, for the first time, he thought about the old man who had been a regular presence in his life for as long as he could remember, and apparently, even longer than that.

TEMPLATE

As he dwelt on the matter of Hallis Tharp he felt a stirring, the first inner rumblings of anger, and automatically invoked the technique that dissipated the emotion. With the exercise came an echo of Tharp's dry and quiet voice—*Never let yourself become angry; he who loses his temper loses all*—and Conn used the sound of the voice in his head to reach for a fuller memory. But the image that came was clouded, diffuse. Instead of the clarity that usually infused his memories, a product of his player's intensive training in observation and recall, all he could recover from a thousand sessions with Hallis Tharp—two hours across the paduay board every Firstday for more than twenty years—was merely an *impression* of their encounters.

The realization sent a shock through him. That was not right, Conn knew. He sought for memories, found that he could remember individual paduay matches, the positions of pieces, the turning points on which the flow of play had hinged, the outcomes. But where the rest of it should have stood in his finely tuned memory—words exchanged, facial expressions noted—there was only a vagueness. And now, as he sought to bring detail out of the fog, he felt a nagging inclination to think of something else. It was as if some part of his own mind had been instructed to watch for the emergence of this line of thought and to deflect it into other.

That realization brought back the anger. Again the automatic response arose, but this time Conn consciously held back from the Lho-tso mantra that calmed the mind. He let the anger rise inside him—he had a mental image of boiling magma filling a volcanic chamber, himself a bubble on its rising surface—and watched as it surged up red and hot in the core of his being. Again, Tharp's voice came, urging restraint, but he tuned it out.

He sensed that the anger was a pry that could break the seal behind which stood the knowledge of what had really happened on all those Firstday mornings. There was clearly something Hallis Tharp had not wanted him to remember, had used some technique of mental editing to keep from Conn's memory. He pushed at the vagueness in his mind, focusing the anger, letting it become a fiery joy that he shaped and drove into the fog.

And the mists parted. He saw Hallis Tharp, not across the paduay board but seated beside him on the divan on the other side of the playing chamber. The man was not so old, in his prime years. And he was big. Conn realized that he was seeing through the eyes of a very young Conn Labro.

His gaze was drawn to Tharp's upraised palm, at its center a disk that spun and swirled and scintillated with flashing colored lines, constantly drawing into a central point, like water rushing into a pinhole drain. He heard the man's voice, younger and firmer: *You will learn and practice. You will become the best player you can be. You need never fear, never worry. But you must not give in to anger. Whenever you feel that you are about to become angry you will perform this exercise*... And Conn heard Hallis Tharp's voice intone the Lho-tso chant, then heard his own child's voice repeating the syllables.

The anger was rising toward rage, but Conn held it in check, focusing it as he had learned to focus so many other aspects of the mind. It became a tool and with it he tore at the shrouds that concealed his memories and stripped away the

157

conditioning, searching for answers to the questions that now defined his existence, questions that had never occurred to him through all his life. He found at least the why behind that mystery: the image of Hallis Tharp's face, the sound of Hallis Tharp's voice telling him, *Lock your mind onto the task ahead of you, banish idle thoughts. The past is not your concern, nor the future. Just do to the best of your ability the work that comes to you.*

Conn found that he had sat up without registering the movement. His teeth ground against each other, his hands had clenched into fists. He could feel the tendons standing out in his neck, a vibration in his limbs and the muscles of his back. *This is how it feels to be angry*, he thought. *And it feels good*. There was a seductive heat to the emotion, a sense of direction, as if he was being carried along on a stream of fire toward some apocalyptic revelation.

But with that sense of impending collision came a warning from his own mind—not cast in Tharp's tones but in his own inner voice—that this was not the moment to let himself go. This force must have a target and must be aimed, else it would become a weapon that would turn in the wielder's hand. He deliberately relaxed his tense and aching muscles, controlled his breathing, spoke the Lho-tso mantra. And felt the rage seep back into its reservoir.

Its cessation left him cool and calm within, paradoxically full of the same empty stillness that had always been the inner Conn Labro. But now, for the first time in his life, he weighed the lightness of his being and thought, *Should I not be more than this? Something has been denied me. Or taken from me*. And once again he had to put down the rising heat.

Hallis Tharp had posed three questions. He now knew the answers to the first and second: he came from Forlor and it was to Forlor that he was going. The answer to the third question—*what are you?*— would be answered there. Of that he was sure.

A buzzer sounded in the corridor. The *Martichor* was approaching the whimsy that would spin them within reach of his home world. A medicinal sac popped out of the dispenser at the head of Conn's bunk. He took it in his hand, lay back and squeezed.

T he Spray was an archipelago of light behind them, the Back of Beyond a swath of darkness in every other direction, broken only occasionally by smudges of distant galaxies and the few lonely stars that lay out here like lost sparks that had whirled too far from a campfire. Even those sources of light were missing in the view directly ahead of the *Martichor*, which was obscured by an immense cloud of interstellar gas into which the yacht was hurtling at so great a speed that the ship's passage through the thinly disseminated molecules of hydrogen caused a faint whisper of sound to be transmitted through the hull.

Conn regarded the great emptiness from the observation port one deck below the space yacht's bridge. A wider view could be had from the panoramic window in the bow, but that was in passenger country and Conn and Erkatchian had agreed that it would be less complicated if the young man avoided contact with the owner and his coterie. Conn did not mind; he

TEMPLATE

preferred his own company to Vullamir's or that of the servants assigned to him. And the yacht's captain made an agreeable traveling companion when duty did not occupy him. He told tales of the Ten Thousand Worlds, especially of the port cities, and particularly the parts of those cities where spacers went in search of diversions and novelties.

Erkatchian had not heard the wind shrieking through the red rock spires it had carved in the heart of the continent-wide desert known as the Swelter on the world called Anvil; but near the planet's sole spaceport was the Blue Egg Café, home to a remarkable female contortionist who could connect parts of her body in a manner that dispensed with the normal restraints of anatomy.

He had not dived beneath the lethargic waves of the tideless ocean on moonless Vermoul to observe the mating rituals of the gravix, a semi-sapient species that came in five sexes, only three of which were involved in conception—the fourth handled the lengthy gestation and the exact role of the fifth had led to beard-pulling debates at conclaves of exobiologists. But the captain could testify to the potency of the spirituous liquor called rack which the locals brewed from pods that washed up on the seashore after seasonal storms. "A fellow jostled my elbow and I spilled a gill or so on the bar's wooden floor," Erkatchian related. "The flunky came to wipe it up and when he was done his gray string mop was bleached as white as virgin snow."

At the captain's urging, Conn told tales from his life at Ovam Horder's house: memorable fights, particularly successful stratagems and ruses, occasions of surprise or satisfaction. The spacer proved as good a listener as a talespinner. "Each is a necessary attribute among those of us who ply the wefts and warps between the stars," he told Conn, "for not all ships move as briskly as a first-class yacht and we can spend many long days penned together in close quarters. It's the stories that lubricate the air between us and keep spacefaring folk from rubbing each other raw."

Conn soon noticed the great difference in their lives. Erkatchian had spread his experiences across the width of The Spray, but without depth. Conn had passed his years on one world, indeed in one building, but he had plumbed the nature of conflict to a degree that few could match. On their third day of motion through the gas cloud that screened Forlor from the sight of The Spray and all the rest of creation, he voiced the comparison.

"Your particular skill may come in handy," said Erkatchian. "I've been thinking about what to do in regard to Magratte."

"I have said I will demand him as part of the price."

"The price was settled before we left Olkney spaceport."

"Then we will have to reopen negotiations, in light of a material change in conditions." It was not an unheard of situation in Transactualism, provided both parties were willing to alter a contract.

"My lord Vullamir would find that a novel proposal," Erkatchian said, in a tone and with a look that said novelty was not a prized quality among the aristocracy. "Even if it weren't, my lord Vullamir did not bring his intercessor with him, nor did you bring yours."

It was not a factor Conn had considered. "He is incapable of simple bargaining?"

"He would be incapable of defining the concept," the captain said, "assuming one could somehow induce him to make the attempt. He is a grand high panjandrum of Old Earth's first-tier aristocracy and as such he is blissfully unaware of any but his peers and near equals."

"Then how do I remove Magratte from under his protection?"

Erkatchian tapped the side of his nose. Conn had not seen the gesture before but he took it to mean that the spacer had high confidence in his own savvy.

"That means you know of a way?"

The captain repeated the gesture. "It does."

At the heart of the immense cloud was a rift and in that rift was a small white star circled by a single great sphere of condensed gas and a number of planets made of more solid stuff. One of these latter, second from the star, had air and water and rudimentary vegetation, according to the *Martichor*'s percepts. It was small, an old world with but a single continent that took up most of the northern hemisphere, a mostly flat expanse of land bounded all about by a sluggish gray ocean that wanly reflected the sun's parsimonious light.

The yacht dissipated speed and looped in to orbit the planet. Erkatchian ordered a more detailed scan which revealed that the few varieties of grass, trees and shrubs were all imported from Loney, a tranquil planet far down The Spray chiefly notable for its innocuous lifeforms. "Whatever was here to begin with, if there ever was anything," the captain said, "was scoured clean away and replanted with little more than stage setting."

The continent had one prominent feature: near its southern edge was a tall hill that fell just short of being a mountain. Its top was capped by a fanciful expanse of domes, blocks, minarets and high-arching bridges, all in white and black, and its lower slopes abruptly became sheer vertical cliffs innocent of cleft, fissure or any handhold that would have made scaling them even remotely feasible. "The whole structure is surely as artificially contrived as the imported greenery," Conn said as the *Martichor* prepared to descend to the great building's illuminated landing area.

The yacht touched down gently at the junction of two intersecting white lines set in a circle of black, just as the sun was sinking below the horizon. As the ship's full weight settled onto the rock the tops of two overlooking towers split open to reveal formidable ison-cannon already rotating to cover the ship. The *Martichor*'s integrator reported that it was receiving a communication.

"Let us hear it," said Erkatchian.

"If you are Conn Labro," said a voice Conn recognized as a younger version of Hallis Tharp's, "you will have thirty minims in which to sing the beginning of the second verse of the old song I often used to sing while I was considering a complex move in paduay. If you are not Conn Labro, please depart before the automatic defenses activate." The message was repeated then the voice began to count down from thirty.

"Do you know the song?" Erkatchian said.

"Yes." Now he could not think about it without calling up a mental image of Jenore Mordene dancing to its sad melody. A pang of sadness went through him, surprising him by its sharp edge.

The spacer interrupted his reverie. "Then sing it before he runs out of numbers."

Conn sang. *"But if you come when all the flowers are dying, and I am dead, as dead I well may be."*

The ison-cannon withdrew back into the spires and an integrator's voice said, "Please follow the indicators."

"I'm glad we brought you," said Erkatchian as the bridge screen showed two parallel rows of lumens leading from the landing area toward the complex of domes and towers. "Shall we go take a look?"

"What about Vullamir?" Conn said.

"It's the Hour of Retrospective Aspersion. He will be fully occupied in cursing the enemies of his ancestors. The activity involves robust and forceful gestures."

"Have the maledictions any practical effect?"

"I haven't considered the question. But the exercise seems to agree with him."

They opened the yacht's mid port and descended to the rock. The air was cold and damp, tinged by a sour odor borne on a north wind. They turned their backs to it and followed the lighted path.

Conn wondered aloud if the place had seasons. Erkatchian replied that the world's axial tilt was scant, but that they were experiencing what degree of summer Forlor could muster. "But I doubt that the Flagit brothers came here for the weather," he said. "Clearly, it was privacy they prized."

Conn looked up at the darkening sky. Though the atmosphere was clear no stars were appearing; the gas cloud obscured the heavens completely. Nor was there a moon. "And darkness," he said.

Their way brought them to a long flight of broad steps, in alternate courses of white and black stone. They mounted, assisted from behind by gusts of the cold rancid wind, and came at last to a wide flagstoned terrace, again checkered in black and white. "Just as clearly, the Flagits did not lean toward great subtlety of decor," Erkatchian said, looking across the wide promenade at a pair of oversized doors, one white, the other black, set in the high and windowless wall of a square building built of more black and white, though this time the alternating monochrome blocks were arranged in chevrons.

There was no who's-there beside the doors, but the portal swung soundlessly open as they reached it. Beyond was uninviting blackness, yet Conn did not hesitate to enter. As he crossed the threshold, lumens set high on the building's inner walls activated, throwing a stark light on the place's interior.

Erkatchian followed him into a great hall whose ceiling and farthest wall were lost in gloom. The mood of the place was austere, with furniture of heavy dark wood—massive tables, high-backed seats, chests and sideboards—all roughly hewn and held together by studs of black iron. The walls were hung with heavy cloths in which images were woven: men heroically posed in fanciful armor, afoot or riding caparisoned warbeasts or at the controls of combat machines, against backgrounds of serried ranks or surging hordes. Everywhere were points and blades and beams of coruscating energies, amid gallant charges and dauntless stands around the battle colors of legendary regiments.

"Do you note that the faces are always the same?" Erkatchian commented.

Conn had. "These, I take it, are the Flagits."

"Aye, the long-nosed one was Ermin. The one with a face like a stale pudding was Blathe."

"Were any of these scenes taken from actual events?"

Erkatchian snorted. "Only vicariously. The Flagits thought of themselves as breach stormers and wall scalers, but they were born to be staff officers, seated comfortably around their maps and figurines well away from the hurly burly. I believe that they could link themselves to the perceptions of their playthings. Not to experience the pain, of course, nor even the smells of fear-sweat nor of spilled intestines—the sights and sounds of battle, remotely channeled to them as they lay upon their dream couches, were as much as they cared to experience."

Conn looked about him. "I have no memory of this place," he said, "not even a child's recollections. Yet this must be where my life began. Were my parents servants here?"

Erkatchian put a hand to his forehead as if rubbing it could improve the function of the organ behind the bone. "I never heard of any servants. If they'd existed, they'd have long since been found and questioned regarding the whereabouts of this place."

"Perhaps they were abandoned here, marooned."

"Perhaps. The Flagits were not renowned for treating their staff particularly well. Though nor had they a reputation for abuse, except of each other."

As they moved farther into the hall increased illumination accompanied them, new lumens lighting up and dispelling some of the gloom. Conn saw the outline of a metal door in the back wall and went toward it, the other man following. As he approached, a beam of light illuminated a spot on the floor beside the door. Out of the illuminated circle of floor rose a narrow column that stopped when its top was waist high.

When Conn reached it he saw that in the center of its top was an armature much like the one he had seen at the Registry of Offworld Properties. He produced the bead from where he kept it and held it ready in his hand. But before he could place it in the hollowed-out space there was a soft hum from somewhere then a projected simulacrum of a man wavered into existence beside the column.

"Hallis Tharp," said Conn. Just as the voice that had warned them of the defenses had been a younger version of the old man's, so were the face and form of the image before them.

TEMPLATE

"So here you are," said the projection. "Which means that I am dead. With luck, I expired from natural causes after a long life and you yourself are now well on in years and at ease in the life I built around you. You'll have come to this dismal place to find out who you are.

"If luck has not been with us," the image continued, "then I am dead because the Flagits and their minions caught up with us and you are here against your will to be pressed back into the horror of the half life from which I released you. Though, to be fair, only after I put you in it to begin with.

"If the first set of conditions pertains, then you may place the bead in its receptacle and go through this door if you feel you must learn the sad truth of where you came from. I have suborned the house's integrator. It will show and tell you all."

Now the simulacrum turned its sightless gaze as if hoping to lock its eyes with Conn's. "But if you are here against your will, then fight them now with whatever strength you can muster and do not stop fighting them until you are either free or dead. Do not let them take you beyond this door."

Chapter 11

The projection flickered then winked out. Conn saw that Erkatchian was looking at him with a peculiar expression. He remembered receiving a similar look from Jenore Mordene and responded as he had to her. "What?" he said.

The captain rubbed his face again and appeared to be weighing up alternative means of answering the question. After a moment he said, "Neither of the conditions Hallis Tharp mentioned applies in this situation. But I think it would be wise for you to come back to the *Martichor* and deliver that bead into the hands of my lord Vullamir. Then we will buy a ship together and wander the Ten Thousand Worlds without your ever having stepped beyond that door."

"You know something?" Conn said. "Tell me."

"I know any number of things that I regret ever having learned," Erkatchian said. "I suspect that behind that door is another unwelcome learning experience. But much worse for you than for me."

Conn felt the bead, solid and warm in his hand. He examined his feelings, felt confusion mingled with curiosity. He had settled his views on Hallis Tharp, at least temporarily: the man had done him harm, though for what gain he still could not fathom. But here was Tharp speaking to him, the recording surely made just before or just after he had seized Conn and was about to take him away, and there was no hint of ill will—indeed, completely to the contrary.

"I am a mystery," he said to the spacer, "and my answer is in there."

"Some mysteries are best left unsolved," Erkatchian said.

"How could I go from here with my questions unanswered?" Conn said. "What could lie beyond the door that I should fear it? Heaps of moldered corpses? Dungeons and chains, bespeaking the dark side of the Flagits' appetites? I am not afraid of what I might find."

"Are you ever afraid?" the captain asked, watching him as if Conn was some newly encountered species of ultraterrene whose dos and don'ts were not recorded in *Hobey's Compleat Guide to the Settled Planets*.

"Of course. Who isn't?"

"How does it feel?"

Conn opened his palm and looked at the bead. "We could have this conversation later," he said. He took the sphere between thumb and finger, extended it toward the aperture.

Erkatchian gently put a hand over the armature. "Humor me," he said. "How does it feel to be afraid?"

"If I answer, can we then get on with this?"

"Yes."

"Very well." Conn thought for a moment. "When I am afraid, my senses sharpen, my circulation alters so that more blood reaches my brain and skeletal muscles but not my skin, and my adrenaline rises, sharpening my reflexes."

"Would you call it an exhilarating sensation?"

"Yes, and very useful since it allows me the better to deal with whatever is making me afraid."

"Has it ever occurred to you that what you call 'afraid' might not be what I call 'afraid'?"

"I don't really have time for a philosophical discussion just now," Conn said. "Please remove your hand."

Erkatchian did not budge. "I don't think you should do this. I think you should walk away."

Conn felt a flash of irritation, automatically suppressed it. "If we were to become partners," he said, "you would have to resist the impulse to tell me what to do. I am coming to realize that others have determined almost the entire course of my life and I believe I am growing tired of it."

He placed the bead in the receptacle. There was a *whir* and a *click* and the door slid up into the wall. Conn stepped through, Erkatchian at his heels.

Beyond was a long hallway, softly lit from sources in sconces on the walls and interrupted by several doors along its length. All were closed. Conn spoke to the air, "Integrator?"

"What do you require?" said a neutral voice.

"Do you know who I am?"

"You are Conn Labro. Cooblor Tonn left instructions that you are to be shown a series of scenes. If you would care to enter the viewing room to your left, I will accommodate you."

One of the nearby doors opened inward on darkness then light glowed in the oblong. Conn entered, again followed by the captain. The room was spacious: two armchairs faced a broad and deep dais with a handful of less inviting chairs in a row behind the two plush seats.

"You may be seated," the integrator said.

Erkatchian shook his head but went and settled himself in one of the two foremost chairs. Conn sat in the other. It subtly conformed to his shape and adjusted its temperature.

"This is obscenely comfortable," Erkatchian said. "Not even my lord Vullamir indulges himself so voluptuously."

Conn paid the chair no attention. "What have you to show me?" he asked the integrator.

A scene appeared on the dais, full-figured. It showed two young boys, one with a pasty complexion and the other with a face that almost seemed to have been artificially elongated to accompany a long, thin nose.

"Blathe and Ermin Flagit," said Hallis Tharp's recorded voice. "From early years, they lived to counter each other."

Conn watched as the boys engaged in games: contests first played on boards or through boyhood integrators, then moving into larger and larger virtual arenas, the scenes tracking the two competitors through their developing years. The conflicts grew more savage, though the skills of Ermin and Blathe never advanced beyond dufferhood. Conn also saw each cheat whenever he thought his brother was not looking.

"Here they are at the end of adolescence," said Tharp's voice. The scene showed a rural estate, lawns and tree-dotted parkland on which ditches had been dug and palisades erected. Banners flew from atop a squat stone tower surrounded by a muddy moat. A horn blew somewhere and a mass of man-sized figures, all in black armor, came out of a stand of trees. Bearing scaling ladders and edged weapons they rushed across the open ground toward the tower. Halfway there they were met by a hail of missiles, fist sized lumps of metal that rang as they struck helms and breastplates. Those that were hit hard fell sprawling and twitching to the grass while their fellow attackers charged on without a backwards glance. They made no sound.

"These are artificial," Conn said. "Mechanisms."

"They are," said the integrator.

Now the angle of view shifted and Conn could see white armored figures atop the tower. They were operating a trio of primitive war engines made of wooden beams and swinging arms that threw the heavy shots out over the lawn like a child throwing gravel into a pond.

More of the black horde fell, then the leading rank ran under the range of the catapults and reached the moat. They laid the ladders they carried horizontally across the water, making narrow bridges across which they streamed while the whites above hurled down spears and blocks of stone, or shot metal bolts from shoulder-aimed weapons.

The assault wavered at the base of the tower, the blacks falling under the rain of missiles as they struggled to position some of the ladders against the wall and ascend. Then a second rank of blacks arrived at the outer rim of the moat and began to shoot up at the defenders with their own bolt throwers, sending coordinated volleys that swept the crenellations clear. The blacks at the base of the tower used the respite to anchor their siege ladders and swarm up. The black bolt throwers dropped their weapons, drew swords and axes and threw down more ladders to cross the moat.

The first few scalers to reach the top of the tower were flung back, falling silently to crash among their fellows. Then, with a clang and a spray of sparks, an ax-swinging black took the head off a white who leaned too far out to strike at him. The ax wielder climbed over the headless body and the first toehold was gained. The whirling ax held the whites at bay while other blacks gained the top of the tower behind him. The attacking force spread themselves into a line and more of their fellows appeared behind them. They began to push the defenders back, step by step.

It seemed that the black assault must carry the day, but now Conn saw a double file of whites, each carrying a repeating-action bolt thrower, emerge from a stairwell that led down into the tower. They arrayed themselves in two ranks, one standing, one kneeling, facing the backs of their beleaguered comrades whose faltering defense must soon give way to the swelling black presence.

Conn expected a signal that would tell the defending line to break off and clear the way. Instead the two firing lines began shooting volleys into the melee, cutting down friend or foe without discrimination. He saw the ax wielder take a bolt through the helmet and drop clattering to the stone floor, while blacks and whites fell all around him. In a few moments, the space before the shooters was heaped with writhing, jerking figures and no more blacks were coming up the ladders.

The view shifted and Conn saw that two white sally parties had come out of the doors on opposite sides of the tower's ground floor to make a pincer attack on the blacks who were bunched around the base of the ladders. The battle was now clearly won and lost, and Conn expected the action to end. Instead it went on until the last black armored mechanism was laid low, at a cost of several dozen whites.

"That was unnecessary," Conn said.

"A waste of good machinery," Erkatchian agreed.

"It was ever the Flagits' way," the integrator said as the scene showed Blathe holding a white standard and standing atop a heap of battered black limbs and torsos to have his image recorded. Ermin sulked in the background.

"Regard," said the integrator and a new scene appeared, a wide and muddy plain sweeping up to a range of low hills. Scores of regiments, great solid masses of black or white, were drawn up in formations and echelons. This time the blacks held the heights and the whites were surging into an attack across the open ground.

"They love the frontal assault," Hallis Tharp's voice said. "Not for Ermin and Blathe the niceties of feint and maneuver. They go at each other in the oldest possible way, grinding and battering to the last man. The mechanical armies grew bigger and they purchased vast tracts of land on which to conduct their campaigns, but the weaponry remained basic and the tactics dull. Until even the Flagits grew bored."

The battle faded out and an image of the younger Tharp appeared on the dais. "That is when they came to me."

Tharp's simulacrum stood with downcast eyes and hands folded before him. The house integrator had positioned the image so that when Tharp looked up his sightless gaze met Conn's eyes. Conn saw a mingling of emotions: regret, shame, resolution.

"I will not spare myself with excuses," Tharp's voice said. "I was as proud in my own way, as wrong-headedly self indulgent, as the Flagit brothers. We deserved each other."

He sighed. "I had a flair for the lost art of making simulated people," he said then smiled ruefully. "Did I say 'lost?' Let me be straight: the art was not lost; it was forbidden. All decent humankind had long ago agreed that it was an immoral practice and no civilized society would tolerate its return.

"But I was fascinated by what I had achieved in my little laboratory on the remote farm I had inherited soon after I graduated from the Institute. And I was entranced by the notion of how much more I might be able to do, had I the resources and no one to tell me that I was plunging myself into evil."

Tharp pinched his nostrils together between thumb and forefinger— it was a habitual gesture, Conn remembered—as if he wished to block the ingress of a foul odor. Then he sighed again. "I don't know how the Flagits found out what I was doing—perhaps through the places where I quietly purchased materials—though I thought I had covered my tracks by spreading my acquisitions around.

"In any case, one day they arrived and told me a tale. They had a world of their own, far out in the Back of Beyond, where they could do what they liked. What they liked was to fight battles, but mechanical warriors had ceased to slake their appetites for mayhem and people would not die for their pleasure, so their thoughts had turned to simulants. And that had led them to me. They were very persuasive. Very flattering. Only I could make them creatures of deep pathos and epic glory, and only I deserved the rewards my work would bring."

Tharp's image flourished his hands like a prestidigitator who was about to make something startling appear from beneath a tented cloth. "And suddenly here I was on Forlor, surrounded by the laboratory of my dreams. I could make sylphs and florigards and the most delicate and fleeting of human ephemera, true works of a recondite discipline that, in a year or two of the full application of my talents, I so mastered that my artist's pride swelled to a skin-splitting tumescence."

Now the hands spread in a show of acquiescence. "And the price of all my overweening happiness? Merely that I fashion some basic types for Ermin and Blathe, some light and heavy infantry, some agile scouts, some engineers and weaponsmen, a few captains and bannermen to direct the action, and some rough beasts to be their cavalry.

"And that is what I did. I made a template from my own plasm, edited it in ways that would suit its intended purpose: more closely packed retinal cells for enhanced vision; a reordered neural net that conferred excellence in some analytical faculties while discarding others—metaphor, artistic subtlety— that are of scant use in combat; a multichambered heart and a more efficient circulatory system to let them fight on after true men would be pallidly dead of exsanguination; enlarged adrenal glands and a redesigned limbic system to diminish fear and allow for the sustained rage that would carry them through a full day of battle without loss of élan. I gave them the capacity for satisfaction in victory, resignation in defeat, loyalty to their comrades."

Conn's armchair no longer seemed so comfortable. He looked over at Erkatchian but the spacer would not meet his eyes.

The projection of Hallis Tharp continued to talk, although he now looked out into the middle distance and seemed to be speaking only to himself. "I installed the template in a generative cradle and brought it to the precise stage of development. Next, I truncated the gestative process and connected the cradle to a serial array of production cauldrons—the vats, to use the vernacular—and created a few simple-minded attendants to carry out the routine tasks of installing feedstock, tending its development, and decanting the products.

"Out of the system came the Flagits' soldiers, in equal legions of white and black, in daily batches of a hundred or so, just as they had ordered. From my private laboratory, I looked in on the business from time to time, but after everything had shaken down to a routine, I left things to run themselves. Meanwhile, I indulged my whims and fancies, creating little bits of human fluff and folly to dance about me and delight my senses. And to flatter my immense self-regard."

And now a haunted look came over Tharp's features, a look Conn realized he had seen from time to time across the paduay board though he had never thought to question its provenance. "And then, one day, Ermin called me to his operations room. He said something about the heavy troopers not functioning as he wished them to.

"I said I would go to the workshop and test the contents of the vats. There might have been some creepage in the replicity matrix.

"Ermin said he had already examined the matrix. He believed the flaw was in the design.

"It did no good to argue with a Flagit. I said I would reexamine the specifications and run some extrapolations. But he said no to that. I would not understand the problem if I came at it from that end of the process; instead I must see the outcome.

"He wished me to accompany him down to the playing area to see some heavy infantry in action. I would understand the problem and could begin to consider remedies.

"Naturally, I responded to my employer's wishes. He summoned his observation platform and we went down to the field."

Again, the image's eyes met Conn's and he saw horror and despair. Though the simulacrum of Hallis Tharp had captured him in his youthful prime, the voice might have been that of the old man he became in Bay City as he whispered, "Here is what I found."

A new scene appeared. Conn realized it must have been recorded by percepts on Ermin's observation platform as it flew low across a wide expanse of level ground, the white sun of Forlor tiny and bleak in the afternoon sky. They passed over three parallel bands of trenches, the outer one bristling with sharp stakes angled into the ground, then went out over a sea of treeless mud, pocked with craters and deep scars gouged out of the gray slime.

Ahead he saw what looked to be large ripples in the mud, as if the saturated earth had thrown up waves that had solidified in the air. It was only as they flew closer and passed over the first of these formations that Conn realized that they were lines of corpses, light and heavy troopers, in places piled up three or four deep on top of one another. The mud had so caked their skin and equipment that they were of the same color as the ground into which they were slowly sinking.

The view continued as the platform passed over another stretch of pockmarked ground, but now that Conn's eyes were tuned to the elements of the scene he noticed the shapes of limbs, heads, torsos. They were everywhere he looked, sunk a little deeper than the bodies heaped up in ranks. Then they came to another line of sodden dead, this one higher and wider, stretching off to either side as far as the platform's forward-facing percepts showed.

Conn noted that he was automatically counting the corpses, estimating the number of dead soldiers in the sections of each windrow that he could see then extrapolating by the estimated width of the battlefield. He realized that he had already moved beyond thousands into tens of thousands, and still the platform flew on.

Ahead was a low ridge with a long slope leading up to its skyline. Against the dark blue of the sky, Conn could see the outlines of spiked barriers. From behind them, all along the top of the ridge, came pinprick flashes of light. And now came a crackling sound, like someone snapping small sticks at a distance, an immense number of small sticks so that the noise was continuous. It grew louder as the view approached, and Conn realized it was the sound of repeating projectile weapons being fired en masse.

The platform slowed as it reached the bottom of the ridge. Here the mud was not so deep and it looked as if heavy drifts of snow coated the lower slopes. But when the projection's point of view drew closer and at last stood still, Conn saw that the drifts were the mounded bodies of Ermin's white soldiers, light and heavy infantry mostly, piled so high that they formed a wall all along the base of the hill. Behind the wall of dead stood and crouched more massed ranks, mud smeared, many of them wounded. Conn could see untended gashes and punctures that bled slowly, broken limbs and some men with parts of their faces shot away.

The projectile fire from the top of the ridge continued unabated. He could hear the rounds thumping into the dead and the impacts caused some of the corpses atop the row to twitch or shift position. But Ermin's recorded voice was drawing Hallis Tharp's attention to those behind the wall.

"They just stand there," the voice was saying. "They do not go forward."

Conn could see a bannerman striding up and down before a long rank of heavy troopers. The infantry stood with their weapons in their hands, ammunition pouches and ration packs slung about their bodies. Their gross faces were slack, their eyes dull as the mud beneath their boots.

The bannerman gestured forcefully toward the wall of dead and the enemy up the slope. His intent was unmistakable but still the troopers did not move to scale the heaped corpses and advance.

"What is *wrong* with them?" Ermin's voice cracked at the question's place of emphasis. "Blathe sits and laughs at me, and your soldiers do not move!"

A captain, distinguishable by the crest on his helmet, pulled a trooper from the line and gestured toward the front. Conn could see the soldier summon an effort, saw a wash of rage pass across the oversized features. But then the emotion faded and was replaced with something like despair. The man stood inert.

The captain drew a hand weapon, placed it at the trooper's temple, just beneath the rim of the helmet. The officer fired, his weapon's discharge sounding sharp and loud above the continuing crackle from upslope. The trooper's head snapped sideways then his knees folded. He seemed to sit down slowly then he fell backwards. The captain called another infantryman forward. The man stolidly advanced two paces and stood, wearing the same look of dull anguish as his dead comrade had before extinction relieved him of all emotion.

But it was not the heavy trooper's face that Conn was looking at. It was the captain's. And now he focused on the bannerman. Their skins, like their uniforms and equipment, were all flat white. But their features were identical, as if cast from the same plaster mold. Conn knew that nose, that chin, the shape of those lips: they were his own.

He looked at the heavy trooper's face as the captain put the muzzle of his weapon to the soldier's head. Pull the cheekbones a little wider, broaden the forehead, deepen the eye sockets, and that was Conn Labro's face enlarged and coarsened. The captain's weapon barked and the soldier collapsed.

"Stop!" Conn heard Hallis Tharp's voice. "Stop this! What have you done?"

"They must go forward," Ermin Flagit said, his voice rising to a nasal whine. "You were supposed to give us troops that went forward. We were months preparing our dispositions, now the game is only half over and I'm stopped. Fix it!"

"I made troops that would advance, energized by fury, eager for victory," Tharp's voice said. "But not day after day without cease. You have worn them out, as if they were machines and you had run them beyond their maximum ratings until they overheated and their parts seized."

Another shot sounded as the captain dispatched another ruined trooper.

"Call off the attack," Tharp said. "Let them rest and recover, purge the toxins from their systems, and they will be renewed to fight again."

"No!" Ermin Flagit made the single syllable an elongated whine. "Blathe sneers at me! Fix them now! Or make me some new ones, better ones!"

"You were supposed to use them for what they are made for," Tharp said, "battle and glory and the dignity of arms. Instead you have used them up, wasted them."

"They are mine. I will do with them as I wish. Now make more and make them better."

Tharp spoke but not to answer Ermin. It was as if he addressed himself, or perhaps the creatures he had made and handed over to the Flagits. "I didn't know," he said. "I didn't know they would do this."

The scene faded and the simulacrum of Tharp reappeared on the dais. "Of course," he said, "I should have known. But the knowledge would have been . . . inconvenient. Thus, I never asked. I never looked."

He sighed. "But now that I *had* seen it, now that I had *smelled* it, I could not let it continue. I turned the platform around and returned to the production facility. I assured Ermin I would fix everything and he slunk back to where his brother gloated. The moment he was gone, I went into the facility and stopped it all. I gently terminated the attendants, emptied the generative vats and let the half-formed contents expire on the floor. Then I smashed the equipment, destroyed the records and purged the process files.

"Soon after my arrival on Forlor I had gained control of the house integrator's command complex. It was not difficult. The Flagits knew only how to give orders; they relied on underlings like me to work the levers that delivered their wishes to them, fully formed. I had thought it a wise precaution in case the brothers reneged on our agreement, leaving me their prisoner in a place where they were the only authorities.

"Now I have instructed the integrator to detain them for several days, then allow them to leave in Blathe's yacht. Ermin's I will take for my own escape and abandon somewhere.

"I have overflown the battlefield and applied a general mortifacient that is even now gently relieving my creations of their suffering. I have seized and will take with me the encrypted bearer deed to this world and I will instruct the integrator to discourage anyone who chances upon this planet. It will allow only one person to land and enter this terrible house."

The simulacrum sighed. It was a sound Conn had often heard when he and Hallis Tharp had sat across the paduay board from each other. "I will go now to my laboratory and terminate my poor ephemerals. They would grow despondent if I left them, and I cannot take them to the Ten Thousand Worlds without risking prosecution.

"Then I will go back to the production facility and retrieve the one piece of equipment I did not demolish: the cradle that contains the template for all of the poor creatures I made and allowed to be fed to the Flagits' cruel appetites.

"I will bring the template to full gestation then take it to a world where it—no, I must say he—can have some reasonable hope of a true and satisfying life. It will not be easy to find a place for such a singular person, but I have an odd little planet in mind that may serve.

"Then I will stay to guide his growth and development as best I can, for as long as I can. Thus will I seek to make one good life come out of the great evil that I did here, and perhaps that will be my atonement. And if he grows into a being who could live at large among other people, and not be a danger to them or to himself, then perhaps in his maturity I will reveal to him his secret and my great shame."

Again the image's gaze came to meet Conn's eyes. "I hope, Conn Labro—for that is what I mean to name you—that you have arrived here as a mature and well-founded man, able to face where you have come from and to go on to whatever may be your fulfillment. I hope that I have been able to train you in the discipline of suppressing the rage that is intrinsic to your matrix, the same rage that burned out the legions I supplied to the Flagits."

Tharp's image performed a solemn gesture and said, "I swear that I will do all that I can to give you a decent life, and I hope that it will be enough."

The simulacrum faded. Conn stared at the air above the empty dais. The old questions posed by Hallis Tharp replayed themselves in his head: *What are you, where do you come from, where do you go?*

He had the answers now. *I am a template*, he told himself. *I come from a vat. I have nowhere in particular to go.*

He heard Erkatchian stirring beside him. He looked over and found the spacer regarding him with an unsettled expression. "I knew someone," Conn said, "who said that all societies are built around one of the seven fundamental sins. I did not believe there could be a world founded on anger. Yet here is that world. And I am its sole remaining citizen."

"That is one way to look at it," Erkatchian said.

"Do you still want to travel the spaceways with me?"

"Why not? You are still the same Conn Labro I have come to know and respect. Now you're just a more knowledgeable version."

"I am not a real human being."

Erkatchian waved a hand. "You're more real than many I've known, and that certainly includes my current employer. People are what they do, not where they come from. If more of us knew the actual circumstances of our conceptions, I am sure it would reduce our self-regard."

Conn rose from the seat. "I do not believe I was designed for philosophical debate."

"All right," said the spacer, getting up as well. "What will you do?"

"I do not know. Perhaps it would be best if I just stay here."

"My lord Vullamir will not welcome your company."

"Nor I his. But he will not be here. This world has been used enough for immoral purposes. I will not sell it."

"What about that girl who is waiting for you on Old Earth?"

"She would be better off with a real human being. What could I give her?"

"A chance to make her own decision."

Conn waved the issue away. A curious stillness had come over him. His resentment of Hallis Tharp had faded. The man had meant him no harm, had taken him to a world where his peculiarities would be least noticeable and where his innate abilities could win him at least the seeming of a meaningful life. Then Tharp had done his best to expiate the sin of pride that had led him to commit the evil of handing his children over to a pair of monsters who would ill use them.

A thought struck him: *He was my father.* Tharp had said he had used his own plasm to make the template. *And my mother, too, I suppose.*

Erkatchian was watching him. Conn said, "Go and tell Vullamir that the transaction is null."

"You are truly no Thraisian, if you can say that without a tremor in your voice," Erkatchian said.

"No, I am not, after all, a Transactualist. I am not a Hauserian, nor a Divorgian, nor an Old Earther. I am unique but I am without purpose. No tasks remain for me to perform."

"On the contrary," the spacer said, "you are free to be whatever you wish, to set your own tasks and perform them to whatever degree satisfies you."

"All of it equally meaningless," said Conn. "I might as well sit here and regard the walls."

Erkatchian wished to offer more arguments, but Conn waved him away. "Go, please, and inform Vullamir," he said.

"He will not take it well. On the other hand, after seeing the result of Hallis Tharp's refusal to ask the questions he should have asked, I find myself less concerned than usual about the degree of my lord's happiness."

Conn said, "If Vullamir's vanity is so grievously offended that he requires satisfaction, I will accommodate him. That is something I do quite well."

Chapter 12

Left to himself in the viewing room, Conn discovered an inclination to explore the rest of the house. He wondered whether Hallis Tharp had instilled in him a predisposition to explore his environment and decided after a moment's reflection that of course he had done so. An urge to know what was around him would be useful in a soldier.

Is this how it is to be from now on? he asked himself. *Will I scrutinize my every impulse to seek the finger marks of Hallis Tharp?* Still, he saw no reason not to give in to the impulse. "Integrator," he said.

"What do you require?"

"A map of the house, with explanatory labels."

A color-coded chart appeared, superimposed on the air. Conn studied it for a few minims then said, "Have it follow me." He set off.

He glanced through an archway that led into the Flagits' sprawling quarters, but declined to enter; their garish, sybaritic extravagance repelled him. He went down the hall and up an ascender to the top of the house. He paused before a simple door then opened it and stepped through. He found himself in a well-apportioned workroom, although all the apparatuses had been smashed. Against one wall was a tiny heap of fragile bones. Conn could make out the outlines of a pair of diaphanous wings. He indicated the remains to the integrator and said, "How did that look in life?"

A second screen appeared beside the floating map and displayed an image of a delicate androgynous creature with two pairs of veined and fast-beating wings, fluttering about this very room. Conn could see Hallis Tharp in the background, bent over a workbench, his hands busy with something.

"Enough," Conn said and the image disappeared. Then he said, "Is this where I was created?"

"It is. Do you wish to see that process?"

"No."

He realized that he had been half hoping that the place would evoke some reaction, perhaps an epiphany that would . . . *do what?* he asked himself. *Provide the rest of my life with the moral equivalent of a full bladder?* But nothing came.

He crossed to the workbench and ran his hand over the tools and instruments scattered there. The cadaver of a partially constructed homunculus sat in a concave armature; by the look of its proportions, it would have been a comical gnome with outsized hands and feet and a face like a mournful tuber. Tharp must have left off tinkering with it to accompany Ermin Flagit to view the battlefield. On the floor beyond the bench were two more oddly formed skeletons, one with a skull that seemed fashioned after a flower's petals.

Conn waited for some emotion to manifest itself. He felt a vague sadness, but could not get it to deepen to anything profound. The place in which he stood, the spot where he had come into existence—birth was not an accurate term—conjured no response from deep within him. Indeed, he was willing to accept that there was no "deep" for Conn Labro, except of course for his unnatural capacity for rage. And that he must avoid, lest it consume him from within until it left him like those heavy troopers in the projection—depleted and spiritless as the hulk of a burned-out star.

For a moment he was tempted to summon up his anger. *At what?* he thought. *The ghost of Hallis Tharp? The even longer dead Flagits? The disinterested universe which could oversee the extinction of a gnat or of a galaxy with the same equanimity?*

And even if he could overcome his conditioning and let the fury take him, what would he do with it? Rampage across the corpse-strewn fields of Forlor, smashing dried bones and raging at phantoms and memories?

The integrator interrupted his thoughts. "I am receiving a signal from the *Martichor*. It is for you."

"Connect me."

He expected to see the face of the spacer. Instead he found himself looking into the eyes of Lord Magratte, a gaze that sparkled with a cold glee. "Erkatchian has relayed your message to my lord," the Old Earther said.

Conn was intrigued to discover that the sight of the aristocrat stirred a faint sentiment in him. He examined it and found it was on behalf of Jenore Mordene. *Of course*, he thought, *Hallis made me loyal to my comrades. She despised Magratte, so her despite became mine.* But the emotion was therefore artificial, therefore pointless. He wanted only to be alone.

"Very well," he said. "You may depart whenever you are ready. My regards to the captain."

"Give them to him yourself. Erkatchian forgot his place. He spoke brazenly and attempted to thwart my lord's intentions. Thus he has been relieved of command. You will find him at the base of the front steps, somewhat the worse for wear. I am now handling matters for my lord Vullamir."

"It does not signify," Conn said. "Take Erkatchian with you and depart. There will be no sale. I wish to be left in solitude. If you attempt to enter the house I will instruct it to fire upon you. And I will do so if your ship remains on the landing apron longer than I think appropriate."

Magratte showed no anxiety. He said, "I invite you to change your mind. Hand over the bearer deed."

"I will not."

A glint of pleasure appeared in the cold blue eyes. Conn saw that the conversation was going in a direction the aristocrat wished for, though he did not know where that direction could lead. "If you agree, I will give you something you want," Magratte said.

"You have nothing that I want."

"Oh?" said the aristocrat, in a tone of practiced malice, "not even this?"

He stepped back from the *Martichor*'s internal percept. Conn heard a rustle and a gasp of pain and then the screen before him filled with the bruised and tear-streaked face of Jenore Mordene. "Conn," she said, "don't let them . . ."

Before she could say more, a hand closed over her mouth and she was pulled from view. Magratte reappeared. "And now?" he said.

Conn paused atop the black and white steps, the anger held in check. The Lho-tso mantra still worked and he repeated it silently in his head as he watched the party descend from the yacht. The coterie of the nobly born wore similar garments to those Vullamir had had on behind the birl field on Five Fingers Key, with wide extravagantly feathered shoulders and six-fingered gauntlets of gleaming metal. They had put on their life masks for the occasion, the dead eyes looking about with vague curiosity.

Magratte had forgone the mask and appeared in more utilitarian garb, a singlesuit of dark metallic mesh that converted the actinic light of Forlor's star into rainbow highlights. He stepped out in front of the others and waited. Behind him were a squad of well-muscled men in coordinated livery, with energy weapons in their hands. Conn assumed they were of Vullamir's household. Two of them held the arms of Jenore Mordene.

"Integrator," Conn said, "carry out step one."

At his command, the two towers overlooking the landing apron divided at their tops and their ison-cannon appeared. The emitters swiveled to cover the party before the yacht. Magratte glanced up at them and moved his head as a player does when his opponent performs an expected move.

"So," the aristocrat said, "we begin."

"Or perhaps, instead, we all end," Conn said. "I am still making up my mind."

"We know what you are," Magratte said. "When we talked with Tharp he told us about you. He didn't want to, but he did."

"The knowledge gives you no advantage. You will do what you will do. I will do what I will do."

"Except that we have the girl."

"I will not deny," Conn said, "that her presence complicates matters."

"She is your comrade. You must aid and protect her."

"Apparently, that is so."

"Then give us the bead, instruct the integrator to accept us and we will let you depart."

Conn let a thin smile show. "Really? How? There is only one ship, and its captain has been dismissed." He glanced down at where Erkatchian was moaning and just beginning to stir at the base of the steps. "And with prejudice."

"I will accompany you, along with these useful men you see here. We will drop the three of you on a world near the edge of The Spray. I will engage a new captain and return."

Conn signaled a negative. "Many things can go amiss in space. Noxious gases can invade parts of a ship, rendering those within unconscious or worse. Or sections can be suddenly exposed to vacuum."

"Trust is out of the question, then?"

Conn made a small but significant gesture.

"Well, we can try the direct and brutal approach," Magratte said. "We could rush you, firing our weapons, hoping some of us will survive. With you dead, the integrator may accept new instructions."

"Except that I have told it to spray the apron at the first discharge of a weapon."

"Which would mean the death of your traveling companion, contrary to the urges and restrictions your maker instilled in you."

"It is a conundrum," Conn said. "But perhaps there is also within me an allowance for a glorious demise in which I take my enemies with me."

"We would certainly want to avoid that," Magratte said. "Have you any proposal to offer?"

Jenore cried out. "You can't bargain with them, Conn! They will kill us no matter what they say." One of the men holding her placed a hand over her mouth. She struggled then subsided.

Conn could feel elements shifting within him. He had reviewed the notes he had found in Hallis Tharp's workroom and now had a good understanding of how the components of his nature fitted together.

"I am a piece of a game," he said, "made for counterfeit wars and artificial battles. I am no longer sure of my judgment, nor am I even confident that I should ever again be set loose in the 'real' world. My standards are peculiar and thus I do not know what to propose."

Magratte put a finger to his chin and made a thoughtful sound from behind closed lips. Conn remembered the subtle tells the man had unknowingly displayed during the game of thrash in the *Dan*'s casino. "Step two," he said, and the whine of the ison-cannon running up to full charge was loud in the silence.

Magratte very slowly drew his finger from his chin while his other hand made deterrent motions to the armed men behind him. "Are we at an impasse?" he said.

"No," said another voice. Yalum Erkatchian was sitting up, leaning back on the first two risers of the black and white steps. He turned his head stiffly to look up at Conn. His face was bruised and his lips split. Conn was reminded of his last view of Hallis Tharp in Skrey.

Magratte regarded the spacer with a skeptical mien. "You wish to add something?" he said.

The captain struggled to his feet, swayed a little then assumed a military posture. "Conn Labro," he said, "I would be honored to speak for you."

Conn recognized the formal phrasing. "The Challenge Exceptional?" he asked.

"Indeed."

Conn saw a stiffness enter Magratte's posture. "Then speak on," he told Erkatchian.

The spacer turned to the margrave and made certain precise motions involving his hands, head and upper torso. His voice was loud. "I have the honor to speak for Conn Labro."

The dead eyes of the several aristocrats' life masks swung toward Erkatchian. When he stopped speaking, they turned to Magratte.

"He has neither rank nor ancestry," the Old Earther said. The life masks turned back to Erkatchian.

"On the contrary," the captain said, "he is the acknowledged offspring of Hallis Tharp, of a respectable landed family of Old Earth. Moreover, his rank derives from his estate on which we stand, it being traditional to ascribe to rulers of entire worlds the presumptive degree of duke when they are at home."

Magratte said nothing. Vullamir's and all the other life masks turned toward the top of the steps. Conn realized that, for the first time, they had him clearly in focus.

Erkatchian spoke. "Therefore, in the name of Duke Conn Labro, I offer you, my lord Magratte, the Challenge Exceptional. We will be interested to hear from your second the choice of weapons."

It was a tidy stroke, Conn realized as he ran through its extrapolations. Vullamir's perceptions would encompass the duel to its nicest degree. If Magratte failed to accept the challenge, he would lose honor. At that point, his patron Vullamir and the other lords would become unable to perceive him. It would be as if he had ceased to exist. Their dismissal of him would extend to their servants; the armed men in livery would obey no orders he might give. He would be lucky to end up stealing food from the kitchens.

On the other hand, if Magratte accepted the challenge, he would have to kill Conn Labro or die in the attempt. There was no blood-or-breakage limit to a Challenge Exceptional. The eyes of the life masks almost seemed alive as they regarded the margrave and awaited his response. The stillness extended and Conn saw Magratte chew the inside of his lip. After a moment, Vullamir tapped his foot.

The margrave swallowed then took a formal stance. "Very well," he said, "I name my second. Step forward, Alwan Foulaine."

Conn contained his surprise though he saw from her reaction that the Tote creator's presence on board the *Martichor* was no secret to Jenore. As he came out of one of the yacht's middle ports and passed her she spat in his direction. Conn saw the way it had gone: Foulaine had eavesdropped on the negotiations at the birl match; he must have contacted the intercessor Opteram and suggested that Jenore's presence on the yacht might prove useful in the event of any last minute hitch; then he and his bullies had snatched Jenore on some deserted stretch of beach and handed her over to Vullamir's minions. But Magratte would not have left Foulaine behind as a loose end. Still, once the two of them were together on a space ship, the margrave's love of card play and Foulaine's facility with numbers could have made some kind of bond between them. *They deserve each other*, Conn thought.

The two conspirators had been whispering together, Magratte demonstrating hand movements. Now Foulaine stepped forward, bowed and made the motions as instructed and called out, "My Lord Magratte accepts the Challenge Exceptional. The weapons shall be . . ."—he paused for effect—"epiniards."

Vullamir spoke to one of his servants. The man stepped forward and said, "My lord Vullamir is honored to offer his brace of epiniards. They are the work of Rhee Vlens."

Weapons by Vlens would be more than suitable. Conn signaled his acceptance to Yalum Erkatchian who formally relayed the information through Foulaine to Magratte. The margrave then spoke again to his second. Foulaine made fresh gestures and said, "We now name the stake: surrender of this world and all its appurtenances."

Conn looked within himself, found a complex of motivations. Magratte was his enemy; it was licit to kill him. The same was true of Foulaine, if the opportunity presented itself. Jenore Mordene was his ally and comrade; he must save her if he could. He found a similar response when he considered Erkatchian, though the attachment was not so deep. For Vullamir, he felt nothing but a distaste, as if he had encountered something unwholesome.

He formed a strategy: to save his friends, he would hand over this world to the Immersionists, then inform the Bureau of Scrutiny of its location and their intent. The Old Earth police could look after the matter, although he had been less than impressed by the way they had handled themselves at the Registry of Offworld Properties.

He gestured approval to the captain, then subtly indicated himself, Jenore and the spacer, too. Erkatchian stood upright and said, "We name the counter stake: safe passage from this world for Conn Labro, Jenore Mordene and Yalum Erkatchian." The captain threw Conn a wry glance, then added, "And title to the yacht *Martichor*."

There was a moment's silence as all eyes turned to Lord Vullamir, then a collective release of breath as the aristocrat waggled one bejeweled finger in acceptance. A footman was dispatched to the yacht and returned with a long, flat case carved from the shovel-like tusk of some offworld beast. He brought it to Vullamir who waved him toward the open space before the steps.

A crowd of people had come out of the yacht in the footman's wake. Conn saw Umlat and Po and even the nameless skivvy with the prominent nose who had cleaned his cabin. They formed a demilune behind the aristocrats and the men who held Jenore, those at the back craning their necks forward to see.

Foulaine and Erkatchian advanced to meet the footman with the ivory case. The latch was snapped and the weapons displayed, two thin spikes of supple gray metal, each razor edged for a hand's breadth below the needle point. They had simple hafts, with four quillions arranged in an "x" and spherical pommels that would exactly balance the weight of the blades.

Erkatchian executed the proper formal gestures and chose one of the epiniards. Foulaine clumsily imitated the spacer's actions and took the other. Now Conn came down the steps to take the weapon from the captain, while Foulaine carried the other to Magratte.

Again, there were gestures to be made. As Conn performed his, he whispered to Erkatchian: "Title to the yacht, too?"

The captain maintained a formal face as he quoted, "In for a zlazni, in for a smov."

"Very well," Conn said and turned to face Magratte. The seconds withdrew to opposite sides of the arena.

Conn flourished the epiniard. It was quite simply the finest weapon he had ever held. As he cut and arabesqued the air, its grip subtly fitted itself to his hand, just as the Flagits' chair had adapted to his body. But where the one had been gross, the other was exquisite perfection. The product of the legendary Vlens's workshop had made itself an extension of Conn Labro, responsive to the slightest microtremors of the nerves and sinews of hand and arm. A masterpiece had found the hand of a master and Conn knew that this fight would be the pinnacle of his career.

And perhaps at this high point he would find not victory but defeat. He watched Magratte adapt to his own weapon and perform a few test strokes, a pensive look on his face. Then the margrave closed his eyes, aligned his body and settled his breathing. *He, too, is a practitioner of the Lho-tso school,* Conn thought. *And he moves very well indeed.*

Conn performed his own preliminary exercises then stilled himself. Magratte advanced halfway across the space between them and Conn did likewise. The aristocrat looked at him levelly and said, "Let us have a neutral opening passage, that the blades may fully acquaint themselves with us. Rhee Vlens deserves no less."

"I agree," said Conn.

They stepped back, performed the final formal gestures appropriate to the situation, and commenced. As the challenged party, Magratte had the option to initiate or reply. He chose the latter and assumed a modified Grievot stance, blade pointing low and forward as he waited for Conn's first move.

Conn advanced and offered a triple Bogiline at moderate speed. Magratte ignored the first thrust, sidestepped the second and parried the third with an economy of motion and precision of form that told Conn he was indeed in the presence of a virtuoso swordster.

Now it was Magratte's turn: he adopted the Flewellyn stance, blade high and angled down, then came forward at a measured pace to execute a double quadriline whose twin epicenters were Conn's eyes and groin. Conn replied with neat, exact strokes that beat each slash aside by no more than a finger's breadth then countered with a spiral bind intended to confine Magratte's blade and divert it to his off side so that Conn's point could reach over the guard and touch the margrave's forearm. But the aristocrat smoothly slipped free of the trap and pressed forward so that his point brushed harmlessly against the bicep of Conn's sword arm. It was a masterful display of precision.

The opening passage concluded, the duelists stepped back and allowed their epiniards to digest what they had learned. Conn felt a subtle shifting in his weapon's response to his grip, a combination of pressure and pulsation that caused the tendons and muscles of his hand and arm to alter their orientation to optimum. He saw that his opponent was entering into his own partnership.

"Are you ready?" Magratte said after a moment.

"I am."

They executed the gestures required to commence the second passage, then Magratte began to circle toward Conn's off side. Conn did likewise. They offered each other stances and exchanged swift but inconsequential attacks, each gauging the other's speed, form and the ineffable quality called *rif*.

The aristocrat's eyes were busy for a little while, his gaze flicking here and there as he measured subtleties and weighed tiny significances. Conn was doing the same and soon came to the conclusion that Magratte was at least his technical equal. The contest would therefore come down to *rif* or, if they proved to be equal in that regard, to simple endurance.

Now Magratte eased back and said, "I regretted that I was not able to meet you that day in the third garden on Ovam Horder's roof."

"You were Hasbrick Gleffen?"

"I was." He stepped in and presented Conn with the attack known as Tetsuro's Bore, thrusting and stabbing with blinding swiftness. Conn countered appropriately but was forced to call up his maximum speed to keep the epiniard's point from his throat. Finally, he stepped into the margrave's attack and clashed guard to guard, driving the man back. But he was surprised at the strength of the aristocrat's resistance before Magratte slipped away and prepared his next attack.

"I had heard of you before I knew what you were," Magratte said. "You were considered one of the best technicians along The Spray."

Conn replied not with words but with a classic Laganz, his blade *snip-snip-snipping* against the other man's, seeking to create that minuscule opening through which the thin length of metal could suddenly slip in and meet flesh. But Magratte threw Conn's Laganz back on him with a brilliant trifoliate riposte, and Conn had to propel himself backwards to miss being spitted on the epiniard's questing point.

"But you see," said Magratte, "I have met and bested almost all of the high technicians in private bouts." And with that he came on in a whirling, stamping storm of an attack, in which his blade seemed to flicker and flash at Conn from two or three directions at once.

Again Conn must call upon his fullest speed to fend off the epiniard's probing tip and cutting fore edge, and again his counterstrokes were contained and rendered innocuous by guards and parries that seemed to cost his opponent little effort.

"I am at least your technical equal," Magratte said.

"It seems so," said Conn.

"Then it comes down to *rif*?"

"Perhaps."

"Then you are lost," the margrave said and came on yet again in what seemed at first to be a repetition of his opening double quadriline, although this time at a cadence that taxed all of Conn's pace and skill.

His training at Horder's Emporium had been exhaustive. From boyhood he had fought experts and superlatives, and had honed individual techniques in practice against machines that simulated the styles and speeds of grandmasters long since gone to dust. He had become a brilliantly proficient swordster, and now he understood that his innate abilities had originated in the workroom at the top of the house behind him, where Hallis Tharp's last project lay moldering on the workbench.

But had Tharp instilled in him that elusive quality called *rif*? Conn thought not. Not even the finest machine simulations could capture giftedness, and giftedness was what he sensed in Magratte.

The Flagits' doomed soldiers needed no giftedness—only strength and speed and the inability to turn their backs on murderous folly until it killed them or wore them out. Thus their template must own only the same virtues. Conn's musings broke off now as the margrave came in fast and perfect, again offering the double quadriline aimed at eyes and groin. But this time, as Conn matched—just barely—the tempo of the attack, Magratte extended the assault past the eighth stroke, moving seamlessly into a repetition of the opening slash, but doing so with an almost imperceptible shift in the rhythm between the first and second quartos, so that Conn was almost caught open and undefended. He managed to cover just in time, but only by aiming an awkward buffet at Magratte's head while leaping backward.

He was thankful to land well because the aristocrat was right on top of him, a thoughtful smile lazing on Magratte's lips as he executed another textbook attack—a grand allevant this time—then modified it by delaying the third thrust by a half-beat followed by a forward rush that caught Conn completely by surprise.

The lord stepped back and flicked a drop of blood from the tip of his blade. It was only then that Conn realized the man's point had entered his shoulder. It was no more than a pinprick, but it was first blood. A sigh went up from the watching Old Earth aristocrats as they saw the red blossom on Conn's shirt, and Jenore made a sound between a moan and a sob.

There were more formal gestures to perform, now that blood had been shed, as well as specific words to be spoken. Conn voiced the phrases automatically, while his mind raced forward. He was no match for Magratte. Technical skill must always yield to genius, and his opponent was clearly more than exceptionally talented. His opponent had true *rif*; Conn did not.

As he prepared to receive the next passage, almost certainly the final one of his career unless Magratte chose to prolong the occasion, Conn felt a flash of incipient anger at Hallis Tharp. Automatically, his mind reached for the Lhotso exercise that would restore his tranquility.

But as the first syllable sounded in his head, another part of Conn said, *No*. Magratte might have *rif* in grand supply, but Conn Labro had rage. It was the founding sin of the small diseased society that the Flagits had produced here on Forlor and it was to be found in its most pure form in the inner landscape of the template.

In all his life, Conn had never allowed his anger to take him. But now his life was almost certainly over if he fought as he always had. The other way would give him at least an interesting match, Magratte's *rif* against Conn's supernal rage. It might even be decisive.

After first blood, it was permissible for the wounded party to call for an interval if he believed that the ensuing passage would bring his death. It was an opportunity for contemplation of the tragic undertones of the duelist's life, perhaps for the creation of a spontaneous quip that the deceased's friends could repeat as his epitaph once the final note was sounded.

Conn raised his off hand in the appropriate signal and stood with eyes downcast. He thought again of Hallis Tharp, then moved on to the Flagit brothers and the monstrous slaughter of—here he allowed the truth of it to flow into him—tens of thousands of Conn's brothers. He thought of his upbringing at Horder's, the deprivations of his childhood, the constrictions of his manhood. Now he thought of Clariq Wallader and the unjust termination of her life as a consequence of Magratte's lust, and that brought him to the question of Jenore Mordene and her fate at the hands of the Immersion, not to mention Alwan Foulaine's foul intent, if Conn Labro failed as her champion.

It was like climbing a series of steps, rising through levels of raw, red emotion he had never experienced. It was glorious and uplifting, so that he felt as if bubbles of elevating gases had been transfused into his veins and arteries, filling him with ecstatic weightlessness. The epiniard, solid in his grip, became as light as a sigh. His lungs filled and rejoiced in the action, as if they could taste the air they encompassed and its flavor was delicious.

He looked up and it was as if the universe was revealing to him new dimensions he had never suspected were there. He saw Magratte limned in red light, the Old Earth lords behind him similarly surrounded by a crimson aura. And Foulaine—he was glowing as if he had been dipped in rosy fire.

Conn flexed the epiniard and looked Magratte in the eye, and saw the margrave's refined features draw into a frown of concentration. "What is this?" said the aristocrat.

"Let us see," said Conn, and heard in his own voice a bestial growl. He took up his stance, shivers of fiery energy rippling across his back and shoulder muscles, and said, "Come at me now."

Magratte's eyes narrowed. He circled right then smoothly reversed his footing to come in from the other side, his epiniard flashing in a complex pattern out of which he suddenly evolved a double thrust at Conn's middle.

Conn twisted and sideslipped, but the second strike scored the flesh of his side just beneath the ribs. He felt the sting of the cut and even the tickle of blood running across the hairs of his belly. But there was no real pain; it was buried beneath the rage and he used the momentum of his sideways motion to initiate a new attack against Magratte's off side.

He saw surprise on his opponent's face as the margrave fell back, fending off a flurry of thrusts and slashes. Conn had never known his speed to be like this: the anger seemed to have lubricated the channels of his nerves, and it was as if his muscles had found a new dimension of power and precision. The Vlens blade sang in his hand.

But Magratte showed no fear. He recovered his footing and assumed a watchful defensive stance, his sword hand low and close to his body, the point of his epiniard making tiny perfect circles in the air before him. His voice held no tremor as he said, "Try that again."

Conn drew air into his lungs. He could feel his diaphragm heaving, his heart racing and the pulse pounding in his ears at a rate he had never known. The world around him faded to deep black except for the figure of Magratte, who glowed red as if cast from molten metal.

Conn took up the stance known as the impelard and threw himself across the space that separated them, his point oscillating as his arm muscles executed a harmonic sequence at greater than human speed.

Magratte remained still, his point still circling even as Conn's attack burst upon him. The Old Earther made no attempt to beat off the onrush with his own epiniard. Instead, as Conn committed his weapon to its final thrust, aimed at the margrave's throat, Magratte thrust up his off hand, the back of his fingers connecting with the shaft of Conn's epiniard just below the razor-sharp edge that lay behind the point, and gently guiding it the small distance necessary to carry it past its target.

At the same time, Magratte's own weapon darted forward and entered Conn Labro's torso beneath his ribs, passing through his heart and exiting his back between his spine and his right shoulder blade.

Conn felt the cold metal transfix his flesh, saw Magratte's face close now to his own, the margrave's expression that of a man who, intent on solving a difficult puzzle, believes he has found the answer. "Those who have it know," the aristocrat whispered, "that there can be no substitute for *rif*."

Conn's heart continued to beat around the tightly contained shaft of Magratte's epiniard.

"Now it ends," said the Old Earther, and smoothly drew the blade free.

Conn felt the metal slide through his body. Again there was little pain. The epiniard came free and a gush of blood followed from the wound it had made. Conn heard a sigh from the lords around Vullamir, a curse from Erkatchian and his own name cried out by Jenore Mordene.

The blackness faded and the red aura that had bathed Magratte in Conn's vision was gone. The margrave stood, his weapon pointed at the ground, waiting for Conn to fall.

Conn's eyes met the other man's. He saw that it took Magratte just a fraction of a minim to understand that his expectations were not about to be gratified. In that so brief a time Conn's sword arm, still extended and holding the weapon out where the lord's fingers had directed it, flicked sideways. The keen fore edge sliced through Magratte's throat, blood and air bubbling out in a crimson froth.

Conn saw the astonishment in the man's eyes yield to a moment of regret. But what the Old Earth lord may have been ruing would never be known, for Magratte had toppled dead to the checkered flagstones.

The Rhee Vlens blade went inert in his hand and he dropped it gently onto the corpse. Blood continued to flow from his chest, but the gush had become a trickle and he estimated that it would soon cease. Hallis Tharp had given him a heart with a complex but robust architecture. Yet the old man had also been right about anger. It drained the energy from Conn. He was tired now.

The fight had turned him around. The steps lay before him and the crowd at his back. Erkatchian had watched the duel from the bottom of the steps and now came toward him. Conn turned to look for Jenore, to order those who held her to set her free.

He saw her near the front of the crowd; the men who had restrained her had relinquished their grips and were now attempting to assemble their faces into arrangements that indicated they had been forced to follow distasteful orders. But Conn's eyes dismissed them and went to the woman. He took a faltering step toward her and she came out of the crowd, her arms extended, her face full of emotions she made no attempt to control. "Oh, Conn . . ." she began.

"Look out!" cried Yalum Erkatchian.

Conn's eyes went from Jenore's face to the people behind her. And there he saw Alwan Foulaine, arm raised, a gleaming length of pointed metal snug against his palm, fingers and thumb holding it in a thrower's grip. An expression of purest hate had contorted his eyes into slits and his mouth into a snarl. His gaze was fixed on the woman who had denied him.

The rage came up in Conn again, but brought only a partial restoration of his strength. Erkatchian was moving forward and Jenore was turning to look behind her. But Conn knew there would not be time. Foulaine's arm was already coming down.

Then from behind the knife thrower an arm snaked around his throat and yanked him sharply back, while another hand reached out and plucked the weapon from his faltering grip. Foulaine fell backwards onto the black and white stones, where he was swiftly rolled over and imprisoned in a holdtight.

Those around the action had pulled back and Conn now saw the person who had performed the disarming and capture stand up. She reached down into a pail that appeared to contain cleaning implements. From it she took a small device and spoke into it.

TEMPLATE

From the dark sky came a thrumming of powerful gravity obviators and a sleek vessel, black with green sponsons and fairings, descended to hover above the scene. The Flagits' ison-cannon swiveled at the tops of their towers to bear upon the new arrival, but twin bursts of incandescent energy broke from emitter ports at bow and stern, and the house's weapons instantly melted into dripping slag.

Jenore came into Conn's arms, then she pulled away to lift his shirt. "Your wound," she said.

"It is not serious," he said. "I was made to withstand worse."

The person with the communicator approached them. Conn saw that it was the woman with the prominent nose who had been assigned to clean his cabin. Now she seized the nose in one hand and twisted it free of her face, bringing with it her brows and a cheek that had borne a bristly wart. Beneath the disguise was the uncompromising face of Directing Agent Odell of the Archonate Bureau of Scrutiny.

"We need," she said, "to talk."

"I am somewhat tired," Conn said.

"It won't take long," Odell said. "Are you the legal owner of this world?"

He displayed the bearer deed. "I am."

"Do you have police services here?"

"I do not."

"Would you like the Bureau of Scrutiny to provide those services for you? Temporarily and at no charge?"

Conn looked at Jenore. "Would that be good?" he said.

"Yes," she said and held him close.

Conn looked at Odell over Jenore's shoulder and said, "Feel free to do as you see fit."

"Right," said the scroot. Her hand signaled to the Bureau cruiser above them. At once a squad of agents in green and black descended on personal obviators, unslung their weapons and took up positions surrounding the crowd from the *Martichor*.

Lord Vullamir and his coterie appeared to have become anxious. Conn saw hands flutter in gestures meant to attract servants, but the attendants were not inclined to move while scroot emitters were aimed at them.

More agents descended on a railed platform. They entered the crowd and began to separate some of its members from the rest, beginning with the men in Vullamir's livery, who had dropped their weapons when the cruiser appeared. The scroots also selected some of the servants—Conn noted Umlat was one of those taken—applied holdtights to the chosen ones and marched them off to where the platform waited.

There was a hubbub and twittering from the aristocrats when Odell approached them. It stilled when she said, "In the Archon's name . . ."

Conn did not listen to the rest of it. Jenore's tears had stopped but she clung to him.

"There are people on that ship," she said. "Stolen people. They brought them so they could . . . ."

187

"It is all over now," Conn said.

"They said they would give me to Foulaine," she said. She shuddered. "He joined them."

"All over."

Later, when the cruiser had taken the Immersionists back to face the justiciars on Old Earth, he showed her the room where he had been created and told her the story of his beginnings. He did not take her down to the viewing room to see what had happened out in the killing fields. He did not want her to see it, nor did he wish to revisit it again.

She looked at the sad heap of bones and the little manling in the armature and cried again.

"So," Conn said. "This is where I am from, and that"—he indicated the cadaver on the bench—"is what I am. So where do I go?"

"You cannot stay here," she said.

"No."

"Then where?"

"Erkatchian wants me to travel the Ten Thousand Worlds. He believes I will find one that suits me, and if I don't I may come to enjoy the search. He promises me there are more worlds than I will ever live to see."

"Will you go with him?"

"I think so."

They were silent. After a while he said, "What about you? Where do you belong?"

"Not where I came from," she said. She put her hand on the wound over his heart. It had already begun to heal over. "I'd like to believe that I belong here."

"In my peculiar heart," he said, "fashioned by Hallis Tharp for peculiar purposes."

"Yes."

"I will never be like other men," he said.

"Then you'll be unusual."

Erkatchian and his crew were readying the *Martichor* for departure when Conn and Jenore came down the steps. "She'll need a new name," the spacer said.

"Why?" Conn said.

"To make a good beginning."

"Then let us call it the *Jenore*."

Erkatchian's face said he could live with that name. He went off to arrange for it to be affixed to the hull.

"That was also good," said the woman, taking his hand in hers. Conn knew he would never understand much of what he would meet in the Ten Thousand Worlds of The Spray. But perhaps it was enough to be understood, at least by one person. The right person.

ABOUT THE AUTHOR

Matthew Hughes (1949-), also published as Matt Hughes and Hugh Matthews, is a Canadian author of science fiction and suspense novels. His Archonate books, of which *Template* is one, have been compared to the work of SF icon Jack Vance, and *Booklist* has referred to him as Vance's "heir apparent." A writer all his life, Hughes began as a journalist and moved up to become a political speechwriter, including a stint as staff speechwriter to the Canadian Ministers of Justice and Environment, before finally moving into fiction writing full time. He is the author of seventeen books, including several nonfiction volumes, as well as nearly fifty short stories, and has been short-listed for the prestigious Nebula Award.

Collect all of these exciting Planet Stories adventures!

THE GINGER STAR
BY LEIGH BRACKETT
INTRODUCTION BY BEN BOVA

Eric John Stark journeys to the dying world of Skaith in search of his kidnapped foster father, only to find himself the subject of a revolutionary prophecy. In completing his mission, will he be forced to fulfill the prophecy as well?

ISBN: 978-1-60125-084-1

ALMURIC
BY ROBERT E. HOWARD
INTRODUCTION BY JOE R. LANSDALE

From the creator of Conan, Almuric is a savage planet of crumbling stone ruins and debased, near-human inhabitants. Into this world comes Esau Cairn—Earthman, swordsman, murderer. Can one man overthrow the terrible devils that enslave Almuric?

ISBN: 978-1-60125-043-8

CITY OF THE BEAST
BY MICHAEL MOORCOCK
INTRODUCTION BY KIM MOHAN

Moorcock's Eternal Champion returns as Michael Kane, an American physicist and expert duelist whose strange experiments catapult him through space and time to a Mars of the distant past—and into the arms of the gorgeous princess Shizala. But can he defeat the Blue Giants of the Argzoon in time to win her hand?

ISBN: 978-1-60125-044-5

NORTHWEST OF EARTH
BY C. L. MOORE
INTRODUCTION BY C. J. CHERRYH

Ray gun blasting, Earth-born mercenary and adventurer Northwest Smith dodges and weaves his way through the solar system, cutting shady deals with aliens and magicians alike, always one step ahead of the law.

ISBN: 978-1-60125-081-0

THE SWORDSMAN OF MARS
BY OTIS ADELBERT KLINE
INTRODUCTION BY MICHAEL MOORCOCK

Harry Thorne, outcast scion of a wealthy East Coast family, swaps bodies with a Martian in order to hunt down another Earthman before he corrupts an empire. Trapped between two beautiful women, will Harry end up a slave, or claim his destiny as a swordsman of Mars?

ISBN: 978-1-60125-105-3

BLACK GOD'S KISS
BY C. L. MOORE
INTRODUCTION BY SUZY MCKEE CHARNAS

The first female sword and sorcery protagonist takes up her greatsword and challenges dark gods and monsters in the groundbreaking stories that made her famous and inspired a generation of female authors. Of particular interest to fans of Robert E. Howard and H. P. Lovecraft.

ISBN: 978-1-60125-045-2

Pick your favorites or subscribe today at paizo.com/planetstories

The Ship of Ishtar
by A. Merritt
introduction by Tim Powers

When amateur archaeologist John Kenton breaks open a strange stone block from ancient Babylon, he finds himself hurled through time and space onto the deck of a golden ship sailing the seas of another dimension—caught between the goddess Ishtar and the pale warriors of the Black God.

ISBN: 978-1-60125-118-3

Before They Were Giants
edited by James L. Sutter

See where it all began! In this exclusive collection, fifteen of the greatest living science fiction and fantasy authors, from Piers Anthony and Ben Bova to William Gibson and China Miéville, present and critique their first published SF stories, offering brand new interviews filled with anecdotes and advice. A must-have for any serious fan, scholar, or aspiring writer.

ISBN: 978-1-60125-266-1

Sos the Rope
by Piers Anthony
introduction by Robert E. Vardeman

In a post-apocalyptic future of barbarians and forgotten science, where duels to the death are everyday occurrences, the exiled warrior Sos sets out to rebuild civilization—or destroy it.

ISBN: 978-1-60125-194-7

The Walrus and the Warwolf
by Hugh Cook
introduction by China Miéville

Sixteen-year-old Drake Duoay loves nothing more than wine, women, and getting into trouble. But when he's abducted by pirates and pursued by a new religion bent solely on his destruction, only the love of a red-skinned priestess will see him through the insectile terror of the Swarms.

ISBN: 978-1-60125-214-2

Who Fears The Devil?
by Manly Wade Wellman
introduction by Mike Resnick

In the back woods of Appalachia, folk-singer and monster-hunter Silver John comes face to face with the ghosts and demons of rural Americana in this classic collection of eerie stories from Pulitzer Prize-nominee Manly Wade Wellman.

ISBN: 978-1-60125-188-6

Robots Have No Tails
by Henry Kuttner
introduction by F. Paul Wilson

Heckled by an uncooperative robot, a binge-drinking inventor must solve the mystery of his own machines before his dodgy financing and reckless lifestyle get the better of him. Collects all five classic "Gallegher" stories by an author hailed as a "neglected master" by Ray Bradbury!

ISBN: 978-1-60125-153-4

PLANET STORIES®

Read How These Men Got Better Books
Then Find Out What Planet Stories Offers You SUBSCRIBE!

> PLANET STORIES SHIPS A BEAUTIFUL NEW SCIENCE FICTION OR FANTASY BOOK DIRECT TO MY DOOR EVERY 60 DAYS AT 30% OFF THE COVER PRICE. ALL I NEED TO DO IS SIT BACK AND READ!
> **ALEXANDER BLADE,** NEW YORK CITY, NEW YORK.

> WITH THE GREAT CLASSIC REPRINTS OFFERED BY PLANET STORIES, I'VE LEARNED MORE ABOUT THE HISTORY OF SCIENCE FICTION AND FANTASY THAN EVER BEFORE. MY FRIENDS THINK I'M AN EXPERT!
> **S.M. TENNESHAW,** BOSTON, MASS.

> THESE BOOKS ARE THE PERFECT COMPANIONS WHEN I'M JET-SETTING ACROSS THE WORLD. ALL MY PASSENGERS ENVY THE TOP-QUALITY FICTION PLANET STORIES PROVIDES.
> **CAPTAIN CURTIS NEWTON,** PATRIOT AIRWAYS, YORBA LINDA, CA.

> I'M A TABLETOP GAMER, AND PLANET STORIES GIVES ME AN EXCITING LOOK AT THE ADVENTURE FICTION THAT INSPIRED MY FAVORITE HOBBY. YOU SHOULD SEE HOW I USE THE MONSTERS IN MY CAMPAIGN!
> **DICK AWLINSON,** LAKE GENEVA, WIS.

> WITH MY PLANET STORIES SUBSCRIPTION, I NEED NEVER WORRY ABOUT MISSING A SINGLE VOLUME. I CAN CHOOSE THE DELIVERY METHOD THAT WORKS BEST FOR ME, AND THE SUBSCRIPTION LASTS UNTIL I DECIDE TO CANCEL.
> **N.W. SMITH,** SCHENECTADY, NEW YORK.

> I CAN COMBINE MY PLANET STORIES BOOKS WITH OTHER SUBSCRIPTIONS FROM PAIZO.COM, SAVING MONEY ON SHIPPING AND HANDLING CHARGES!
> **MATTHEW CARSE,** KAHORA, MARS

Fine Books For Fine Minds
Subscribe Today

Explore fantastic worlds of high adventure with a genuine Planet Stories subscription that delivers the excitement of classic fantasy and science fiction right to your mailbox! Best of all, you'll receive your bi-monthly Planet Stories volumes at a substantial 30% discount off the cover price, and you can choose the shipping method that works best for you (including bundling the books with your other Paizo subscriptions)!

Only the Finest SF Books
The Best of Yesterday and Today!

Personally selected by publisher Erik Mona and Paizo's award-winning editorial staff, each Planet Stories volume has been chosen with the interests of fantasy and science fiction enthusiasts and gamers in mind. Timeless classics from authors like Robert E. Howard (Conan the Barbarian), Michael Moorcock (Elric), and Leigh Brackett (*The Empire Strikes Back*) will add an edge to your personal library, providing a better understanding of the genre with classic stories that easily stand the test of time.

Each Planet Stories edition is a Paizo exclusive—you cannot get these titles from any other publisher. Many of the tales in our line first appeared in the "pulp era" of the early 20th Century that produced authors like H. P. Lovecraft, Edgar Rice Burroughs, Fritz Leiber, and Robert E. Howard, and have been out of print for decades. Others are available only in rare limited editions or moldering pulp magazines worth hundreds of dollars.

Why Spend $20, $50, or even $100 to Read a Story?
Smart Readers Make Smart Subscribers

Sign up for an ongoing Planet Stories subscription to make sure that you don't miss a single volume! Subscriptions are fixed at a 30% discount off each volume's cover price, plus shipping. Your ongoing Planet Stories subscription will get you every new book as it's released, automatically continuing roughly every 60 days until you choose to cancel your subscription. After your first subscription volume ships, you'll also receive a 15% discount on the entire Planet Stories library! Instead of paying for your subscription all at once, we'll automatically charge your credit card before we ship a new volume. You only need to sign up once, and never need to worry about renewal notices or missed volumes!

> BEST OF ALL, AS A SUBSCRIBER, I ALSO RECEIVE A 15% DISCOUNT ON THE DOZENS OF BOOKS ALREADY PUBLISHED IN THE PLANET STORIES LIBRARY!
> **WILL GARTH,** CHICAGO, ILL.

Visit paizo.com/planetstories
to subscribe today!

PLANET STORIES AUTHORS

PIERS ANTHONY   ROBERT E. HOWARD
LEIGH BRACKETT   OTIS ADELBERT KLINE   MICHAEL MOORCOCK
GARY GYGAX   HENRY KUTTNER   C. L. MOORE

PLANET stories — STRANGE ADVENTURES ON OTHER WORLDS